DEMONGLASS

A HEX HALL NOVEL

DEMONGLASS

A HEX HALL NOVEL

RACHEL HAWKINS

HYPERION
NEW YORK

All rights reserved. Published by Hyperion, an imprint of Disney Book Group. No part
of this book may be reproduced or transmitted in any form or by any means, electronic or
mechanical, including photocopying, recording, or by any information storage and retrieval
system, without written permission from the publisher. For information address Hyperion,
114 Fifth Avenue, New York, New York 10011-5690.

First Edition
1 3 5 7 9 10 8 6 4 2
V567-9638-5-10349
Printed in the United States of America

Library of Congress Cataloging-in-Publication Data on file.
ISBN 978-1-4231-2131-2

Reinforced binding

Visit www.hyperionteens.com

SUSTAINABLE FORESTRY INITIATIVE
Certified Fiber Sourcing
www.sfiprogram.org

THIS LABEL APPLIES TO TEXT STOCK

For John, who said, "You know what this book needs? More fire. And maybe some swords." This one time, honey, you were right.

Still she haunts me, phantomwise,
Alice moving under skies
Never seen by waking eyes.

—Lewis Carroll

CHAPTER 1

At a normal high school, having class outside on a gorgeous May day is usually pretty awesome. It means sitting in the sunshine, maybe reading some poetry, letting the breeze blow through your hair. . . .

At Hecate Hall, a.k.a. Juvie for Monsters, it meant I was getting thrown in the pond.

My Persecution of Prodigium class was gathered around the scummy water just down the hill from the school. Our teacher, Ms. Vanderlyden—or the Vandy, as we called her—turned to Cal. He was the school's groundskeeper even though he was only nineteen. The Vandy took a coil of rope from his hands. Cal had been waiting for us at the pond. When he'd seen me, he'd given me a barely perceptible nod, which was the Cal version of waving his hands over his head and yelling, "Hey, Sophie!"

He was definitely the strong and silent type.

"Did you not hear me, Miss Mercer?" the Vandy said, twisting the rope in her fist. "I said come forward."

"Actually, Ms. Vanderlyden," I said, trying not to sound as nervous as I felt, "see this?" I gestured to my mass of curly hair. "This is a perm, and I just got it done the other day, so . . . yeah, probably shouldn't get it wet."

I heard a few muffled giggles, and next to me, my roommate Jenna muttered, "Nice one."

When I first came to Hecate, I would've been too terrified of the Vandy to talk back to her like that. But by the end of last semester, I'd watched my great-grandmother kill my best frenemy, and the boy I loved had pulled a knife on me.

I was a little tougher now.

Which was something the Vandy apparently did not appreciate. Her scowl deepened as she snapped, "Front and center!"

I muttered a few choice words as I moved through the crowd. When I reached the shore, I kicked off my shoes and socks to stand next to the Vandy in the shallows, grimacing at the slimy mud under my bare feet.

The rope scratched my skin as the Vandy first tied my hands together, then my feet. Once I was all trussed up, she rose, looking satisfied with her handiwork. "Now. Go all the way into the pond."

"Um . . . how, exactly?"

I was afraid she was going to make me hop out into the water until it was over my head, an image too mortifying to even contemplate. Cal stepped forward, hopefully to come to my rescue.

"I could toss her off the pier, Ms. Vanderlyden."

Or not.

"Good," the Vandy said with a brisk nod, like that had been her plan all along. Then Cal leaned down and swept me into his arms.

There were more giggles, and even a few sighs. I knew most girls would give up a vital organ for Cal to hold them, but my face flamed red. I wasn't sure this was any less embarrassing than flopping out into the pond on my own.

"You weren't listening to her, were you?" he asked in a low voice.

"No," I replied. During the part where the Vandy had been explaining why someone was about to go into the pond, I'd been telling Jenna that I had *not* flinched just because some kid had called me "Mercer" yesterday, the way Archer Cross always did. Because I hadn't. Just like I hadn't had a dream last night that re-created in vivid detail the one kiss Archer and I had shared last November. Only, in the dream, there was no tattoo on his chest, marking him as a member of L'Occhio di Dio, so there was no reason to stop kissing, and—

"What were you doing?" Cal asked. For a second, I thought he was talking about my dream, and my whole body flushed. Then I realized what he meant.

"Oh, I was, uh, talking to Jenna. You know, making monster small talk."

I thought I saw that ghost of a smile again, but then he said, "The Vandy said that real witches escaped trial by water by pretending to drown, then freeing themselves with their powers. So she wants you to sink, then save yourself."

"I think I can manage the sinking part," I muttered. "The rest . . . not so sure."

"You'll be fine," he said. "And if you're not up in a few minutes, *I'll* save you."

Something fluttered inside my chest, catching me by surprise. I hadn't felt anything like that since Archer had disappeared. It probably didn't mean anything. The sun was shining through Cal's dark blond hair, and his hazel eyes were picking up the light bouncing off the water. Plus, he was carrying me like I didn't weigh anything. Of course I'd feel butterflies when a guy who looked like that said something so swoon-worthy.

"Thanks," I said. Over his shoulder, I saw my mom watching us from the front porch of what had been Cal's cabin. She'd been staying there for the past six months while we waited for my dad to come get me and take me to Council Headquarters in London.

Six months later, and we were still waiting.

Mom frowned, and I wanted to give her a thumbs-up to let her know I was okay. All I could manage was raising my bound hands in her general direction, clocking Cal on the chin as I did so. "Sorry."

"No problem. Must be weird for you, having your mom here."

"Weird for me, weird for her, probably weird for you since you had to give up your swinging bachelor pad."

"Mrs. Casnoff let me install my heart-shaped Jacuzzi in my new dorm room."

"Cal," I said with mock astonishment, "did you just make a joke?"

"Maybe," he replied. We'd reached the end of the pier. I looked down at the water and tried not to shudder.

"I'll be pretending, of course, but do you have any advice on how I'm supposed to not drown?" I asked Cal.

"Don't breathe in any water."

"Oh, thanks, that's super helpful."

Cal shifted me in his arms, and I tensed. Just before he tossed me into the pond, he leaned in and whispered, "Good luck."

And then I hit the water.

I can't say what my first thought was as I sunk below the surface, because it was mostly a string of four-letter words. The water was way too cold for a pond in Georgia in May, and I could feel the chill sinking all the way into my bones. Plus my chest started burning almost immediately, and I sunk all the way to the bottom, landing in the slimy mud.

Okay, Sophie, I thought. Don't panic.

Then I glanced over to my right, and through the murky water, made out a skull grinning back at me.

I panicked. My first impulse was a human one, and I bent my body, trying to tear at the ropes across my ankles with my bound hands. I quickly realized this was profoundly stupid, and tried to calm down and concentrate on my powers.

Ropes off, I thought, imagining the bindings slithering off me. I could feel them give a little, but not enough. Part of the problem was that my magic came up from the ground (or something beneath the ground, a fact I tried not to think about too often) and it was hard to get my feet on the ground while I was trying not to drown.

ROPES OFF, I thought again, stronger this time.

The ropes snapped violently, unraveling until they were nothing more than a big ball of floating twine. If I hadn't been holding my breath, I would have sighed. Instead, I untangled myself from what was left of the ropes, and made to kick for the surface.

I swam up about a foot, and then something jerked me back to the bottom.

My eyes went to my ankle, half expecting to see a skeletal hand grabbing me, but there was nothing. My chest was on fire now, and my eyes were stinging. I pumped with my arms and legs, trying to swim up, but it was like I was being held underwater even though nothing was holding me.

Real panic set in as black spots danced before my eyes. I had to breathe. I kicked again, but just bobbed in place. Now the black spots were bigger, and the pressure in my chest was agonizing. I wondered how long I'd been down here, and if Cal was going to make good on that promise to save me anytime soon.

I suddenly surged upward, gasping when I broke the surface, the air burning as it rushed into my chest; but I wasn't done yet. I kept flying until I was completely out of the water, landing on the pier in a heap.

I winced as my elbow connected painfully with the wood. I knew my skirt was probably hiked up too high on my thighs, but I couldn't bring myself to care. I just took a second to enjoy breathing. Eventually, I stopped gulping air and started to breathe normally again.

I sat up and pushed my wet hair out of eyes. Cal was standing a few feet away. I glared at him. "Awesome job with the saving."

Then I realized Cal wasn't looking at me, but up toward the head of the pier.

I followed his gaze and saw a slender, dark-haired man. He was standing very still, watching me.

Suddenly, it was hard to breathe all over again.

I rose to my feet on shaky legs, tugging my soaked clothes back into place.

"Are you all right?" the man called out, his face clearly worried. His voice was more powerful than I would've expected from such a slight man, and he had a soft British accent.

"I'm fine," I said, but the black spots were back in front of my eyes, and my knees seemed too wobbly to hold me. The last thing I saw before I fainted was my father walking toward me as I crashed back to the pier.

CHAPTER 2

For the second time in six months, I found myself sitting in Mrs. Casnoff's office, wrapped in a blanket. The first time had been the night I'd discovered that Archer was a member of L'Occhio di Dio, a group of demon hunters. Now my mom was next to me on the couch, one arm wrapped around my shoulders. My dad was standing by Mrs. Casnoff's desk, holding a manila folder overflowing with papers, while Mrs. Casnoff sat behind that desk in her great purple throne of a chair.

The only sounds were Dad flipping through all that paper and my teeth chattering, so I finally said, "Why couldn't my magic get me out of the water?"

Mrs. Casnoff looked up at me like she'd forgotten I was even in the room. "No demon could escape from that particular pond," she answered in her velvety voice.

"There are protection spells in it. It . . . holds anything it doesn't recognize as a witch, faerie, or shifter."

I thought of the skull and nodded, wishing for some of that spiked tea I'd had last time I was here. "I kind of figured that. So the Vandy was trying to kill me?"

Mrs. Casnoff's lips puckered a little. "Don't be ridiculous," she said. "Clarice didn't know about the protection spells."

She might've been a little more believable if her eyes hadn't slid away from mine as she'd said that, but before I could press the issue, Dad tossed the folder down on Mrs. Casnoff's desk and said, "Quite an impressive file you've amassed, Sophia." Clasping his hands, he added, "If Hecate offered classes in complete mayhem, I have no doubt you'd be valedictorian."

Nice to see where I got my snarkiness. Of course, that seemed to be all I'd gotten from him. I'd seen pictures of him before, but this was the first time I'd seen him in person, and I was having a hard time not staring. He was so different from what I expected. He was definitely handsome, but . . . I don't know. In a fussy way. He looked like the kind of guy who had a lot of shoe trees.

I glanced over at Mom and saw that she was having the opposite problem from me. She was looking anywhere but at Dad.

"Yeah," I said, turning my attention back to him. "Last semester was intense."

Dad raised both eyebrows at me. I wondered if that was on purpose, or if, like me, he couldn't lift just one. "'Intense?'" He picked up the file again and studied it over the top of his glasses. "On your first day at Hecate, you were attacked by a werewolf. . . ."

"It wasn't really an attack," I muttered, but no one seemed to pay any attention.

"But of course, that's paltry compared to what came after." Dad flipped through the pages. "You insulted a teacher, which resulted in semester-long cellar duty with one Archer Cross. According to Mrs. Casnoff's notes on the situation, the two of you became 'close.'" He paused. "Is that an accurate description of your relationship with Mr. Cross?"

"Sure," I said through clenched teeth.

Dad turned another page. "Well, apparently you two were . . . close enough that at some point you were able to see the mark of L'Occhio di Dio on his chest."

I flushed at that, and felt Mom's arm tighten around me. Over the past six months, I'd filled her in on a lot of the story with Archer, but not all of it.

Specifically, not the whole me-making-out-in-the-cellar-with-him part.

"Now, for most people, nearly being murdered by a

warlock working with the Eye would be enough excitement for one semester. But you also became involved with a coven of dark witches led by"—he ran his finger along the page—"ah, Elodie Parris. Miss Parris and her friends, Anna Gilroy and Chaston Burnett, murdered the other member of their coven, Holly Mitchell, and raised a demon who just happened to be your great-grandmother, Alice Barrow."

My stomach twisted. I'd spent the past six months trying not to think about all that had happened last fall. To have it all read out to me in Dad's emotionless voice . . . well, let's just say I was beginning to wish I'd stayed in the pond.

"After Alice attacked Chaston and Anna, she killed Elodie, and then you killed her."

I saw his eyes drift from the paper and to my right hand. A puckered scar ran across my palm, a souvenir of that night. Demonglass leaves quite a mark.

Clearing his throat, Dad dropped the papers. "So yes, Sophia, I would agree that you did have quite the intense semester. Ironic considering the fact that I sent you here to be safe."

Sixteen years' worth of questions and accusations flooded my brain, and I heard myself snap, "Which I might have been if someone had filled me in on the whole my being a demon thing."

Behind Dad, Mrs. Casnoff frowned, and I thought I was about to get a lecture on respecting one's elders, but Dad just watched me with those blue eyes—my eyes—and gave a tiny smile. "Touché."

The smile threw me, and I looked at the floor when I said, "So are you here to take me to London? I've been waiting since November."

"We can discuss that at some point, yes. But first I'd like to hear about the events of last semester from your perspective. I'd like to hear about the Cross boy."

Resentment surged up in me, and I shook my head. "No way. You want those stories, you can read the accounts I wrote up for the Council. Or you can talk to Mrs. Casnoff, or Mom, or any of the other people I've told the story to."

"Sophia, I understand that you're angry—"

"It's Sophie. No one calls me Sophia."

His lips thinned. "Very well. Sophie, while your frustration is perfectly valid, it's not helpful at this moment. I'd like to spend time talking with you and your mother"—his eyes flickered to Mom—"as a family before we proceed to the subject of your going through the Removal."

"Too bad," I retorted, tossing off the blanket and Mom's arm. "You've had sixteen years to talk to us as a family. I didn't ask you to come here because you're my dad and I wanted some kind of tearful reunion. I asked you to come here as head of the Council so I can get my stupid powers removed."

All of that came out in a rush. I was afraid if I slowed down, I might start crying, and I'd done enough of that over the past few months.

Dad studied me, but his eyes had gone cold, and his voice was stern when he said, "In that case, in my capacity as head of the Council, I reject your request to go through the Removal."

I stared at him, dumbfounded. "You can't do that!"

"Actually, Sophie, he can," Mrs. Casnoff interjected. "Both as head of the Council and as your father, he's well within his rights. At least until you're eighteen."

"That's over a year away!"

"Which will give you enough time to understand the implications of your decision to the fullest," Dad said.

I whirled on him. "Okay, first of all, no one talks like that. Secondly, I *do* understand the implications of my decision. Removing my powers will keep me from potentially killing someone."

"Sophie, we've talked about this," Mom said, speaking for the first time since we'd come into Mrs. Casnoff's office. "It's not a foregone conclusion that you will kill someone. Or that you'll even try. Your father has never lost control of his powers." She sighed and rubbed her eyes with one hand. "And it's just so drastic, honey. I don't think you should risk your life for a 'what if?'"

"Your mother is right," Mrs. Casnoff said. "And bear in mind that you decided to go through the Removal less than twenty-four hours after watching the death of a friend. More time to weigh your options might be a good thing."

I sat back down on the couch. "I get what you guys are saying. I do. But . . ." I looked at the three of them, settling finally on my dad, the only person I thought might understand what I was about to say. "I saw Alice. I saw what she was, what she did, what she was capable of." I dropped my eyes to the faded cabbage roses on Mrs. Casnoff's carpet, but I was seeing Elodie, pale and streaked with blood. "I don't ever—*ever*—want to be like that. I really would rather die."

Mom made a choked noise, and Mrs. Casnoff suddenly became fascinated by something on her desk.

But Dad nodded. "All right," he said. "I'll make you a deal."

"James," Mom said sharply.

Their eyes met and something passed between them before Dad continued. "Your year here at Hecate Hall is almost over. Come spend the summer with me, and at the end of that time, if you still want to go through the Removal, I'll allow it."

My eyebrows shot up. "What, like at your house? In England?" My pulse sped up. There had been three sightings of Archer in England.

Dad paused, and for one awful moment I wondered if he could read minds. But he just said, "England, yes. My house, no. I'll be staying with . . . friends for the summer."

"And they won't care if you bring your daughter?"

He smiled at some private joke. "Trust me. They have room."

"What exactly is this supposed to accomplish?" I was trying to sound haughty and disdainful, but I'm afraid it just came off as petulant.

Dad began fishing in his coat for something, but when he pulled out a thin brown cigarette, Mrs. Casnoff made a disapproving cluck. He sighed and put the cigarette back.

"Sophie," he said, sounding frustrated, "I want to get to know you, and have you get to know me, before you decide to throw your powers—and possibly your life—away. You don't even fully comprehend what it means to be a demon yet."

I thought about Dad's offer. On the one hand, I was not exactly his biggest fan right now, and I wasn't sure I wanted to spend time on a whole other continent with him.

But if I didn't, I'd be stuck as a demon for a lot longer.

Also, my mom had given up the house she'd been renting in Vermont, so I'd probably be spending all summer at Hecate with just her and the teachers. Ugh.

And then there was England. Archer.

"Mom?" I asked, wondering if she had some motherly input. She seemed pretty shaken up, which was understandable, what with watching me nearly get killed, then having to deal with Dad.

"I'd miss you like crazy, but your dad makes a good point." Her eyes were bright with tears, but she blinked them back and nodded. "I think you should go."

"Thank you, Grace," Dad said quietly.

I took a deep breath. "Okay," I told him. "I'll go. But I want to bring Jenna."

She didn't have anywhere to go this summer either, and I wanted at least one friendly face if I was going to spend a whole summer embracing my demon-ness or whatever.

"Fine," Dad said, without hesitation.

That took me by surprise, but I tried to seem nonchalant as I said, "Awesome."

"That reminds me," Dad said to Mrs. Casnoff. "I was wondering if it would be all right for Alexander Callahan to come with us as well."

"Who the heck is Alexander Callahan?" I asked. "Oh, right. Cal."

It was weird to think of him as *Alexander*. It was such a formal name. Cal suited him a lot better.

"Of course," Mrs. Casnoff said, all business again. "I'm sure we can manage without him for a few months. Although without his healing powers, we'll certainly have to invest in more bandages."

"Why do you want to bring Cal?" I asked.

Dad's fingers strayed to his suit pocket again. "Council business, mostly. Alexander's powers are unique, so we'd like to interview him, possibly run a few tests."

I didn't like the sound of that, and something told me Cal wouldn't either.

"And it will give the two of you a chance to get to know one another better," Dad continued.

A sense of dread slowly began creeping up my spine. "Cal and I know each other well enough," I said. "Why would I want to know him better?"

"Because," Dad said, finally meeting my eyes, "you and he are betrothed."

CHAPTER 3

It took me a good thirty minutes to find Cal. That was actually a good thing, because it gave me plenty of time to come up with something to say to him that wasn't just a string of four-letter words.

There are a lot of freaky things witches and warlocks do, obviously, but the arranged marriage thing was one of the grossest. When a witch is thirteen, her parents hook her up with an available warlock, based on things like compatible powers and family alliances. The entire thing is so eighteenth century.

As I stomped across school grounds, all I could see was Cal sitting with my dad in some manly room with leather chairs and dead animals on the wall, chomping on cigars as Dad formally signed me away to him. They probably even high-fived.

Okay, so it's not like either of them are exactly the cigar-and-high-fives type, but still.

I finally found Cal in the potting shed behind the greenhouse, where our Defense classes were held. His talent for healing extended to plants, and he was running his hands over a browned and drooping azalea when I flung open the door. He squinted as a shaft of late afternoon sunlight flooded in behind me.

"Did you know I'm your fiancée?" I demanded.

Cal muttered something under his breath and turned back to the plant.

"Did you?" I asked again, even though I clearly had my answer.

"Yes," he replied.

I stood there waiting for him to say something else, but that was apparently all Cal had to say.

"Well, I'm not going to marry you," I said. "I think this whole arranged marriage thing is gross and barbaric."

"Okay."

There was a bag of potting soil by the door, and I scooped up a handful to fling at his back. Before it hit, he raised his hand and the dirt froze in midair. It hovered there for a moment before floating slowly back to the bag.

"I just can't believe you knew and didn't tell me," I said, sitting on an unopened bag.

"I didn't see the point."

"What does that mean?"

He dusted his hands off on his jeans and turned to face me. He was streaked with sweat, and his damp T-shirt was clinging to his chest in ways that would have been interesting if I wasn't so irritated with him. As usual, he looked more like an all-American high school quarterback than a warlock.

His face was blank, but Cal always held his cards pretty close to his chest. "It means that you didn't grow up in a Prodigium family, so I knew you'd think arranged marriages were—what did you say?"

"Gross and barbaric."

"Right. So what was the point in making you all freaked out and hostile?"

"I'm not hostile," I protested. Cal gave a pointed look to the potting soil, and I rolled my eyes. "Okay, yes, but I was mad that you didn't tell me, not that we're . . . engaged. God, I can't even say it. It sounds too weird."

"Sophie, it doesn't mean anything," he said, leaning forward and resting his elbows on his knees. "It's like a business contract. Didn't anyone explain that to you?"

Archer had. He'd been betrothed to Holly, Jenna's old roommate, before she died. Of course, now that I knew he was an Eye, I wondered how legit that had ever been. But I didn't want to think about him right now.

"Yeah," I said. "And we can, you know, break it off, right? It's not a done deal."

"Exactly. So are we cool?"

I drew a pattern on the dirt-covered floor with my toe. "Yeah. We're cool."

"Great," he said. "So there's no need for things to be awkward."

"Right."

Then we sat there awkwardly for a moment before I said, "Oh! Almost forgot. Dad wants you to come to England with us this summer." Briefly, I told him everything that had happened in Mrs. Casnoff's office. He looked surprised when I told him about the Vandy, and he scowled when I mentioned the interview-and-testing part of his summer vacation, but he didn't interrupt me. When I was finished, he said, "Well, that sucks."

"A bunch," I agreed.

He got up and walked back to the azalea, which I guess was my cue to leave. Instead, I said, "Sorry I tried to throw dirt at you."

"It's fine."

I waited for him to say something else. When he didn't, I pushed myself off the bag of soil. "See you back at the house, honey," I muttered as I left. He made a sound that might have been a laugh, but it was Cal, so I doubt it.

The sun was beginning to set when I walked up the front steps of the crazy half-antebellum mansion, half-stucco institution that was Hecate Hall. Crickets were already chirping, and frogs croaked around the pond. A gentle breeze that smelled like honeysuckle and the sea breeze nudged the vines that climbed the walls of the school. I turned and looked back at the lawn. I'd hated this place when I first came here, but I was actually going to miss it this summer. So much had happened to me since Mom had steered that rental car up the drive for the first time, and, as impossible as it would have seemed then, Hecate Hall almost felt like home.

Something furry brushed my arm. It was Beth, a werewolf I'd met my first night at Hecate.

"Full moon," she growled, nodding her muzzle toward the darkening sky.

"Right." Weres got the run of the place during the full moon. Glancing behind me, I could see a handful of them gathering in the foyer.

"Can't believe the school year is almost over," Beth said, in that voice that sounded like a teenage girl who had a throat full of broken glass and lug nuts.

"Tell me about it," I replied.

Her eyes were bright yellow, but I could see the affection in them as she said, "I'm gonna miss you this summer, Sophie."

I smiled. Just a few months ago, Beth hadn't trusted me, thinking I had to be a spy for the Council or something. Luckily, nearly dying had cleared me of that suspicion. I reached out to pat her shoulder. "I'll miss you too, Beth."

Then she leaned forward and licked the side of my face.

I waited until she had loped off before wiping my cheek with the back of my hand. "Yeugh."

Okay, so I wouldn't miss everything about Hecate Hall.

I headed up to the third floor, where all the girls were housed. There were a few people gathered in the lounge on the landing, but for the most part, things were pretty quiet tonight.

Taylor, one of the shifters, saw me and waved. "Hey, Soph! Heard you went for a swim today," she said, taking in my still-bedraggled appearance. "Why didn't you change your clothes?"

I tucked a strand of hair behind my ear. "I, uh, didn't really have time."

Taylor laughed, the sound surprisingly throaty for such a delicate-looking girl. "I meant with magic," she said.

Oh, right. "With the way things have been going lately, I didn't wanna risk it."

She nodded sympathetically. "Oh, I understand. Especially after the Bed Thing."

The Bed Thing had happened two months ago. I'd wanted to move my bed, and decided to use magic to do it. Instead of scooting over a few feet, the bed had gone flying out the window, taking out a big chunk of the wall with it.

Mrs. Casnoff had not been amused.

Especially since the Bed Thing had followed the Doritos Incident. Jenna had wanted chips; when I'd tried to make them appear, I'd flooded the hallway with Doritos. There were still traces of cheese dust in the floorboards. Before that, there was That Time With The Lotion (the less said about that, the better). Ever since Alice and Elodie, my magic had definitely been . . . off. As a result, I'd pretty much stopped using it.

After saying good-bye to Taylor, I continued on to my room. A few more students called out greetings, or commented on my date with the pond. It still caught me off guard, this newfound popularity. At first I thought that word must've gotten out that I was a demon, and everyone was being nice to me because they were afraid I'd eat them. But according to Jenna, who was a champion eavesdropper, everybody still thought I was just a superpowerful dark witch. Mrs. Casnoff had done a bang-up job covering up the truth of Elodie's death, which meant there were all kinds of rumors about what happened to her. The most popular one had Archer sneaking back onto Graymalkin Island and me and Elodie trying to fight him off with our mad magic skills, Elodie dying in the attempt.

Too bad the truth was a lot more complicated. And a lot sadder.

I was nearly at my door when I caught a movement out of the corner of my eye. Hecate Hall was full of ghosts, so we were always catching glimpses of them like that. But when I saw who it was, I froze.

Even as a ghost, Elodie was still beautiful. Her red hair waved around her face, and her skin was translucent. It sucked that she had to spend eternity wearing her school uniform, but then again, Elodie made even that look good.

She was doing what all the ghosts seemed to do: wandering around, looking confused. They weren't technically in our world, but they weren't in the afterlife either, so they were just . . . stuck.

I'd seen Elodie's ghost a lot, and every time I did, a wave of sadness washed over me. Her death had been her own fault. She and her coven had raised a demon in the hopes that they could bind it and use its power. They'd even sacrificed Holly for it. Still, Elodie had given me her last spark of magic. Without it, I never would have been able to kill Alice.

Now Elodie drifted past me, her eyes searching for something, her feet not touching the ground.

It seemed wrong that someone as vibrant as Elodie would be reduced to this pale, sad spirit, forever wandering the place where she died. "I wish you could just go on to wherever you're supposed to be," I whispered in the silence of the hallway.

The ghost swung around and looked at me.

My heart lodged in my throat.

That was impossible. Ghosts couldn't see or hear us. That was why I should've known right away that Alice wasn't a ghost like she claimed. But Elodie was staring at me, the expression on her face no longer lost and bewildered, but annoyed, with just a touch of disdain.

The way she'd always looked at me in life.

"Elodie?" I barely murmured the word, but it sounded deafening in the quiet. She kept studying me, but she didn't reply. "Can you hear me?" I asked, slightly louder this time.

A pause. Then, to my disbelief, she made a tiny nod.

"Soph?" My door opened, and Jenna peeked out. "Who are you talking to?"

I whipped my head around, but Elodie had already vanished.

"No one," I said, trying hard not to seem irritated. It wasn't Jenna's fault she'd interrupted me in the middle of talking to a ghost, a ghost who wasn't supposed to be able to communicate at all.

"Where have you been?" Jenna asked as I slumped on my bed. "I was worried."

"It's been a really long afternoon," I answered before launching into the Tale of Casnoff's Office again. Unlike Cal, Jenna had a lot of questions, so the story took a lot longer to tell. I left out the part about Cal and I being betrothed. Jenna was already practically wearing a Team Cal T-shirt. I didn't want to give her any more ammunition. By the time I was finished, I felt too tired even to go down to dinner, usually my favorite time of day.

"England," Jenna breathed when I was done. "How awesome will that be?"

I laid an arm over my eyes. "Honestly, Jen? I have no idea."

She tossed a pillow at me. "It's going to be superawesome. And thank you."

"For what?"

"For letting me come too. I thought maybe you'd want some time alone with your dad."

"Are you kidding? You were the deal breaker, my friend. No Jenna, no England. Those were my conditions."

She smiled brightly, shaking her head so the pink stripe in her bangs fell over one eye. "I'm not sure that island is big enough for the two of us. Oh! Do we get to use some sort of sweet witchy transportation to get there? Like, a traveling spell or a magical portal?"

"Sorry," I said, forcing myself to get up and change. After all, my uniform still had the distinct odor of Nasty Pond. I would need at least a thirty-minute shower before going to bed tonight. "I asked Dad. We're taking a plane."

Jenna's face fell. "That's such a . . . human thing."

"Look on the bright side," I told her, tugging on a clean Hecate-blue skirt. "It's a private plane, so at least it's a rich-human thing."

That cheered her up, and we started planning our entire wardrobe for the summer as we made our way toward the dining hall.

But once our plates were filled and we were sitting at our usual table, Jenna's face grew serious. "Sophie," she said.

"What?"

She pushed her food around and seemed to be debating what to say. Finally, she just decided to be blunt.

"Archer's in England."

The piece of ham I'd been chewing turned to sawdust in my mouth, but I forced my voice to be light as I said, "Allegedly. I'm not sure the word of two warlocks—who were drunk off their butts, from what I hear—can be taken as fact." Except that that hadn't been the only sighting. There was the werewolf who'd seen a guy matching Archer's description when The Eye raided a den in London. And the vampire who'd fought with a young dark-haired Eye three months ago a few blocks from Victoria station.

Mrs. Casnoff had a file on Archer in her bottom desk drawer. Her desk was protected from spells, but apparently not from nail files and elbow grease.

"Anyway," I said to Jenna, lowering my eyes to my plate. "That sighting was months ago."

"It was last month," Jenna corrected, and her tone suggested I had known that. "And people have been saying he was in England since he disappeared. I overheard those two witches in Savannah."

"It's a big island, Jenna," I said. "And even if Archer is there, I seriously doubt he's anywhere near Prodigium. That would be stupid. Archer's a lot of things, but he's not an idiot."

Jenna turned her attention back to her food, but when her green beans had made their third circuit around her plate, I pushed my dinner away and said, "Spit it out."

She put down her fork and looked into my eyes. "What would you do, though, if you did see him?"

I held her gaze for as long as I could. I knew what she wanted me to say. She wanted me to tell her that I'd turn him in to the Council—who would almost certainly execute him—or maybe even that I would kill him myself.

For the first time in a long time, I let myself remember Archer, really remember him. His brown eyes and slow smile. His laugh, and how I felt when I was with him. How his voice sounded when he called me "Mercer."

The way he had kissed me.

I lowered my eyes to the table. "I don't know," I finally said.

Jenna sighed, but she didn't say anything more about it. After a moment we started talking about the trip again, and I made Jenna laugh by wondering aloud if there was such a thing as vampire high tea. "And when you ask for Earl Grey, you actually get Earl Grey," I summed up, sending Jenna into another fit of giggles.

I felt better as we left the dining hall, and Jenna must have too, since she looped her arm through mine to walk up the stairs.

But the thought she'd put in my mind refused to die, and I fell asleep that night seeing Archer's eyes and hoping with most of my heart he wasn't in England.

Even as a not so tiny part of it hoped that he was.

CHAPTER 4

Three weeks later, I left for England.

Mom and Mrs. Casnoff walked down to the ferry with the four of us late in the afternoon. Mom's eyes were red, so I knew she'd been crying, but she tried to seem cheerful as she helped Jenna and me load our luggage. "Make sure you take lots of pictures," she told me. "And if you come back using words like 'queue' or 'lorry,' I'll be very upset."

We stood on the deck, the sea breeze ruffling our hair. Jenna had already claimed a bench in the shade, and Cal was talking in a low voice to Mrs. Casnoff. I saw her look over his shoulder at me, and wondered how she felt about me leaving for the summer. She was probably pumped, or as pumped as Mrs. Casnoff got. God knows, I'd brought nothing but trouble to Hecate Hall.

I also wondered if I should have told her about Elodie's ghost. Actually, I *knew* I should have. If I'd told her about Alice when she first appeared to me, maybe Elodie wouldn't be a ghost. It was a thought that had burned at the back of my brain for months, and here I was making the same mistake all over again.

Before I could think about that any more, Mom wrapped her arms around me. We were about the same height, and I could feel her tears at my temple when she said, "I'm going to miss your birthday next month. I've never missed your birthday."

My throat was so tight that I couldn't speak, so I just hugged her closer.

"Sophie," Dad said, appearing at my elbow. "It's time to go."

I nodded and gave Mom one last squeeze. "I'll call lots, I promise," I told her as we pulled apart. "And I'll be back before you know it."

Mom wiped her cheeks with the back of her hand and gave me one of her dazzling smiles. Dad drew in a sharp breath next to me, but when I glanced over at him, he had turned away.

"Good-bye, James," Mom called after him.

Cal, Jenna, and I stood at the railing as the ferry pulled away from the dock. Mrs. Casnoff stood on the shore, watching us go, but Mom was already walking back into the woods that surrounded the beach. I was glad. It was a miracle I hadn't started sobbing already.

The ferry chugged out into the brown water. Over the trees, we could make out the very top of Hecate Hall.

"I haven't been away from this place since I was thirteen years old," Cal said softly. "Six years."

I'd never asked Cal what he'd done that had landed him at Hecate Hall. He just didn't seem like the type of guy to do the dangerous spells that usually got warlocks sent to the school. He'd decided to stay on after his eighteenth birthday, although I'd never been clear on whether that had been by choice. But the farther we got from the school, the more troubled he looked.

Even Jenna, who usually acted like she was composing a thesis on all the ways Hecate sucked, looked wistful.

I stared at the bit of roof I could see against the blue sky, and a strong sense of foreboding came over me, as though the sun had gone behind a cloud.

The three of us will never come back here.

The thought was so startling that I shivered. I tried to shake it off. That was ridiculous. We were going to England for three months, and we'd be back at Hecate by August. Premonition isn't one of my powers, so I was just being paranoid.

Still, the feeling stayed with me long after Graymalkin Island had faded in the distance.

"Being a demon should make you immune to jet lag," I mumbled hours and hours later as a sleek black car carried us through the English countryside.

The long flight from Georgia to England had been pretty uneventful. Except that Cal had sat next to me.

Which was fine. Really.

It wasn't like I'd been hyperaware of his presence and jumped the three times his knee bumped mine. And after that third time, he definitely hadn't shot me a kind of disgusted look and said, "Chill out, will you?"

And when Jenna gave us both a quizzical look, we hadn't snapped, in unison, "Nothing!" Because all of that would have been weird, and Cal and I weren't weird. We were cool.

"You'll feel better soon," Dad said. For the first time since I'd met him, his eyes were bright and he actually looked relaxed. I guess being back in the motherland will do that to a guy.

Jenna was practically bouncing with excitement, but Cal looked as tired as I felt. I hadn't been able to fall asleep on the plane, and I was paying for it now. My eyes felt gritty and hot, and all I could think about was collapsing into a bed. After all, my poor body thought it was six a.m., but in England it was nearly lunchtime. Plus, we'd been driving for what felt like hours.

When the plane had landed in London, I'd assumed the car would take us to a house in the city, or maybe to Council Headquarters so Dad could do business stuff. But the car had driven out of the crowded streets and past small houses all clustered together that reminded me of a Dickens story. Gradually, the brick buildings had given way to trees and rolling green hills. I saw more sheep than I thought existed.

"So we came all the way to England just to hang out in the middle of nowhere?" I asked, leaning my aching head on Jenna's shoulder.

"We did," Dad replied.

Cal smiled. Well, of course he'd be thrilled to be stuck on some British farm all summer long, I thought grumpily, my visions of Big Ben and Buckingham Palace and Tower Bridge crumbling. Probably all sorts of English plants to heal—

Then I caught sight of a house.

Although, calling it a house was like calling the *Mona Lisa* a painting, or Hecate Hall a school. The term was technically correct, but it didn't even begin to sum up the reality of the object.

This house was one of the biggest buildings I'd ever seen, and made of a light, golden-colored stone that looked warm to the touch. It sat nestled in a lush valley, an emerald green lawn stretching in front of it, while a forested hill rose in the back. A thin, shining ribbon of water curved gracefully along one side of the property. Literally hundreds of windows glittered in the sunlight.

"Wow," Cal said, leaning over to look out the window.

"This is where we're staying?" I asked.

Dad just smiled, looking way too satisfied with himself. "I told you there would be room for all of us," he said, and I caught myself smiling back. We held each other's eyes for a second, but I broke away first, nodding toward the house. "Don't houses like that always have a name?"

"More often than not," he answered. "This is Thorne Abbey."

Something about that name was familiar, but I couldn't think why. "It used to be a church?"

"Not that actual house. It wasn't built until the late sixteenth century. But there was an abbey on the land."

He went into lecture mode, talking about how the abbey had been razed under Henry VIII, and the land given to the Thorne family.

But to be honest, I wasn't really listening. I was watching several people walk out the front door of the house. Then I spotted a pair of wings and wondered who exactly Dad's friends were.

The car rumbled over a stone bridge and pulled into

a circular drive. Dad got out of the car first, and as he opened my door, I suddenly wished I'd worn something nicer than a faded pair of jeans and a plain green T-shirt.

Impossibly wide steps led up to a terrace made of the same golden-colored stone as the rest of the house. There were six people standing there, two dark-haired kids who looked about my age, and four adults. I guessed they were all Prodigium. Well, the faerie was obvious, but I could sense magic hovering around the rest of them, too.

The day was warmer than I'd expected, and I felt a few beads of sweat pop out on my brow. The gravel crunched under my feet, and in the distance I heard birds singing. Jenna appeared at my elbow, her earlier excitement gone, her fingers moving over her bloodstone.

Dad placed a hand on the small of my back and steered me up the steps. "Everyone, this is Sophie. My daughter."

Suddenly I felt something surge in my blood. Something like magic, but darker, more powerful. It was coming from the two teenagers near the back of the crowd. They were the only ones not smiling, and the boy—who looked weirdly familiar—was glaring at me.

Realization slammed into my chest, and it was all I could do not to gasp.

They were demons.

CHAPTER 5

I stared at the demon kids, numbness seeping through me. Dad and I were supposed to be the only demons in the world, so how—

A sudden, horrifying thought came to me: holy hell weasel, were these kids my half-*siblings*? Had Dad dragged me all the way to England to play out some twisted version of the Brady Bunch?

"What is this?" I choked out, meaning the other demons.

But Dad smiled proudly. "This is Council Head-quarters."

Behind me, I heard Cal let out a long breath, like he'd been holding it, as a woman with dark blond hair stepped out from the group and offered her hand. "Sophia, we're so thrilled you'll be with us this summer. I'm Lara."

I shook her hand, even as I shot a glance at the demon kids. They were whispering to each other.

"Lara is a Council member, and my second-in-command, you might say," Dad said.

Lara didn't let go of my hand right away. "I've heard so much about you, both from your father and from Anastasia."

"Mrs. Casnoff?" Oh, God, if that's where this woman had gotten her Sophie Mercer gossip, I was surprised she'd greeted me with a handshake instead of an exorcism.

"Lara and Anastasia are sisters," Dad said.

"Okay," I replied, trying to process that. Then something else occurred to me. "I thought Council Headquarters was in London."

A deep vertical line appeared between Lara's brows. "It is. Due to some unforeseen events we've decided to relocate for the summer." Now that I knew she was Mrs. Casnoff's sister, I could see—and hear—the resemblance. I wondered if the demon teenagers were the "unforeseen events," or if there was *more* messed up stuff happening. Wouldn't have surprised me.

I turned to Dad, "You said we were going to a friend's house. Why didn't you tell me you were bringing me here?"

He met my gaze. "Because if I had, you wouldn't have come."

Out of the corner of my eye, I saw the demon kids break away from the group and head for the massive double doors just past the terrace. The girl shot me one last look before they slipped inside.

"Sophie, this is the Council," Dad said, drawing my attention back to the Prodigium standing there.

"That's it?" I heard Cal say under his breath, and I had to admit, I was surprised, too. All this time I'd imagined the Council as this huge, shadowy group of Prodigium who wore long black robes or something.

I don't know if he heard Cal, or if he could just read the looks on our faces, but Dad said, "There are normally twelve members, but now there are just the five of us currently at Thorne."

"Where are—" Jenna started to say, but she was interrupted as one of the men stepped forward. He was older than Dad, and his white hair gleamed in the sunlight. "I'm Kristopher," he said, his voice thick with an unidentifiable accent. "It is a pleasure to meet you, Sophia." His eyes were icy blue instead of gold, but he was definitely a shifter. I could feel it.

Wondering if he turned into a husky dog, I turned to the next guy, craning my neck to look up at him. He must've been nearly seven feet tall, and his huge wings reminded me of water in oil: they were black, but they still swirled with every color, from green to blue to pink.

"Roderick," he said as my hand disappeared into his. The woman was Elizabeth, and with her soft gray hair and little round glasses, I thought she looked like someone's nana; but when I went to shake her hand, she yanked me to her and sniffed my hair.

Great. Another werewolf.

Dad said something about speaking with all of them later, and then, finally, we headed inside.

Jenna gasped as we moved into the foyer, and if I hadn't still been reeling from the one-two punch of the Council on the steps, plus the demon teenagers, I probably would have too. It was one of those spaces where you felt like you could look forever and still not see everything. Hecate could be overwhelming as well, but it was nothing like this. The black-and-white marble floor underneath my feet was shiny enough to make me glad I hadn't worn a skirt, and I was nearly blinded by the acres of gilt that covered every surface. Like Hecate, the main entrance was dominated by a staircase, but this one was a lot bigger, and carved from white limestone. The steps were covered in a carpet as red as spilled blood.

Overhead, the curved ceiling was covered in a mural, but I couldn't quite make out what was being depicted. From the looks of it, it was violent and tragic. Other paintings around the room showed the same kind

42

of scene: stern-faced men pointing swords at weeping women, or men charging into battle while their horses' eyes rolled in fear.

I shivered. Even in June, it was impossible to believe you could ever be warm in a room like this. Or maybe my goose bumps were from all the magic, as though five hundred years' worth of spells had seeped into the stone and wood.

"They have statues," Jenna said. "In a *hallway*." Sure enough, two bronze statues of veiled women guarded the massive staircase, where even more people were now lining up. They were all wearing black uniforms, and had nearly identical smiles plastered on their faces.

"What are those people doing?" Jenna whispered to me.

"I don't know," I replied through a frozen grin, "but I'm afraid a musical number might be involved."

"This is our household staff," Dad said, sweeping his arm toward the group. "Anything you need, they'll be happy to help you with."

"Oh," I said weakly, feeling like my voice echoed in the cavernous room. "Great."

Beyond the crowd, at the top of the stairs, was a large marble arch. Dad nodded toward it and said, "Our temporary offices are through there, but we can see those later. I'm sure you'd like to see your rooms now."

I caught the edge of Dad's sleeve and pulled him away from the group. "Actually," I whispered, "I'd like to know where those other demons came from. Are they— they're not my brother and sister, are they?"

Dad's eyes widened behind his glasses. "No," he said. "Dear Lord, no. Daisy and Nick are . . . We can talk more about them at another time, but no, they're no relation to us."

"Then why are they here?"

Dad frowned and rolled his shoulders. "Because they have nowhere else to go, and this is the safest place for them."

That made sense. "Right. Because you guys could take them out if they went all super-demon."

But Dad shook his head, puzzled. "No, Sophie, I meant it's safer for *them*. Nick and Daisy have already had several attempts made on their lives."

He didn't even give me time to react before raising his hand and waving Lara over. Her heels clicked on the marble as she strode toward us. "Sophie, Lara has pre-pared some lovely rooms for you and your guest. Why don't you go get acclimatized? We can talk later."

It obviously wasn't a request, so I just shrugged and said, "Sure."

Lara led us across the foyer to a tall stone doorway housing yet another set of steps. As she led us up the dim passageway, I couldn't shake the feeling that I was walking into a tomb.

As we walked, Lara rattled off statistics that I only half listened to. They were unbelievable anyway.

Over a million cubic feet of living space. More than three hundred rooms, thirty-one of which were kitchens. Ninety-eight bathrooms. Three hundred and fifty-nine windows. Two thousand four hundred and seventy-six lightbulbs.

Jenna was shaking her head by the time we reached the fourth floor, where the three of us would be staying. Cal was shown to his room first, and Jenna burst into giggles when we peeked over his shoulder. The room could not have been less Cal. I mean, I guess the hunter-green bedding and drapes were kind of masculine, but the spindly gold-and-white furniture was definitely not. Nor was the giant ruffled canopy over his huge bed.

"Wow, Cal," I said, feeling a little bit like myself for the first time since I'd walked into this crazy house. "You will be able to have some awesome slumber parties in here. All the other girls are gonna be so jealous."

Cal shot me a half smile, and I felt some of the weirdness between us dissipate. "It's not so bad," he said. Then he flopped down on the bed, only to sink out of sight in the middle of it. As Cal drowned in a sea of fluffy coverlets and throw pillows, I couldn't help but crack up.

Lara looked offended. "That bed originally belonged to the third Duke of Cornwall."

"It's great," Cal said, his voice muffled. He gave her the thumbs-up, which only made me and Jenna laugh harder.

Frowning, Lara led us down the hall a little ways. She opened a door, and there was no doubt this room had been set up for Jenna. There were pink drapes, pink furniture, and even a deep rose-colored bedspread. The room overlooked a small, private garden. A breeze from the open window carried the scent of flowers. I had to admit, I was impressed. And a little surprised.

"It's perfect," Jenna told Lara. Her smile was bright, but her face was chalky, and I suddenly realized that Jenna hadn't fed since we'd left Hecate. Lara must have been thinking the same thing, because she crossed the room and opened a cherrywood armoire. Inside, there was a mini-fridge stacked high with blood bags.

"O-negative," Lara said, gesturing to the blood as though Jenna had just won a prize on a really gruesome game show. "I was told that's your favorite."

Jenna's eyes darkened, and she licked her lips. "It is," she said, her voice thick.

"Then we'll leave you to it," Lara said smoothly, taking my arm. "Sophie's room is just down the hall."

"Awesome," Jenna replied, but she was still staring at the blood.

"See you later," I called as we left. Jenna just shut the door and, I assumed, chowed down.

"We prepared a very special room for you," Lara said, and her voice sounded nervous. "I hope you'll like it." She opened a door a few feet away from Jenna's.

For a moment, all I could do was stand in the doorway and gape. The room wasn't just special, it was . . . amazing.

A series of three floor-to-ceiling windows looked out on another garden, this one larger than Jenna's. In the center of the garden, a fountain sprayed sparkling showers of water into the soft afternoon air. The drapes around the windows were white satin with a delicate green pattern that I thought were supposed to mimic leaves. Likewise, the wallpaper was white with long green stems of grass, like a jungle, punctuated by the occasional brightly colored flower.

The bed itself was snow white, with a pale silk canopy overhead. I had my own fainting couch, and two chairs, all covered in apple-green velvet. There were even a couple of my favorite books stacked on the nightstand, and a picture of my mom on a low bookcase by the window.

"I love it," I told Lara, and a grin practically split her face.

"I'm so glad," she said. "I wanted you to feel as welcome as possible."

"Well, you did a great job," I told her. And she had, although I thought it had less to do with me and more to do with Dad. Cal's and Jenna's rooms had been nice, but extra care had gone into mine. Maybe she just wanted to impress her boss.

Then I realized that she could be sucking up to me because *I* might be her boss one day. Suddenly, all I wanted to do was lie down. But before I could do that, I needed to talk to Mom and let her know we'd gotten here safely. "Is there a phone around here?" I asked Lara.

She pulled a cell phone out of her jacket and handed it to me. "Actually, your father wanted me to give this to you. His number is programmed in at number one, and your mother's is number two. If you need to talk to anyone at Hecate Hall, they're number three."

I stared at the phone. It had been nearly a year since I'd even seen a cell phone, much less held one. They weren't allowed at Hex Hall. I wondered if I still remembered how to text. Then Lara pointed to a gorgeous rolltop desk, and for the first time, I noticed the sleek silver laptop sitting on its surface. "Your father has also set up an e-mail address for you, so you're welcome to communicate that way as well."

Computers were also forbidden at Hecate, at least for students. Mrs. Casnoff supposedly had one in her private quarters. Jenna and I had spent one very boring Magical

Evolution class speculating on what her e-mail address might be. Jenna thought it was probably something dull, like just her name, but my personal vote (and a ten-dollar bet) was for HexyLady@hecatehall.edu. I guess now I could find out.

"I'll let you call your mother," Lara said, heading for the door, "but if you need anything else, please just let me know."

"Will do," I said, but I was distracted. I'd just noticed the door leading to my private bathroom, and from what I could see, it was about three times the size of my dorm room back at Hecate.

Once Lara had slipped from the room, I called Mom. When I told her that we were at Thorne Abbey, her voice immediately turned suspicious. "He took you *there*? Did he say why?"

"Uh, no. I'm guessing it has to do with embracing my destiny as future head of the Council and all. You know, Take Your Demon To Work Day."

Mom just sighed. "Okay. Well, I'm glad you're there, safe and sound, but please tell your father to call me as soon as he gets a chance."

I promised that I would, but as I hung up, I was suddenly overwhelmed by a wave of exhaustion. I didn't really want to deal with parental drama on top of everything else I was trying to process.

I was in England. With my dad. At some ridiculously huge house that was also serving as Council Headquarters, and home to two other demons. And on top of all that, I still couldn't shake that weird feeling, almost like a premonition, that had been with me ever since leaving Hecate Hall.

Then, of course, there was the fact that my sort-of-ex-crush might be lurking around the same country, all monster-killing.

Yeah, I was definitely gonna need a nap before dealing with any of that.

I flopped on my new bed. It may never have belonged to a duke, but it had apparently been stuffed with baby angel feathers. Kicking off my shoes, I settled into the cool sheets. Everything smelled faintly of sunshine and green grass. I figured I could nap for an hour or so before I went and talked to Dad. And maybe I could ask Lara if she had a map, or better yet, a GPS for this place. I closed my eyes, and fell asleep still wondering why the name Thorne sounded so familiar to me.

CHAPTER 6

The next thing I knew, someone was shaking me, and a shout was echoing in my ears. I had a feeling it had come from me. Disoriented, I sat up, my heart thrumming in my chest.

"Sophie?" Jenna was sitting next to me on the bed, her eyes wide.

"What happened?" I asked, my voice husky. The room was darker than it had been when I'd laid down, and for just a second, I thought I was back at Hex Hall.

"You must have been having a nightmare. You were yelling. Screaming, actually."

Well, that was embarrassing. And also weird. I never had nightmares, not even after all that had happened last semester. I searched my brain for any image or memory from the dream, but it was like my head was stuffed with cotton. All I could remember was that I had been running, that I'd been scared of . . . something. Weirdly, my throat was aching too, like I'd been crying. Other than that, all I was left with was that same feeling of dread I'd felt on the ferry, and a strange odor in my nostrils.

Smoke.

I took a deep breath, but even the sunshine smell of my sheets couldn't block the acrid stench.

I tried to smile. "I'm fine," I said. "Just a stupid dream."

Jenna looked less than convinced as she wrapped her arms around her knees. "What was it about?"

"I don't really know," I told her. "I was running, I think, and there was a fire somewhere nearby."

Jenna twirled her pink streak. "That doesn't sound too bad."

"It wasn't, but the feeling that came with it . . ." I shuddered, remembering that awful sense of loss. "It's like I was scared, obviously, but I was also sad. More than sad. Devastated." Sighing, I leaned back against the headboard. "I felt something similar when we left Hecate. Like, I had this super-strong sense that we'd never go back there. Not all three of us, at least."

One of my favorite things about Jenna is that she's pretty much unshockable. Maybe that comes with being a vampire, or maybe she was that way before she changed.

Either way, she didn't freak out about my maybe being psychic all of a sudden. She just chewed her thumbnail with a thoughtful expression before saying, "Is that a demon power? Seeing or sensing the future?"

"How the heck would I know? Alice was the only demon I've ever been around. The only thing she seemed to do that regular witches don't is suck people's blood, and that's not particularly impressive. No offense."

"None taken. Well, maybe you could ask your dad. Isn't that the point of this vacay? Learning what it means to be a demon?"

I made a noncommittal sound, and Jenna wisely dropped the subject. "Okay, so you had a dream about fire and possibly a psychic sense that we're all going to die in England."

"I feel so much better now; thanks, Jenna."

She ignored me. "Maybe it doesn't mean anything. Sometimes dreams are just dreams."

"Yeah," I agreed. "You're probably right."

"And if those are the only weird things that have happened to you lately, then why . . ." She trailed off at the expression on my face. "Those aren't the only weird things that have happened."

At that moment, all I wanted to do was slide back down and pull the covers over my head. Instead, I told Jenna about seeing Elodie.

And apparently, that was the one thing that could surprise Jenna. "She looked at you? Like, right at you?"

When I nodded, Jenna blew out a long breath, ruffling her bangs. "What did Mrs. Casnoff say?"

I fidgeted. "I, uh, haven't exactly told her yet."

"What? Soph, you have to tell her. That could mean something, and after Alice . . . Look, I get that living in the regular world for so long gave you major trust issues, but you don't need to keep any more secrets from Mrs. Casnoff. Or me."

There was that familiar stab of guilt again. Jenna and I had never really talked about it, but we both knew that if I had just told someone about seeing Alice, then Jenna might never have been accused of the attacks on Chaston and Anna. And, of course, Elodie might still be alive.

"I'll send her a letter tomorrow. Oh! Or, duh, I can call her. Lara gave me a cell phone."

Jenna perked up. "Really? What kind? Can we download music and—" She broke off and shook herself. "No. Do not try to distract me with shiny, sexy technology, Sophie Mercer. Promise," she said, squeezing my arm.

I held up my hand and did what I thought was the Girl Scout salute. Or it could have been that *Star Trek* thing. "I solemnly swear to tell Mrs. Casnoff that Elodie's ghost looked at me. And if I do not tell her, I swear to buy Jenna a pony. A *vampire* pony."

Jenna tried not to crack a smile, but no one can resist a vampire pony.

I felt about a million times better as we both started to laugh. Jenna was right. There were people I could trust now, people who deserved to know what was going on with me. My heart suddenly seemed lighter, and I decided that, Demon Central or not, Thorne Abbey was as good a place as any to turn over a new leaf, and clean the slate, and all those other clichés about starting over.

I was done with secrets.

"I hate that you had a bad dream, but I'm glad you're awake," Jenna said when we were done giggling. "I wanted to talk to you."

"About what?"

"Oh, I don't know, maybe about how your dad brought us to Council Headquarters?" Her expression softened as she added, "I could tell something freaked you out."

"Was it that obvious?"

"No, but as a vampire, I'm able to detect subtle shifts in emotional energy."

I just stared at her until she rolled her eyes and said, "Okay, you got really pale and looked like you were gonna hurl. I thought you might faint there for a second." Then her face brightened and she sat up straighter. "Oh my God, you so should have fainted, and then Cal could have caught you, and, like, carried you up the stairs." She punctuated that last bit with a little squeal and clutched my arm.

"I liked you so much more when you were sulky and angsty, Jenna."

She just kept grinning and wriggling around the bed like a four-year-old until I laughed. Shoving off my covers, I begrudgingly said, "Okay, I admit that the image of Cal carrying me up that fancy staircase is . . . nice."

Jenna gave a happy sigh. "It is, isn't it? And I don't even like dudes."

I snorted at that as I leaned down to fish under the bed for my sneakers. I knew I should probably tell Jenna about the betrothal, but I wasn't really ready to talk about it with anyone else until I worked out how I felt.

"It wasn't just the Council thing," I called up to Jenna. "Did you see those kids at the back of the welcoming committee?"

"Yeah, the black-haired girl, and the guy who looks like Archer."

I sat up too fast, hitting my head on the bed frame. "What?" I said, rubbing my scalp.

"That guy. He looked a lot like Archer. In fact, I thought that might be part of the reason you looked all vomitish."

Sitting back on my haunches, I tried to remember the

guy without the haze of "Oh, dear God, that's another demon" clouding my vision. "Yeah," I said finally. "I guess he did look like him. Similar hair. Tall. Kind of smirky." My stomach twisted a little, and I wished Jenna hadn't brought up Archer. "Anyway," I said, sliding my shoes back on, "that's not what freaked me out. He's a demon. Both of them are."

Jenna's mouth dropped open. "No way. But I thought you and your dad were the only ones in the whole world."

"So did I. Hence my puking face."

"What do you think they're doing here?"

"No idea."

We were quiet for a minute before Jenna said, "Well, they're probably lame demons anyway. I'm sure you and your dad are much better at demoning."

I grinned at her. "Jenna, how are you so awesome?"

She smiled back. "Yet another one of my special vampire powers." She pushed herself off the bed. "Now come on. I did a little exploring while you took that epic nap. You were out for like three hours. Anyway, I was scared to go too far by myself."

"You scared? You know you could probably take out anything that goes bump in the night?"

Jenna shrugged. "Yeah, but being a vampire doesn't protect you from getting lost. I really didn't feel like wandering around this spooky house for all eternity."

"Thorne Abbey isn't spooky," I said. "*Hecate* is spooky. This place is just . . . different."

"It's huge," Jenna said, her eyes wide. "Didn't you hear what Lara said? Thirty-one kitchens. Just *kitchens*, Soph."

My mouth watered at the thought of food. "I wonder which one is making dinner tonight."

Jenna and I stepped out into the hallway. There were several lamps affixed to the walls, but it was still gloomy. "It's weird to think of one family living in this house," I said.

"This wasn't even the Thorne family's primary residence," Jenna said, like she was quoting from a guidebook. "They had a mansion in London, a castle in the north of Scotland, and a hunting lodge in Yorkshire. Unfortunately, they lost most of their wealth after World War II, and in 1951, they were forced to sell all of their properties except for the Abbey. It still belongs to the Thorne family."

"Dude. How do you know all of this?"

Jenna looked a little sheepish. "I told you. You were napping for a long time and I got bored," she said. "There's this insane library downstairs, and they have a whole bunch of books about the history of the house. Some really fascinating stuff happened here. Like those big statues in the foyer? They were commissioned by Philip Thorne in 1783 after his wife committed suicide by throwing herself down the stairs."

"Gruesome," I replied, but something was bothering me. It was that name, Thorne. I knew I'd heard it somewhere before, but where? And why did I feel like it was so important?

As we walked downstairs, Jenna rattled off more history about the house. "Oh! One thing I read was really neat. In the late 1930s, Thorne Abbey was a school for girls."

A faint alarm bell began ringing in the back of my head.

"Really?"

"Yeah. During the Blitz, they had to evacuate a bunch of kids from London, including whole schools. The Thornes figured girls make the least mess, so they opened the Abbey to nine 'ladies' colleges."

And just like that, it all clicked. I knew exactly where I'd heard the name before.

CHAPTER 7

My stomach rolled. "Oh my God."

"It's not that interesting," Jenna said, but I shook my head.

"No, not that. Did the book have any pictures of those girls?"

"Yeah. I think I saw a few."

I could hear the blood rushing in my ears as I said, "Okay, I need to see that book. Now."

Jenna looped her arm through mine as we walked down one of the many hallways branching off the main foyer. "I left it sitting on the window seat in the library," she said. "I bet it's still there."

We passed countless closed doors and turned down three different halls before reaching the library. Like the rest of the house, it was gorgeous. And gigantic.

I actually froze in the doorway for a second. I wasn't sure I'd ever seen so many books in my life. Shelf after shelf stretched out before me, and twin spiral staircases curled up to the second level, where there were even more books. Low couches were scattered throughout the room, and Tiffany lamps cast soft pools of light on the hardwood floor. Large windows at the other end of the room looked out over the river and let in the last few rays of the setting sun.

The window seat was empty.

"Crap," Jenna sighed. "I swear I left it there like twenty minutes ago."

"Do you remember where you found the book?" I asked. "Maybe someone came in and reshelved it."

Jenna bit her lip. "Yeah, I think so. It was upstairs by this really weird cabinet."

I followed her as she headed to the second floor. "Weird how?"

"You'll see. Okay, I was near the back, by the painting of some dude on a horse. . . ."

I could see where Jenna would have trouble remembering which shelf was which. Downstairs, the books had lined the walls, leaving the floor open. Up here, there were roughly thirty bookcases vying for space, some of them so close together I had to turn sideways just to pass between them.

"Aha!" I heard Jenna exalt from somewhere to my left.

I found her standing on tiptoes, scanning a shelf that was indeed next to a painting of a dude on a horse. I thought he looked awfully irritated for a guy in such a spiffy ermine cape.

Jenna was wearing an equally annoyed expression. "It's not here," she said. "Maybe we should look downstairs again."

I bit back disappointment. I wasn't sure why I wanted to see the book so badly. I already knew where I'd heard Thorne before, and why it was so important.

Thorne was the last name of the woman whose spell had made Alice a demon. Who had, inadvertently I guess, made *me* a demon. There was no doubt in my mind that Alice had been one of those girls sent here during the Blitz, and that Thorne Abbey was where everything had started.

Still, I wanted to see a picture of Alice here. Before she'd been changed.

"Yeah," I told Jenna. "We can look again later. It's not that big a deal."

Jenna wasn't an idiot. She'd known me long enough to know when I was lying. But she let it go and said, "Oh, check this out."

Shoved in the corner, just under Pissy Guy on a Horse,

was a small black bookcase that only came up to my chest. It was covered in dust, and I saw immediately why Jenna had said it was weird. There was only one book on the shelf, but it was under a thick glass cube. Scratched into the glass were symbols I'd never seen before.

"Try to open it," Jenna said.

There wasn't any handle that I could see, so I curled my fingers around the edge of the glass, trying to see if it could be pried open.

I immediately jerked my hand back. "Whoa."

"I know, right? That thing is covered in some serious mojo."

Serious mojo was an understatement. My fingers were burning. The sensation was similar to what I'd felt when I'd touched Archer's chest and felt the mark of The Eye sear into my palm. "Whatever that book is, someone really didn't want anyone to look at it."

"No, they didn't."

Jenna and I both jumped and whirled around.

My dad stood behind us, a small smile on his lips. His hands were clasped behind his back. "That book is the Thorne family's grimoire. A spell book."

"I know what a grimoire is," I said irritably, but he continued like I hadn't spoken.

"It contains some of the darkest magic ever known to Prodigium. The Council locked it up years ago."

"They were witches, then? The Thornes?"

Dad ran a hand over the top of the cabinet. I flinched for him, but he didn't even seem to feel the shock of magic. "They were," he replied. "Dark witches, of course. Very powerful and very adept at concealing their true identity from humans."

"They're the ones who made Alice a demon, right?"

Jenna made a little surprised noise next to me, but Dad just studied me for a moment before saying, "Yes. And aren't you clever for putting that together so quickly?"

He sounded genuinely pleased, and a little surge of happiness went through me. Still, I said, "Jenna actually helped me figure it out. She read something about a bunch of girls being sent here during the Blitz, and I remembered Mrs. Casnoff saying that the lady who, uh, changed Alice was named Thorne. That's why we were in here, actually. I was going to see if I could find Alice's picture in one of the books Jenna was reading."

"If you want a picture of your great-grandmother during her time at Thorne, I have one. Why didn't you just come ask me in the first place?"

A sarcastic comment sprang to mind, but I immediately bit it back. He was right. Asking him would've been the logical thing to do instead of playing cloak-and-dagger in the library.

Thank God for Jenna, who looked up at my dad and

said, "Mr. Atherton, Sophie's spent the last sixteen years of her life having people lie to her about one thing or another. At Hecate, she got pretty good at finding things out on her own. Hard habit to break."

Jenna may have been a tiny blonde with a nearly pathological love for pink, but she was still a vampire, and that meant she could be pretty intimidating when she wanted to be. Right now, I kind of wanted to pick her up and hug her.

Dad looked back and forth between us. "Mrs. Casnoff said the two of you were a formidable team. I see now what she meant. Well, if there's nothing else you ladies need in the library, Sophie, would you care to accompany me on a walk about the grounds?"

I wondered if there were ever times when Dad didn't sound like he'd just escaped from a Jane Austen novel. It was weird to think of my superpractical mom falling for a guy like him. She'd never struck me as the type to go for a smooth talker. Of course, I never thought I'd fall for a pretty boy who was secretly a Prodigium-killer, so what the heck did I know?

"It's getting dark," I said to Dad.

"Oh, I think we still have plenty of light left. And the view of the house at this time of day is quite spectacular."

In the few weeks since I'd met Dad, I'd learned to read his eyes and not his tone of voice. And right now, his eyes said I was going on a walk with him whether I wanted to or not.

"Okay," I said. "Why not?"

"Excellent! You'll be fine on your own for a little while, won't you?" he asked Jenna.

She glanced at me. "Sure, Mr. Atherton," she said. "I'll, uh, just go see what Cal is doing."

"Wonderful idea," Dad replied. He held his elbow out to me. "Shall we?"

CHAPTER 8

We made our way to the front door, passing one of the servants. She was dusting a marble-top table in the hallway, but instead of using a feather duster or Pledge, she just held her hands above the surface. The dust swirled up in a tiny cloud, vanishing as it rose. Watching it was every bit as jarring as the computer and cell phone had been. At Hecate, no one was that . . . well, *casual* with magic. Mrs. Casnoff certainly wouldn't have let us use our powers to dust.

Dad and I didn't speak until we were outside. "Look," I said, "I'm really sorry I touched your magical bookcase or whatever that was. I didn't know."

Dad just took a deep breath as we walked down the gravel drive. "Lovely. Can you smell that, Sophie?"

"Um . . . smell what?"

"Lavender. Thorne Abbey has it planted in every garden on the premises. It's especially fine on evenings like this."

I took an experimental sniff. It *was* nice, and the evening was beautiful; the air wasn't too warm or too cool, and there were shadows creeping across the green lawn. I probably would have enjoyed it a lot more if I hadn't been at the Home for Wayward Demons.

We kept walking in silence. My hand rested lightly in the crook of Dad's elbow, which was equal parts nice and weird. As we walked, all I could think was, This is my *dad*. I'm hanging out with my dad, and we're acting like he hasn't been the World's Most Absentee Father for nearly seventeen years.

Dad led us over the stone bridge and up a small hill. We stopped at the top and turned to look down at the house.

Dad was right. The view was amazing. Nestled in its valley, Thorne Abbey was bathed in soft, golden light. In the distance, the forest seemed to curl around the building, protecting and sheltering it. I wanted to think it was beautiful, but looking at it, all I could think about was how different my life would have been if Alice had never come here.

"I've loved this house from the moment I set eyes on it," Dad said quietly.

"I just wish it were a little bigger," I said. "I need at least five hundred bedrooms to keep from feeling cramped, you know?"

It was a lame attempt at a joke, but Dad chuckled anyway. "I hoped you would like it. It's our birthplace, in a manner of speaking. Would you like to hear the story?"

Even though my mouth was dry and my knees were shaky, I forced myself to sound nonchalant. "Might as well."

"Members of the Thorne family were dark witches and warlocks. For hundreds of years they managed to keep their true identities secret from humans, all the while using their powers to increase the family's wealth and influence. They were ambitious and clever, but not particularly dangerous. At least not until the war."

"Which war?"

Dad looked at me, surprised. "You didn't learn about the war at Hecate?"

I thought back over all my classes last year, but I had to admit I'd spent a lot of that time thinking about other things, like Archer, and Jenna, and how girls were getting mysteriously attacked. Who could blame me if I hadn't paid that much attention in class? "We might have. I just don't remember."

"In 1935, a war broke out between L'Occhio di Dio and Prodigium. It was a particularly grim time in our history. Thousands were killed on both sides."

He paused to clean his glasses with his handkerchief. "At that time, there were only two members of the Thorne family left, Virginia and her younger brother, Henry. Virginia was apparently the one who came up with the idea of raising a demon to fight The Eye. No one had ever been able to do that before in the history of Prodigium, but Virginia decided to try. It took her years, but she finally found the ritual she was looking for in an archaic grimoire."

"I'm guessing that's the one in the locked cabinet?"

"Yes. According to Council records, she wanted to perform the ritual on herself, but the head of the Council refused to allow that. He thought it would be safer to attempt it on a regular human. Luckily for Virginia, there were hundreds of girls staying at the Abbey."

I shivered. "And she picked Alice."

"She did."

"Why? I mean, you said there were hundreds of girls here. Did she draw Alice's name out of a hat or something?"

"I honestly don't know, Sophie. I've always believed the fact that Alice was pregnant at the time had something to do with it. Perhaps she and Henry . . . Well, in any case, Virginia never told anyone, and after the ritual, Alice was in no position to say anything."

I rubbed my nose with the back of my hand and said, "In stories like this, there's usually a magical diary hidden in a trunk that gives you all the answers. Any chance of that happening here?"

"I'm afraid not. Anyway, I think you know the rest of the story. Virginia performed the ritual, but something went wrong. We'll never really know what happened that night, but the end result was that Virginia and her brother were both dead, and Alice had become a demon."

"A monster," I muttered, thinking of those silver claws sliding into Elodie's neck. I plopped down on the lawn and drew my knees up to my chin. Dad sighed and, after a long moment, sat next to me.

"You'll get grass stains on your suit."

"I have other suits. You know, that's not the first time I've heard you use that word to refer to us. May I ask why?"

I raised both eyebrows. "Seriously? You have to ask why demon means monster to me?"

"When you thought you were just a witch, did you use the word 'monster' to describe yourself?"

"Of course not."

"And yet witches, faeries, shapeshifters, demons . . . we all have the same origins."

"What do you mean?"

Dad plucked a piece of grass and began shredding it

absentmindedly. "We all started out as angels."

"I know that regular Prodigium did," I said. "They're descended from the angels who didn't pick a side in the war between God and Lucifer."

Dad met my eyes. "Well, demons are the angels who did pick a side. The wrong one, as it turned out."

"So what? Just because they used to be angels doesn't make them—us—the good guys."

"No, but it does make us a little more complex than monsters. For example, you weren't particularly disturbed to find out you were a dark witch, and their powers are remarkably similar to ours. In many ways, a demon is nothing more than a very strong dark witch."

"Or Hogaroth the Slimy," I muttered.

"What?"

"I just mean . . . when Virginia called that demon to possess Alice, did that mean Alice—like, actual, real Alice, her soul or whatever—was gone, and it was just some monster wandering around in her body?"

Dad gave a startled laugh. "Oh, God, no. Is that what you've thought this whole time?"

I crossed my arms over my chest. "Well, how was I supposed to know? It's not like anyone was in a big hurry to answer all my burning, demony questions."

He stopped laughing and actually looked a little sheepish. "You're right. I'm sorry. No, when a demon is called forth, it's really nothing more than a large dark . . . force, basically. That's what being exiled to hell does to an angel. It strips it of everything but its power. They don't have names, or personalities, or even bodies. They're nothing but pure, undiluted magic."

"Wow."

"Possession isn't even really the right word for what happens," Dad said. "It's more like a *meshing*. The demon alters everything about that person, even their blood, their DNA. That's why it can be passed down through families. That's why if we're ever grievously injured we don't die. Our powers heal us." He nodded at my scarred hand. "Unless, of course, someone uses demonglass on us. But for all that, a demon who was changed during a possession ritual is still essentially the person they always were."

"Only now they have the darkest, most powerful magic in the world literally flowing through their veins," I added.

"Exactly." Dad smiled proudly, and I suddenly remembered Alice standing in the clearing, exclaiming, "You did it!" right before I cut off her head.

My throat was tight when I said, "So if Alice was still Alice, why did she have claws and start drinking blood?"

Dad shrugged and held up his right hand. Long silver claws sprang up in place of his manicured fingernails, and then disappeared just as quickly. "Any witch or warlock could do that if they wanted to. Try it yourself."

I looked down at my ragged nails, still splotched with Iced Strawberry polish from the last time Jenna had tried to give me a manicure. "No thanks."

"As for the . . . other part, blood magic is a very strong, very ancient practice. Again, many witches and warlocks have used it in the past. Your friend Jenna certainly benefits from it. In fact, that's how vampires were created. Nearly a thousand years ago, a coven of witches were performing a very complicated blood ritual, and—"

"Alice killed people," I said, my voice breaking on the last word.

"Yes, she did," Dad said calmly. "That much dark magic can drive a person insane. That's what happened to Alice. It doesn't mean it will happen to you."

He looked at me, his expression intense. "Sophie, I understand your hesitation to embrace your heritage, but it's vital that you stop thinking of demons as monsters." He reached out and covered my hand with his. "That you stop thinking of *yourself* as a monster."

Struggling to keep my voice level, I said, "Look, I get that you're big into this whole Up With Demons thing, but I watched one kill a friend. And Mrs. Casnoff told me that your mom demoned out and killed your dad. So don't stand there and expect me to believe that being a demon is all sunshine and kittens."

"It's not," Dad said. "But if you're willing to listen to me, and to learn more about what it means to be a demon, you'd understand that the Removal is not your only option. There are ways of . . . well, fine-tuning your powers. Of lessening the chances of hurting someone."

"'Lessening'?" I repeated. "But not *removing*, right?"

Dad shook his head. "I'm going about this all the wrong way," he said, sounding frustrated. "I just want you to understand that . . . Sophie, have you given any thought to what it will be like once you've gone through the Removal? Provided you survive it, of course."

I had. It sounds dumb, but one of the first things I'd thought of was that I'd look like the Vandy: covered in swirling purple markings, even on my face. It wouldn't be an easy thing to explain away in the human world, but I was hoping "crazy spring break" might work.

When I didn't answer Dad right away, he said, "I'm not sure you understand what really happens in that ritual. It's not just that you won't be able to do magic anymore. You will be destroying a vital part of yourself. The Removal gets into your blood. It rips out something that's as much a part of you as the color of your eyes. You were *meant* to be a demon, Sophie, and your body and soul will fight to keep you that way. Possibly to the death."

There's nothing you can say to a speech like that. So I just stared at him until he finally sighed and said, "You're tired, and this was a great deal to tell you on your first night. I can understand if this is overwhelming."

"It's not that," I said, but he just kept on talking, something I was beginning to learn was an annoying habit of his.

"Hopefully, after a good night's sleep, you'll be more receptive to what I have to tell you." He glanced at his watch. "Now, if you'll excuse me, I was supposed to meet with Lara fifteen minutes ago. I trust you can find your way back to the house."

"It's right in front of me, so yeah," I muttered, but Dad was already walking down the hill.

I sat in the gathering darkness for a long time, watching Thorne Abbey, trying to absorb everything Dad had just told me. I'd been sitting there for about ten minutes before it occurred to me that I hadn't asked him anything about the demon kids and what they were doing here. Or how they even existed. Finally, I got up, dusted off my jeans, and headed back toward the house.

As I walked, I thought about what Dad had said. I'd only had my powers for a few years, but they were a part of me. For the first time, I admitted to myself that the thought of slashing the magic right out of myself—and maybe dying in the process—scared the heck out of me.

But I couldn't go through life as a ticking time bomb either, and no matter what Dad said about "fine-tuning" my magic, as long as I had powers, exploding would always be a very real possibility. Somehow, my whole existence had become a really complicated word problem.

I'd always sucked at those.

There was no sign of Dad when I got back to Thorne, and I trudged up to my room. Earlier, I'd been starving, but the conversation with Dad had killed my appetite. Despite my long nap, all I wanted to do was take a hot bath and crawl into bed.

But when I got to my room, I saw that my bed had already been made up. Had it been servants, or did they now have some sort of tidiness spell?

Then I saw the photograph propped on the pillow.

I wondered briefly if Dad had put the photo there himself as I reached down and picked it up. My hands trembled a little. It was a black-and-white shot of about fifty girls in the front garden of Thorne. Half of them were standing, while the other half sat on the ground, their skirts pulled demurely around their legs. Alice was one of the seated girls.

I studied her face for a long time. Somehow, it had been easier to think of Alice as really possessed, a soulless creature using my great-grandmother's body as a tool.

It was harder to think of Alice's soul still being in her body when I sliced through her neck with that shard of demonglass.

I traced her features. What had she been thinking the day this photograph was taken? Had she thought Thorne Abbey was overwhelming, too?

For all I knew, she'd stood in this very room more than sixty years ago. The thought sent a shiver down my spine. I wanted to ask her if she'd had any sense of the horrible thing that was about to happen to her, if she had wandered the halls of Thorne feeling the same sick feeling of dread that coiled inside me.

But Alice, frozen in 1939, smiling and human, didn't have any answers, and there was nothing in her face to suggest that she'd had any hint of what the future would hold for her.

For me.

CHAPTER 9

Dad wasn't around the next morning. I woke up early and took a marathon shower. Trust me: if you'd spent the last nine months sharing a bathroom with all manner of supernatural creatures, you'd be pretty psyched about a private shower too. Sometime the evening before, all of my bags had been unpacked, and my clothes were neatly folded in the painted dresser. Remembering how nicely everyone at Thorne had been dressed yesterday, I briefly considered digging out the one dress I'd brought. In the end, I settled on another pair of jeans and a cranberry-colored T-shirt, although I did wear a nice pair of sandals instead of my ratty tennis shoes.

I stopped by Jenna's room before heading downstairs, but she wasn't there. Cal's door was closed, and I thought about knocking on it before reminding myself that it was kind of early, and he was probably asleep. For just a second, the image of a sleepy, shirtless Cal opening his bedroom door popped into my head, and my face flushed as red as my T-shirt.

I was still kind of flustered when I practically ran into Lara Casnoff in the main hallway. She was wearing another dark suit and was somehow holding on to a sheaf of papers, a cell phone, and a steaming mug of coffee that smelled so good my mouth started watering. "Oh, Sophie, you're awake," she said with a bright smile. "Here"—she handed me the coffee—"I was just bringing this up to you."

"Oh, wow, that's really nice of you," I replied, mentally adding Lara to my list of People Who Are Awesome. At Hex Hall, we were practically blasted out of bed in the morning by an alarm that was somewhere between a foghorn and the baying of hell hounds. People bringing you coffee in bed was a way nicer way to wake up.

"Also, your father wanted me to tell you that he's been called away on business today, but he should be back later this evening."

"Oh. Um . . . okay, thanks."

"He hated to miss your first day," she said, frowning slightly.

I couldn't hold back a sarcastic laugh. "Well, Dad's missed a lot of my first days, so I'm pretty used to it."

I think Lara was going to rush in to defend Dad, but before she could, I asked, "So in which of the nine thousand kitchens could I maybe find some cereal? I skipped dinner last night."

Immediately, Lara was all business again. "Oh, of course. Breakfast is being served in the east dining room."

She gave me directions that included three right turns, another flight of stairs, and a "conservatory," whatever *that* was. When I stared at her blankly, she waved her hand and said, "I'll just show you myself."

"Thanks," I said, trailing behind her. "Maybe by the end of the summer I'll actually get the layout of this place down."

Lara laughed. "I've been coming to Thorne Abbey for decades, and I still get turned around."

"Wow," I said as we proceeded down a long hallway lined with pictures. I did a double take as I passed them. There were portraits of werewolves in eighteenth-century costumes, their silvery fur poking out from underneath knee breeches, and one image showed a family of witches from what looked like the 1600s—lots of lacy ruffs around their necks—all of them levitating underneath a tree, silvery sparks of magic dancing around them.

Then what Lara had said sunk in. "Decades? So you've known my dad since you were kids?"

She nodded. "Indeed. Your grandmother gifted

Thorne Abbey to the Council before . . . before she passed away. Anastasia and I spent many summers here with our father." She paused and gave me a fleeting smile. "Something we have in common, Sophie. My father was also head of the Council."

"Wait, what?"

"Alexei Casnoff. You've never heard of him?"

All I could do was shake my head, so Lara continued. "Casnoffs ruled the Council for nearly two hundred years. However, my father made the decision very early on to pass his title to your father, due to his powers."

I took that in. "But the title is hereditary. So if your dad hadn't done that, you would have been the head?"

She gave an elegant shrug, like it was a subject that didn't even warrant discussion. "Anastasia, actually. She's the eldest. But we both agreed with Father's decision, and Anastasia felt she could be of the most use at Hecate anyway." She smiled at me and squeezed my arm a little. "Neither of us have ever regretted it. James has done an excellent job as the head, and I'm sure you'll do just as well."

I tried to smile back at her, but I think it came across more as a grimace.

"So . . . if you and Mrs. Casnoff are sisters, and your dad was a Casnoff, why is she a Mrs.?" I asked. "Makes it sound like she married into the family."

"Anastasia was married," Lara said, gesturing for me to walk down another corridor. "But we've always kept the name Casnoff. Her husband even took it."

I want to know more about that, but by then we'd reached the dining room. I followed Lara inside.

I wondered if there were any rooms in all of Thorne Abbey that wouldn't leave me gawking in wonder at the doorway. The east dining room was probably three times the size of the dining hall at Hecate. Like every other room I'd seen at Thorne, there didn't seem to be a square inch of wall that wasn't covered in paintings or gilt. Even the chairs were upholstered in gold brocade.

A long table that could have seated whole armies dominated the room, so I guessed this is where most meals at Thorne were served. But Cal was the only person there now. He glanced up as we came in and gave a tiny nod. "Morning."

Lara practically beamed at him. "Mr. Callahan! So nice to see you this morning. How are you enjoying Thorne Abbey?"

Cal took a long sip of orange juice before replying. "It's great."

I don't think it was possible for Cal to sound less enthusiastic, but either Lara didn't pick up on it, or she didn't care, because she sounded awfully perky as she said, "Well, I'm sure the two of you are welcoming the chance to spend some time together."

Cal and I both stared at her. I tried to will her to stop talking, but apparently that power wasn't in my repertoire. Lara flashed us a conspiratorial grin. "Nothing makes me happier than seeing an arrangement that's a real love match."

All the awkwardness that had vanished between me and Cal yesterday seemed to swoop back into the room with an audible *whoosh*.

I dared a quick look in his direction, but Cal, as usual, was doing his whole Stoic Man thing. His expression didn't even waver. But then I noticed his hand tightening around his glass.

"Cal and I aren't . . . we don't . . . there's not any, um, love," I finally said. "We're friends."

Lara frowned, confused. "Oh. I'm sorry." She turned to Cal, eyebrows raised. "I just assumed that was the reason you turned down the position with the Council."

Cal shook his head, and I think he was about to say something, but I beat him to it. "What position with the Council?"

"It was nothing," he said.

Lara gave a delicate snort before saying to me, "After his term at Hecate ended, Mr. Callahan was offered a position as the Council's chief bodyguard. Correct me if I'm wrong, but didn't you initially accept the assignment?" she asked Cal.

It was the closest I'd ever seen Cal to angry. Of course, on him, that meant that his brow furrowed a little. "I did, but—" he started to say.

"But then you heard Sophie was coming to Hecate, and you decided to stay," Lara finished, and her lips twisted in the triumphant smile I'd seen on Mrs. Casnoff's face dozens of times. I stood there, frozen in place, as she turned back to me and said, "Mr. Callahan gave up a chance to travel the world with the Council so that he could be little more than a janitor on Graymalkin Island. For you."

CHAPTER 10

After that, I didn't hear much more of what Lara said. I know she mentioned something about a meeting and being late, and then suddenly she was gone, leaving me and Cal alone.

Cal turned his attention back to his plate, so I crossed the room to the buffet. There were dozens of silver trays steaming with eggs, fried potatoes, bacon, and a whole bunch of other foods I wasn't sure I could name. My heart was jumping around nervously, but I tried not to let it show as I filled my plate.

Then it occurred to me that I had no idea where to sit. The table could easily fit over a hundred people, so I didn't want to sit right next to him, obviously. But it would also look weird if I picked one of the seats far down the table. I finally just sat across from him, and for a while, Cal and I sat in silence, munching on our respective breakfasts. The sound of our forks scraping across the plates echoed in the cavernous room.

Cal shifted in his chair, and I thought he was about to leave without saying anything. Then, quietly, he said, "I didn't stay just for you."

I kept my eyes down. "Right. Of course you didn't. Duh."

His foot nudged mine under the table, and I finally looked up at him. He was leaning forward, his face intense. "I mean it. I like Graymalkin. I like being close to the ocean and working outside. Working for the Council would've meant . . ." He sighed, lifting his eyes to the ceiling. "Offices and planes. And wearing a tie. It wasn't for me."

"Cal, it's fine," I insisted, even as my cheeks burned. "I didn't actually think you were hanging out at Hex Hall because of your burning love for me. But that's what I'm telling all the girls back at school," I said, stabbing a forkful of eggs. "I'm thinking 'heartbreaker' might be a nice addition to my 'avenging witch' reputation."

He looked like he was going to say something else, so I hurried on, even though it meant talking around a mouthful of food. "So, what do you think of Thorne Abbey?"

Cal blinked at the subject change, but then said, "This place freaks me out."

"Me too," I said. "Which is weird, seeing as how Hex Hall is technically a million times creepier."

Cal shrugged. "Yeah, but it's home."

"For you, maybe. Have you *really* never left since you were thirteen?"

"Never. Not even to go to the mainland."

I shook my head and broke off a piece of my toast, slathering it with orange marmalade. "That's insane. Why?"

He put down his fork, his eyes on a spot somewhere over my shoulder. "I don't know. As soon as I set foot on that island, I never wanted to leave it. Like I said, it's home. Haven't you ever felt that way about a place?"

I thought about all the houses Mom and I had lived in over the years. Some of them had been nice, but none of them had ever felt permanent. I'd always known better than to get too attached to a place. All the word "home" conjured up for me was Mom and the vague impression of suitcases. "No. One of the benefits of being a nomad. You never feel homesick."

Cal studied me in that quiet, intense way of his before saying, "How did it go with your dad last night?"

I sighed. "Not great. Apparently I should be way more psyched about being a demon. And of course he's dead set against my going through the Removal."

"Huh," was his only reply, but Cal could put a world of meaning behind one syllable.

"Let me guess. You're joining the legions of people who think it's a bad idea for me to go through the Removal."

To my surprise, I saw that angry look cross Cal's face again. "You say it like everyone is against the idea just to be jerks. But Mrs. Casnoff, your parents, me . . . can you blame any of us for not wanting you to *die*?"

Something shifted in the air, and suddenly I felt like I was on very shaky ground. "Can you blame *me* for not wanting to be a demon? Alice killed people, Cal. So did her daughter, Lucy. She killed her own *husband*."

He didn't react to that, so I added—with way too much venom even for me—"Bet you didn't know that when you agreed to be 'betrothed' to me, huh? Husband-eviscerating apparently runs in my family."

Still no reaction, and I felt shame curl in my belly. "Of course, you also didn't know you were getting a demon bride," I added in a softer tone. Very few people knew what my dad really was. I'd always assumed Cal had found out the same night I did.

That's why I was really surprised when he raised his head and said, "I knew."

"What?"

"I knew what you were then, Sophie. Your dad told

me before the betrothal. And he told me about your grandmother, and what happened to your grandfather."

I shook my head. "Then, why?"

Cal took his time before answering. "For one thing, I like your dad. He's done good things for Prodigium. And it—" He broke off with a long exhale. "It felt like some kind of honor, you know? Being asked to be the head of the Council's son-in-law. Plus, your dad, he, uh, told me a lot about you."

My voice was barely above a whisper. "What did he say?"

"That you were smart, and strong. Funny. That you had trouble using your powers, but you were always trying to use them to help people." He shrugged. "I thought we'd be a good match."

The vast dining room suddenly felt very small, like it consisted only of this table and me and Cal. "Look, Sophie," he started to say.

But before he could finish, Jenna walked in. "I am so glad I still get to eat human food, because that bacon smells *insane* . . ." she said, and then froze. "Oh!" she exclaimed, her earlier bounciness draining out of her. "Sorry! I didn't mean to interrupt . . . whatever. I c-can . . . leave?" She gestured with her thumb over her shoulder. "And then come back, uh, later?"

But the moment was broken. Cal sat back, and I

pushed my hair behind my ears. "No, it's fine," I said quickly, concentrating harder on my eggs than I had on my SAT. "We seem to be the only people up yet."

"Everyone's awake. They're just quiet," a voice said from the doorway.

I looked up and tried very hard not to choke on my food. It was the demon girl. Her black bob was messy and she was still wearing pajamas—cute ones, too, made of dark blue silk and covered in little silver moons and stars. She was watching me with an expression I couldn't read.

She moved into the room with an easy grace, but her shoulders were up, and she kept her head tilted so that her profile was hidden by her hair. She took a piece of toast and an orange before coming to sit next to me. Her power set my teeth on edge, but I made myself smile.

"Hi. I'm Sophie."

She plucked at the orange's peel. "Yes, I know," she said, her accent every bit as crisp as Dad's. "And you're Cal, and you're Jenna. I'm Daisy."

They murmured hello, then Jenna shot me a look and mouthed, "Daisy?" I knew what she meant. With her jet-black hair and translucent skin, this girl looked a lot more like a Lilith or a Lenore than a Daisy.

We all sat in silence while Kristopher, Roderick, and

Elizabeth came in. I was kind of surprised to see the other three Council members. I figured they'd already be at work, like Lara.

Once everyone was seated, Kristopher looked down the table. "I'm glad to see you and Daisy getting to know one another, Sophia." His bright blue eyes practically gleamed. Like Lara, he seemed way too enthusiastic for so early in the morning.

"Yeah, maybe later we can all sing a demon version of 'Kumbaya,'" I said. As far as jokes went, it wasn't exactly stellar, but the three Council members laughed like it was the funniest thing they'd ever heard.

"Daisy, didn't we tell you Sophie had a wonderful sense of humor?" Roderick, the tall faerie said, his wings fluttering.

But before she could reply, the demon guy walked into the dining room. Jenna was right: he did look a little like Archer. He wasn't quite as handsome, and when he glanced my way, I saw that his eyes were blue instead of brown, but there was definitely a resemblance.

"Good morning, Nick," Kristopher said, patting his mouth with a napkin. "I trust your new room was to your liking?"

Nick headed over to the buffet, flashing a wink at Daisy, whose lips curved in response. "Very much so, Kris. Thanks for that," he said before helping himself to breakfast. Unlike Daisy, he was American. He sat down on Daisy's other side and leaned across her to say to me, "Got tired of the view in my old room. I mean, how many times can you look at a pond, right? Kris here was nice enough to hook me up with digs overlooking one of the gardens." He grinned as he broke open a muffin. "Guess it'll do for now."

Kristopher smiled again, but it was strained. "We strive to keep our guests happy," he said.

"What about you, Daisy?" Elizabeth, the grand-motherly werewolf asked, reaching out to pat Daisy's hand. "Are your rooms still all right, dear?"

"They're fine, thank you," she said softly, and I could've sworn Elizabeth sighed with relief.

"So, Sophie," Nick said. "I'm guessing you've worked out that Daisy and I are your siblings in demonhood?"

"Right," I said, straining for nonchalant. I cleared my throat and asked, "So were you guys born demons, like me, or made?"

Elizabeth answered for them, her voice warm and sympathetic. "They don't remember, poor things. When we found the two of them, they were both in mental institutions. They didn't even have names."

"Yes, and we're ever so thankful for the rescue, Liz," Nick said, slurring his words slightly. I looked closer at him. His eyes were kind of red, but not in the demon way; in the drunk way. Holy crap, who started drinking first thing in the morning? And *why*?

"So," Nick said to me, "how do you like Thorne?"

"Love it," I replied, but I sounded unconvincing, even to myself.

"Well, it's gotta be better than that dump you guys call a school," Nick said with a snort.

Cal's expression turned positively stormy at that, so I rushed in to say, "Hecate's not that bad. It just has, uh, character."

"Didn't L'Occhio di Dio raid Hecate last year?" Daisy asked, reaching across me for the marmalade. That's when I noticed the jagged, purplish scar running along her inner arm. It looked a lot like the scar on my hand. I remembered what Dad had said about both Daisy and Nick nearly being murdered, and tried not to stare.

"No, it wasn't a raid. There was a warlock there. Archer Cross." It was the first time I'd said his name out loud in a long time. "He was working for The Eye. But he didn't hurt anyone."

Everyone fell silent, and I really hoped that that was the end of this particular conversation. Then Nick said, "I heard he tried to cut your heart out in a cellar."

If everyone hadn't been hanging on my every word, they certainly were now. "That's not true," I said evenly. I could feel Cal's gaze on me, but I kept my eyes on

Nick. "We fought, but he never pulled a knife on me."

"You fought?" Roderick asked. "With your hands?"

"Um, yeah," I replied, confused. "I think I might have kicked him somewhere in there, too, but—"

"What Roderick means is why didn't you use your powers?" Kristopher said, folding his arms on the table. "You are a demon. You could have vaporized him if you'd wanted to."

My mouth went very dry and I stammered a little as I said, "I-I wouldn't have any idea how to do something like that."

"Well, if you ever learn, I don't think I want to be your roommate anymore," Jenna chimed in. But if she'd thought joking was going to change the subject, she was wrong.

Nick leaned forward, his eyes practically burning. "Or maybe the rumor is true. Maybe you didn't kill him because you're in love with him."

CHAPTER 11

My heartbeat pounded in my ears. I quickly put my fork down so that no one would see that my hands were shaking. But I met Nick's gaze across the table and said, "No. I'm not. But we were friends. He had a girlfriend, Elodie Parris. She was one of the girls killed by a demon at Hecate."

My words hung in the air for a minute while Nick and I stared each other down. He broke first. "Okay, well good, then," he said, his voice jovial. "Glad we got that cleared up. Just wanted to be sure your boyfriend wouldn't be dropping by with any of his buddies." He smiled at me, and it was easily one of the scariest things I'd ever seen.

Roderick cleared his throat. "Nick, please remember your manners," he said. "Sophie is our guest."

"I'm just making conversation, Rod," Nick said. "After all, involvement with The Eye is something me and Sophie have in common."

"What do you mean?" I asked.

"Oh, just that they tried to kill me too." He leaned back in his chair and tugged his shirt up, revealing a vicious purple scar that snaked from his waistband to just below his sternum.

Everyone at the table was deathly silent, and next to me, Daisy shuddered.

"I was fifteen when they found me. Living in a foster home in Georgia, not knowing why I could make things happen with my mind. Not knowing much of anything, for that matter."

"Nick doesn't remember anything before he was thirteen," Daisy interjected, her voice so quiet I could barely hear her.

Nick nodded. "I was homeless for a while, but then the great state of Georgia took me in. Shuffled me off to the Hendricksons' house." He snorted. "Which ended up really sucking for the Hendricksons. The Eye killed all four of them while they were trying to kill me."

"How did you get away?" Jenna asked. Her shoulders were tense, and I know she was remembering her own escape from The Eye.

Nick shot another look at me. "Used my powers.

Figured that made more sense than attempting hand-to-hand, you know?" Something crackled against my skin like electricity, and Daisy's hair ruffled. There was a distant look on Nick's face as he continued. "One of the guys caught me as I was trying to get out a window. He had this black knife." The china on the table began to rattle, and I saw Kristopher and Elizabeth shoot each other worried looks. "I didn't know what demon-glass was then," Nick said, "but I knew it hurt like a mother—"

Suddenly, Lara reappeared in the doorway. "Nick," she said, her tone just a little too sharp. "Perhaps that story can wait for a more appropriate time. If you're finished with breakfast, why don't you and Daisy go practice the exercises Mr. Atherton taught you?"

Just like that, the surge of power evaporated, and I let out the breath I hadn't known I was holding.

"Sure thing, Lara," Nick said, smiling that creepy smile again. He rose from the table, and Daisy followed suit. "Oh yeah," he added. "Meant to ask if Daisy and I can take Sophie and her friends out tonight."

I started at that. After what I'd just seen, the last thing I wanted to do was go anywhere with these two.

"Out where?" Lara asked.

"Just to the village. Isn't she here this summer to spend more time with her own kind?"

Lara hesitated, and Nick went in for the kill. "James asked me specifically to take Sophie under my wing, Lara," he said, laying a hand on my shoulder. It took everything I had not to throw it off.

Still not totally convinced, Lara said, "I'll talk to James this afternoon and see what he thinks. Now go on."

Nick gave my shoulder a squeeze before he and Daisy headed out of the room. Cal, Jenna, and I sat in silence, staring at each other. At least now I knew how Elodie, Chaston, and Anna had pulled off that three-way glance thing. Finally, the other Council members and various underlings trickled out of the room until it was just the three of us.

It was Jenna who spoke first. "So that was creepy as all get-out."

I shivered. "No lie. Captain Mood Swing totally gives demons a bad name, which is quite an accomplishment."

But Jenna shook her head. "It wasn't him. Well, I mean, it was him, but not *just* him. It was the Council members. Did you see how weird they were with Nick and Daisy? Nick looked like he was seconds from blowing us all away, and no one said anything. And that stuff about changing his room?"

"Makes sense that they're scared of him," I said. "I'm a demon and *I'm* scared of him."

"How can those two be demons?" Cal asked, leaning

back in his chair. "I thought that ritual had been destroyed after Alice."

"Apparently not," I said. "But it's not so much the *how* that bugs me as the *why*. I mean, it's not like demon raising went so well for them the last time they tried it."

I got up from the table, carrying my plate to the buffet. The others had used magic to dispose of their dishes.

"If your dad says it's okay, do you want to go out with them tonight?" Jenna asked, rising to stand beside me.

"Not really. But I still think we should. Might give us a good chance to learn more about what's going on here."

Jenna bumped her hip against mine. Or at least she tried to. She's so short that it was more like her hip against my thigh. "I love when you think all deviously, Soph."

Cal smiled at us, and my face flushed. Seriously, what was going on with me?

Jenna looked back and forth between us. "Oh! I just remembered, I need to, uh, unpack some more stuff, so I'm . . . gonna go do that. Come find me in a little while, and we can do some more exploring." By which of course she meant, *Come find me when you're done talking to and/or making out with Cal, then tell me everything.* Jenna may have been a vampire, but she was still a girl.

But as soon as she left the room, Cal rose to his feet. "I promised your dad I'd check out one of the gardens this morning." He wiggled his fingers, and little silver sparks flew between them.

"Right," I said, relieved. "Go work your plant mojo, and we can, uh, talk or whatever later."

"Sounds like a plan." His voice was low, and I felt a shiver race up my spine. I think he could tell, because he kind of laughed before saying, "I'll see you later, Sophie."

Once he was gone, the room felt bigger again, and I sagged back against the buffet.

Lara stuck her head in the door. "Sophie? Everything okay?"

"Yeah, fine. Just, you know . . ." I waved my hand. "Adjusting."

"It is a lot to take in, I know," she replied, her voice sympathetic. "When your father—"

I didn't want to hear anything about Dad, so I cut her off, even though I felt bad doing it. "It's fine. I've had lots of experience dealing with new places."

And, I thought, I'm already doing better than I had my first day at Hex Hall. No one's slobbered on me, I haven't developed an inappropriate crush, and I haven't made any enemies yet. Well, there's Nick, but he's nothing compared to Elodie—

Suddenly I remembered my promise to Jenna to tell

Mrs. Casnoff about Elodie. I really didn't want to have to find a vampire pony. I *could* use the cell phone Lara had given me to call Hecate, but no one could put you on the spot like Mrs. Casnoff, and I knew she'd have a bajillion questions. From me, there would be stuttering and lots of "ums," and "I don't knows," and I wasn't in the mood to deal with it. Then I remembered the sweet, shiny laptop in my room. "Lara, do you know Mrs. Casnoff's e-mail address?"

"Certainly. It's ACasnoff at Hecate dot edu."

Great. I may not have to give Jenna a vampire pony, but now I *would* have to give her ten bucks.

Fifteen minutes later, I was sitting in front of my computer, typing out an e-mail to Mrs. Casnoff. I tried to make it sound as casual as possible, and I used the phrase "it's no big deal" twice. Still, I hesitated before sending it. What if Elodie acknowledging me actually *was* a big deal? I wasn't sure I could handle much more weirdness. Besides, that feeling was back, and when I took a deep breath, trying to make it go away, I caught the faint whiff of smoke.

But I'd promised Jenna.

So I sent it.

CHAPTER 12

I spent the rest of the day exploring Thorne Abbey with Jenna, and even though we spent hours wandering through its rooms, we didn't come anywhere close to seeing it all. Every room was filled with bizarre, dusty treasures, including one bedroom that contained five complete suits of armor, and another that held nothing but taxidermied animals. I told Jenna about e-mailing Mrs. Casnoff—and paid up my ten bucks—and that seemed to make her happy.

At lunch, Lara brought us sandwiches in the conservatory—which, it turned out, was a large sunlit room that housed the biggest piano I'd ever seen, as well as about a thousand ferns—and told us that she'd talked to Dad. He would be home later that evening, and we had his permission to go to the village with Nick and Daisy.

"But," Lara added, "you're to be home by midnight, and you're only to go to the village. Anything farther afield is absolutely forbidden."

Yeah, that sounded like something Dad would say. "How much 'farther afield' could we go?" I asked Jenna once Lara had gone. "We're in the middle of nowhere."

I found out that night. We were supposed to meet Nick and Daisy by the back entrance (wherever that was) at eight. At 7:45, I was in the bathroom putting on some mascara when Jenna slipped in wearing an outfit that I can only describe as Hello Kitty Goes Goth.

"Isn't that a bit much for strolling through the village?" I asked, eyeing her hot pink go-go boots.

She shut the door and hoisted herself up on the counter. "We're not going to the village," she replied. "I asked Daisy. They're taking us to London."

I nearly poked my eye out with the mascara wand. "London is like three hours away. Are we going to steal a car or something?"

Jenna shook her head. "Sophie, when are you going to start remembering that we have magical powers? We're not driving, we're . . . well, I don't know how we're getting there, exactly, but it'll be, you know." She waved her hands in the air. "Maaaaaagic."

"Great," I muttered, fishing in my makeup bag for some lip gloss. My stomach lurched nervously. If Daisy expected me to perform some sort of awesome demon traveling spell . . . yeah, that wasn't happening. "Why exactly are we going to London?"

Jenna grinned. "There's this club that's just for Prodigium. Daisy says it's pretty awesome."

Ugh. A club for Prodigium? That conjured up images of way more velvet and dry ice and angst than I was up for.

"I don't know," I said. "That sounds awfully 'afield' to me."

"Yeah, but if we wanna find out more about Daisy and Nick . . ."

"I know. It's so obnoxious when you're right about stuff. Still, there's no way Cal is going to be cool with this," I said, hoping that might put an end to the whole thing.

Jenna looked confused. "Cal's not coming."

"What? Why not?"

She shrugged. "He got caught up in dealing with some sort of botanical emergency. Apparently there were a lot more sick plants here than he thought."

"Huh," I said, turning back to the mirror.

"Why, Sophia Mercer! Is that disappointment I detect with my super-special vampire powers?"

"No, I just . . . I just wish he'd come to tell me himself."

"Uh-huh," Jenna said with way too much smugness. "And you wore that low-cut shirt and those high-heeled boots for my benefit, right?"

I tossed a compact at her. "No one likes a nosy vampire, Jenna."

Nick and Daisy were waiting for us by the back door once we finally made it downstairs. Nick shot me a surly glance, but didn't say anything.

"I take it Jenna filled you in on our plans for this evening?" Daisy asked me in a low voice. Her gray eyes were lined with kohl and practically glittering.

"Yeah," I said, trying to feign some excitement. "Can't wait!" There was nothing I wanted less than to hang out with a bunch of Prodigium and two demons, one of whom was obviously unstable.

"You know if you narc on us to your dad, he'll probably kick us out," Nick said, opening the door.

"Wow, I sure would hate that after you've been so friendly and welcoming to me," I replied brightly.

"She's right," Daisy admonished, pulling on Nick's sleeve. "Be nice."

He studied me with those unnerving blue eyes.

"I'll try," Nick said finally.

We stepped out into the damp night. Just outside the door, a gravel path led to a long row of shoulder-high hedges. It disappeared into the darkness near the edge of the forest that surrounded the back of Thorne Abbey.

We followed the path as it wound its way toward the woods. Jenna clutched my arm, our shadows stretching out before us in the moonlight.

Up ahead, Daisy lit a cigarette, and I could see its tip glowing bright red. Nick walked next to her, hands in his pockets, and I could hear the two of them talking, his voice low and clipped. I was pretty sure I heard my name.

"They're not so bad," Jenna whispered. "And it's like they don't even care that I'm a vampire. Apparently they've met lots of them at this place where we're going tonight, Shelley's."

"Shelley's?"

"Yeah, you know. As in Mary. Frankenstein, monsters . . ."

"Cute."

We reached the edge of the forest, and I saw that the gravel path continued through the trees, although it was a lot narrower. My heels sank into the damp ground, and soon Daisy, Nick, and Jenna were pretty far ahead of me. I shoved my hands deep into my pockets, wondering if I was ever going to be able to walk through a forest at night without thinking of Alice, and all of the time Elodie and I had spent learning spells.

The path came to an end just in front of a large stone building. Nick was nowhere in sight, but Daisy was standing in the doorway. "Come on," she said, waving us forward before disappearing inside.

We followed her. Even though the night was warm, the stone structure felt damp and gloomy. The musty scent of age and disuse hung in the air. I heard a flutter of wings and looked up to see a large dark bird fly out of a giant hole in the roof. "What is this place?" I asked.

"It used to be a corn mill for the estate," Daisy replied. She pointed toward the destroyed roof. "A tree fell on it during a storm about sixty years ago."

"So why not tear it down?" Jenna asked.

Even in the dim light, I could make out Daisy's incredulous look. "Because," she said, "it houses an Itineris."

"That's not some kind of hideous Latin monster, is it?" I asked, trying to raise an eyebrow.

Daisy laughed as she picked her way over fallen beams to lead us deeper into the mill. "It *is* Latin, but it means journey, or road."

I stumbled over a pile of broken stone. "Well, that sounds equal parts fun and terrifying," I muttered, but Daisy was already too far ahead to hear me.

Nick stood at the back wall. There was a tall opening, probably about eight feet high. It looked like a doorway. Inside, all I could see was darkness.

"Oh, man, I really hope we're not crawling all the way to London," I said, but as I got closer, I could see that it wasn't the opening of a tunnel like I'd originally thought. The doorway led to a shallow alcove, no more than three feet deep.

Daisy smiled shyly at me. "I take it you've never traveled by Itineris."

"I'm not even sure I could spell it."

To my surprise, Nick graced me with a tiny smile, one that actually looked genuine and not unhinged. Then he walked into the opening. There was no flash of light or surge of magic. One minute he was there, the next he wasn't. Somehow, that was so much scarier than if there'd been a big light show, or maybe some smoke. Daisy went next. It was the same way with her, like she just blinked out of existence.

Jenna and I stood there, staring at the passageway. "We could go back," I suggested weakly. "Tell them their magical road thingie didn't work for us."

But Jenna shook her head. "It can't be that bad," she muttered.

"We could try to go together," I said. "I think we'd both fit, and that way, if we end up transported to another dimension or morphed into a wall, at least we'd have company."

Jenna laughed. "All right, then. Let's do this."

Hand in hand, we walked toward the opening.

CHAPTER 13

The second we stepped into the alcove, I felt Jenna's hand slip from mine. Then everything went dark, and I cried out as a vicious pounding started in my temple. It felt like a migraine, only about a hundred times more intense. Dimly, some part of my brain registered that I should stop being surprised when magic stuff sucked way harder than I thought it was going to. God knows I ought to be used to it by now.

But I wasn't prepared for the awful twisting in my skull, or the overwhelming darkness. There wasn't even the sensation of flying, another thing I'd kind of expected from magical travel. Instead, everything was very still as the blackness pressed down on me.

And then I was standing outside. Well, kneeling outside, actually, taking big gasping breaths while someone patted my back.

It was Daisy. "The first time is always the worst," she said soothingly.

"Yeah, Daisy puked all over my shoes after her first 'road trip.'" Nick laughed, earning him a swat from Daisy.

"That's because you took me too far, you tosser! *Spain*. Idiotic. Anything more than a hundred miles is insane for a first trip."

Jenna staggered to my side. She looked paler than normal, which was saying something. "I had no idea maaaaaagic would be that intense," she tried to joke, but her voice was high and slightly breathless.

I tried to ask her if she was okay, but talking was still beyond me, so I tried to smile. That hurt too, so in the end, I just slumped against the nearest wall until the pain eased a little.

As the headache subsided, I took in my surroundings. We were in an alley, surrounded by several nondescript brick buildings. Overhead, low-hanging clouds reflected the orange glow of streetlights. There was also a strange smell in the air, a mix of exhaust fumes, old stone, and, I thought, water somewhere nearby.

When I felt like I could speak again, I asked Daisy, "So what exactly was that? A portal or something?"

She fished in her purse and pulled out another ciga-rette. "Basically. But portals can only go from one specific place to another specific place. An Itineris can go . . .

well, anywhere. You just create the entrance and then tell it where you want to go. That's why Nick went first, so he could tell it we were going to Shelley's."

"If it only goes one way, how are we getting back?" I asked.

"There's another road opening about a block from here," Daisy said, pointing to her left.

"So, wait, we could go in that opening and tell it *anywhere* we wanted to go?" Jenna asked.

"Anywhere," Nick answered with a shrug. "But like Daisy said, the farther you go, the harder it is. So while I could get in there and say I wanted to go to, like, Madagascar, the trip would probably kill me."

Next to me, Jenna shuddered. "I can't imagine being in that thing for any longer than we were."

"Itineris travel can be especially tough on vamps," Nick replied.

Then maybe you should have told her that before you dragged us on this little outing, jackass, I thought irritably.

Suddenly I wished Cal were here, and not just because he could have cured my headache in about two seconds.

"They can only be created by very powerful witches," Daisy continued while I tried to keep my skull from exploding. She flicked open her lighter, her face briefly illuminated in the glow. "Or demons, obviously."

"So who made the one at Thorne?" Jenna asked.

Nick answered her. "We don't know." He grinned. "But since it's so kickass, I'm gonna say it was a demon."

I wondered if Alice had made it, but before I could ask any more questions, Daisy broke in. "Okay, as fascinating as this conversation is, we only have a few hours, and I'd like to spend them in Shelley's, not in an alley. Can we go inside now, please?" I did my best not to gape at her, but seriously. What had happened to the introverted, delicate girl from this morning?

We trailed out of the alley and around to the front of the building. From the outside it looked like a regular, if kind of seedy, nightclub. There was a small awning over the entrance that read SHELLEY'S in white cursive, and people had scratched their initials and insults on the black door.

I looked around for a scary monster bouncer, but there was no one. There wasn't even one of those cool panels that slides open so you can whisper a password. Then I realized the door was wavering slightly.

Daisy saw me studying it, and smiled. "It's glamoured," she said. "Only Prodigium can find it. To humans, it just looks like a particularly drunk and fragrant homeless guy leaning against the wall."

Well, that was lovely. But she was right. If I squinted just right, I could make out a ghostly figure slumping where the door was.

Then Daisy stepped in front of me, and the door was just a door again. Daisy knocked and it swung open almost immediately. I was assaulted by the smell of smoke and a nearly deafening wave of techno. The light pouring from the entrance was blue and pulsed slightly.

I'd only gone to a club once, back in ninth grade. That had been when Mom and I were living in Chicago, and I'd had a brief flirtation with rebelliousness. I'd gone to some gross black hole of a room with a girl named Cindy Lewis, who'd worn way too much eyeliner and smoked clove cigarettes. My main memories of that night included music that was so loud I was sure I'd done some permanent damage to my eardrums, and some guy who smelled like a brewery grabbing my leg and attempting to slobber all over my face. So yeah, clubs were not exactly my favorite places.

But then, Shelley's was nothing like that smoky pit in Chicago.

Okay, so there was smoke. And really, really loud music. But other than that, the two places could not have been more different. For one thing, the interior of Shelley's was huge, much bigger than it had appeared from the outside. There were two levels, the bottom one made up almost entirely of a glossy black dance floor. It was crowded with bodies, and the magic coming off of them was so strong that my skin crawled. I saw lots of Prodigium our age, but there were just as many older people here too. In fact, there was an ancient bearded guy in the corner who looked like he'd probably palled around with Mary Shelley. I saw a werewolf dancing with what I assumed was a witch, his claws making small tears at the waist of her dress. Above the crowd, several faeries floated in the air, their wings beating in time with music, their shiny, pale hair reflecting the colored lights.

In the very middle of the dance floor, a guy wearing a purple velvet smoking jacket was dancing, surrounded by several witches. He looked familiar, and when he turned around, I realized it was Lord Byron.

Yeah, *the* Lord Byron. He'd been our English teacher at Hecate before all the attacks started. Since he was a vampire, people had been suspicious of him. Even after he was cleared, he still hadn't wanted to come back to Hex Hall. Not like I could blame him.

I thought about going over to say hi, but then he spotted us. I'm not sure, but I think he flipped us off before limping away.

Neither Jenna nor I had been exactly stellar students.

Nick jerked his head toward the back. "Let's go grab a seat."

We moved away from the dance floor, to where it was dimmer and less crowded. The music also seemed a good deal softer, so my brain no longer felt like it was leaking out of my ears. Daisy led us to a booth in the back and flopped down on a velvet banquette. Nick sat next to her, leaving Jenna and I to scoot into the seat opposite them.

Daisy pulled out yet another cigarette, this time offering the pack around. Nick took one, but I shook my head when he held the box out to me. "No thanks. Don't smoke."

"Fair enough," Nick replied.

A tall woman with auburn hair came up to the table. She was wearing a bright purple dress that was so short, I thought it might have started its life as a shirt. She would've been pretty if her face hadn't looked like she'd just taken a big swig of sour milk. "You two again," she said.

Daisy rolled her eyes, but Nick looked totally unruffled. "Ah, Linda, my sweet. I was hoping you'd be our waitress tonight. I've missed that sunny smile of yours."

Linda folded her arms across her chest. "Bite me, freak."

Nick grinned, and for just a second, he looked so much like Archer that I clenched my teeth.

"Who's to say I won't, Linda?" Nick asked, raising his eyebrows. Daisy elbowed him in the side. Linda just glared until Nick waved his hands. "Truce, truce," he said. "All right then, Daisy and I will have our usual."

I wondered what that might be. Evil Juice? Some kind of demonic energy drink?

Linda's surly gaze flicked to Jenna, who uncharacteristically blushed.

"They have any kind of blood you could want on tap," Daisy offered.

I really didn't want to think about what that meant.

Jenna gave a nervous smile. "Then a, uh, glass or whatever of O-negative."

"Fine," Linda said. "And you?"

"Uh, water is fine," I said.

"Oh, come on," Nick said, draping his arm across the back of the banquette. "At least let me buy you a drink." He flashed that unsettling grin again. I scooted a little closer to Jenna.

"I don't drink."

As Linda stalked off, Nick laughed. "Oh my God, a straight-edge demon! I freaking love it!"

"Yeah, I figure occasionally ripping people's internal organs out is vice enough for me," I quipped.

It was the wrong thing to say.

Nick's laugh abruptly ended, and even Daisy bristled.

"Sorry," I said quickly. "I didn't mean—" I blew out a breath. "Self-deprecation is like my second language. It was nothing against you guys."

Daisy seemed placated by that, but Nick was still watching me with an unreadable look.

"We've never hurt anyone, Sophie," he said. "Neither has James, neither have you."

"Yeah, but we could," I replied. "Mrs. Casnoff said that demons can be fine for years, and then suddenly monster out."

Nick's gaze flicked away from mine. "Isn't that what they're hoping we'll do?" he muttered darkly.

"What does that mean?" Jenna asked, but Daisy leaned forward, cupping her hand around Nick's knee.

"Let's not get into all of this tonight," she said. "We have the whole summer to teach Sophie about demon-hood."

Nick grumbled, but Daisy caught his chin and gently pulled his face to hers. He kissed her with surprising tenderness, and I felt my face grow hot. I hadn't realized they were together, at least not like that.

Daisy and Nick finally pulled apart. "Okay." Nick slouched against the wall, his fingers flirting with the hem of Daisy's skirt. "If we're not going to talk about demon stuff, what are we going to talk about?" Even though his tone was friendly, his eyes were hard when he said, "After all, isn't that why you're here, Sophie? To get a crash course in all things demon?"

Suddenly I wished I did drink. Why was it that

everyone here wanted to get all intense with me right away? "I guess."

Linda reappeared, setting down Jenna's glass of blood with a thunk that sent some of its contents slopping over the sides. I think she would have slammed down Nick's and Daisy's drinks just as hard, but Nick took them from her before she could. A look of disgust flickered over her face when their hands touched. I guess I should have been offended at that, what with her slighting my demon brethren and all, but I couldn't really blame her. There was something about Nick and Daisy that made my skin crawl. I could only imagine how creepy they seemed to regular Prodigium.

Especially when I noticed that the liquid in Nick's and Daisy's glasses was pitch black and oily looking.

"Um, what is that?" I asked after Linda tossed me a room-temperature bottle of water and huffed away.

Nick quirked his eyebrows at me and raised the glass in a kind of toast. "And so the education begins! This, Sophia, is Cassandra's Elixir. It's a potion they brew here at Shelley's."

I twisted the cap off my water bottle. "A potion? Like with eye of newt and all that?"

Laughing, Nick dipped a finger in his drink and licked it. Ew. "No, no eye of newt. Just water from the Aegean Sea, a couple of shots of hundred-year-old brandy, and a whole lot of magic. Oh, and a dash of faeries' blood."

I took a sip of water to keep my mouth from puckering in disgust.

"What does it do?" Jenna asked, turning her glass of blood around in her hands.

"They say it puts you in the right frame of mind to receive visions of the future," Daisy said. Then she took her drink from Nick and threw it back like it was water. My esophagus burned in sympathy as Nick did the same thing.

Daisy put down her empty glass, her eyes brighter and cheeks flushed. "But really it just makes everything in here"—she pointed to her temple—"go all . . . hazy. It's nice. You should order one."

"Yeah, I think I'll pass on hazy for tonight."

Nick shrugged. "Your loss." He leaned back in the booth, wrapping his arm tighter around Daisy. She snuggled against him as he said, "So should we get to the bonding part now?" He nudged Jenna's foot with his own. "Why don't you tell us how you got vamped? That's probably an interesting story."

It wasn't. It was a sad story, and one that Jenna hadn't told me until we'd been rooming together for months. I waited for Jenna to tell them that she didn't want to talk about it.

Instead, she took a deep breath and said, "I fell in love

with a vampire. I let her turn me because I bought into that whole eternal love spiel. Then The Eye staked her, and I . . . I killed someone because I was starving. Eventually the Council took me in and sent me to Hecate."

Her voice was flat and emotionless, but I could see how much it cost her to tell that story, even such a condensed version of it.

"Oh, wow," Daisy breathed. "I'm so sorry." For a second, I thought she was making fun of Jenna, and my hands tightened into fists in my lap. But then I really looked at her, and saw that her sympathy was totally genuine. There might have even been tears in her eyes.

"Yeah," Nick said, sounding completely sincere. "That's rough."

No one at Hex Hall had known about Jenna's past except me and, I guessed, Mrs. Casnoff. Still, nearly everyone there had treated Jenna like a freak and a killer. But the two demons across from us were looking at Jenna with nothing but compassion.

The music had changed, going from that thumping techno to something softer and slower. It was a welcome relief. "So you two really have no idea how you became demons?" I asked. Hey, if they were gonna pry into Jenna's personal monster business, I could pry into theirs.

They didn't seem offended, though. Daisy laid her

head on Nick's collarbone. "We really don't." Her face got distant as she said, "Not even dreams. It's like everything before is just this big black hole." She waved her fingers dreamily in front of her face, and I saw Nick's fingers tighten on her shoulder.

"All we know is that someone did this to us," he said, his voice tight.

Jenna shot me a look before saying, "How could you know that?"

"We can feel it," Daisy said, closing her eyes. When she opened them, they nearly glowed with unshed tears. "It's like we were . . ."

"Violated," Nick finished, and Daisy nodded slowly.

"Yeah, exactly," she said. "It's like everything inside us is different. Our brains, our souls, our blood . . ."

I found myself nodding. After all, hadn't Dad said demonhood was literally in our DNA? And I'd been born this way. How weird would it feel to just wake up a demon one day?

"It's awful," Daisy continued, her words coming out a little slurred. "All this magic just pounding inside your skull every single day."

Her words sounded strangled, like she was trying hard not to cry. I had no idea what to say. I mean, I wasn't exactly thrilled about being a demon either, but I certainly didn't feel like *that*. If that's what being demons was like for Nick and Daisy, no wonder they drank all the time.

I cleared my throat. "So do you guys actually use your powers?"

But before they had a chance to reply, a loud cracking sound echoed through the room.

"What was that?" Jenna asked, nearly dropping her glass of blood.

"Thunder?" I guessed, even though the sound had been more like the crack of a whip, or wood breaking.

The music cut off abruptly, just as a chorus of howls started up from somewhere on the dance floor.

"Don't worry about it," Nick said with a wave of his hand. "Probably just a shifter fight. Happens like every night."

But then someone—or something—screamed, and suddenly the room was full of shrieks and guttural cries and pounding feet.

"Sounds like more than a shifter fight to me." I stood up, trying to see the dance floor. It was hard to make out anything through the smoke. All I could see were hazy forms that seemed to be running toward the door. Then a purpled-winged faerie shot above the crowd, her wings beating furiously. There was a flash of silver as something curled around her ankle. She shrieked with pain and fell back into the throng.

Then I saw them. Moving in and out of the smoke, like they were made of it, were dozens of dark figures. One moved near enough for me to see the blue lights gleaming off the dagger he held in his hand.

My mouth went dry, and my heart plummeted to somewhere south of my toes.

"What is it?" Daisy asked, looking more curious than worried.

I could barely get the words out. "It's The Eye."

CHAPTER 14

"What?" Jenna cried, leaping to her feet. Nick stood up too, but slowly, shaking his head. "That's impossible."

A bright flash of blue illuminated the room, like a bolt of lightning, as the witch I'd seen dancing with the werewolf earlier struggled with three of the dark figures. Nick's eyes widened. "Oh my God."

"The Eye can't get in here," Daisy said, shaking her head. "And they've never tried to raid Shelley's before. Ever."

Nick blinked like he still couldn't believe what he was seeing. The dance floor was utter chaos now. There was so much magic flying around that my skin ached with it, but none of the spells seemed to be doing any good. The Eye just kept coming, more and more of them, spilling into the cramped club. They were outnumbered, but they had the element of surprise on their side, not to mention that most of the Prodigium in Shelley's had been drinking. That "hazy" feeling Daisy had talked about didn't make for stellar magic.

"How do we get out of here?" Jenna asked. She was breathing hard, and her fangs were poking out from under her top lip. "Is there a back door or something?"

Nick finally tore his gaze away from the front of the club. "No," he said. "But we can make one." He reached down and grabbed Daisy's hand, pulling her to her feet.

"Wait!" I yelled. All three of them froze, staring at me. "It's just . . . we could do something." Off to my right, I saw another faerie trying to fly above the fight. He was struggling, though, thanks to a large rip in one of his iridescent wings. "We should help them."

Nick looked at the faerie, his mouth set in a grim line. "They wouldn't do it for us. And we need to get you out of here. Now come on."

"Nick," I said, but Jenna grabbed my hand.

"Sophie, he's right. Let's go. Please."

I hesitated for just a second before squeezing her hand in return and following Nick as he turned toward the back of the club, tugging Daisy behind him.

The back wall was solid brick, but Nick simply raised his hand and flicked his fingers. A section of the wall crumbled, and I don't think I'd ever seen anything as beautiful as that opening.

But we weren't the only ones who'd run for the back, and as soon as the hole opened up, a crush of Prodigium gathered around it, trying to squeeze themselves through.

The screams got louder behind us, and I knew without looking that The Eye was headed our way. The pushing at the hole got more intense, and I watched as a werewolf snarled and bit a warlock who was trying to shove his way to the front.

"Oh my God," Jenna whimpered. Her eyes were bloodred and her fangs were out.

"It's going to be okay," I told her, even though I was pretty sure we were all going to be skewered on L'Occhio silver daggers any minute now. For a split second I wondered if Archer was out there, hacking his way through Prodigium. The thought made me nauseous, so I shook it away and held Jenna tighter.

More bodies pressed in on all sides of us, so close I was afraid I'd be lifted off my feet. I shut my eyes, my body shaking.

Move, I thought, as my chest tightened with panic.

And then I felt it. Magic rose up from the ground beneath me. I didn't even have to lift my hands.

I focused all my concentration on the Prodigium in front of me, even as I pictured a sort of shield around

Daisy, Nick, and Jenna. *Move*, I thought again, stronger this time.

I'd only meant to knock them out of the way, like my spell was a bowling ball and they were the pins. But as usual, my power was too much. As one, the Prodigium were flung into the wall before sliding to the floor. Only Daisy, Nick, and Jenna were left standing.

"Nice one, Sophie," Nick said, clapping me on the shoulder as he and Daisy stepped over the dazed Prodigium and out the door. Even Jenna smiled at me as she went by.

The exit led to the alley we'd been in earlier. I was shocked by how cool the night air felt compared to the humidity in the club, and shivered as the sweat began to dry on my skin. Daisy and Nick were already running down the street in the direction of the Itineris, but I turned to look back into Shelley's. Jenna was waiting next to me.

A few Prodigium had staggered to their feet, but the rest still lay inert on the ground. One, a witch who was about my age, blinked at me in confusion. And behind her, I could see a group of Eyes rushing toward the exit, daggers drawn.

"Jenna, go with Daisy and Nick," I said, without taking my eyes from the hole.

"Sophie—"

"Go!" I said, more sharply than I'd intended. "I'll catch up."

She hesitated for a second before turning and following Daisy and Nick.

I didn't know how much magic I had left in me, but I gathered up all my strength and raised my hands toward the men in black. There was no spark or flash of light, but I could feel the attack spell—one of Alice's—surge from my fingertips. The Eyes dropped like rocks, and my knees hit the pavement. No magic in six months, then two heavy spells within seconds of each other. How stupid could I be?

Even though my head was fuzzy with magic and exhaustion, I forced myself to my feet. I had to get to the others, had to make it to the road. I could see the three of them just ahead as they passed under a streetlamp. Jenna glanced over her shoulder and skidded to a stop when she saw how far back I was. I managed to lift my arm and wave her on. She stood still, but Nick nodded at me and grabbed her arm, pulling her out of the alley. I noted that the three of them headed left, and struggled to catch up. Running was out of the question, but I walked as fast as I could, my heels slipping and sliding on the damp street.

Still, I was too slow.

I was nearly to the end of the alley when an arm snaked around my waist and yanked me backward, out of the light. I wasn't sure if it was an Eye or a Prodigium, or just your run-of-the-mill rapist/scumbag type, but it was definitely a guy. He was several inches taller than me, and I could hear his ragged breathing in my ear as he struggled to hold me. There was no way I'd be able to do a spell on him: I was too tired and too frazzled. But while I didn't have magic, I did have a whole bunch of the Vandy's Defense classes on my side.

Skill Nine, you asshat, I thought as I drove my elbow back, while at the same time attempting to drive my boot heel as hard as I could into his instep.

He blocked both easily, pulling his torso back from my elbow even as he tightened his grip on my waist, lifting me slightly off the ground so my heel came down harmlessly on thin air.

For a second I felt real panic. Anyone who could block Prodigium Defense moves was a lot more dangerous than some random pervert. I was about to try Skill Fifteen, which involved both breaking his nose and potentially ending his chances of ever having kids, when my captor bent down and whispered in my ear, "Don't even think about it, Mercer."

CHAPTER 15

This is not happening.

That was the only thought in my mind as Archer set me on my feet and released my waist.

This was some kind of mistake. There was some other guy running around England who just happened to know Defense and called me Mercer. Because there was no way that tonight, of all nights, could also be the night I came face-to-face with—

I turned around.

The light was dim in this section of the alley, but it was definitely Archer Cross standing there. He looked a lot rougher than he had the last time I'd seen him. There was dark stubble covering the lower half of his face, and his hair was longer. More than that, though, he looked older. Tired. And still, seeing him again was like being punched in the chest.

There were so many emotions rushing through me that it took me a while to identify them: fear, definitely. Shock.

But underneath those, there was something else, a feeling I wasn't sure I wanted to give a name to.

It felt a little bit like joy.

But I stamped that right the heck down. The shock was wearing off, and I remembered that the last time I'd been alone with Archer, he'd pulled a knife on me. I wasn't going to stand around and see what he had this time.

I gathered up my last reserves of strength to do some kind of magic. I may not have been able to manage a transportation spell, but a quick lightning bolt would probably be pretty effective. I could feel the magic start to creep up from the soles of my feet, but it was weak. I'd be lucky to throw a couple of sparks at him.

But before I could even do that, he grabbed my arms and pulled me farther into the shadows, spinning me so my back was pressed against the wall.

I brought my knee up. It was less of a defense skill and more of a girl instinct, but it didn't matter. He dodged that too. Then he stood in front of me, his hands clamped around my wrists as I tried to get away.

"I'm not going to hurt you," he muttered through

clenched teeth. "But I can't say the same for the others."

I stopped struggling as I remembered just how many members of L'Occhio had been in Shelley's. Just then, I heard a young-sounding voice yell out, "Cross!"

Archer glanced over his shoulder and angled his body so I was hidden from view. "It's not her," he called back. "Just a human girl, wrong place, wrong time."

The guy rattled off a string of words in a language I guessed was Italian. At least it sounded like it. I couldn't understand what he said, obviously, but whatever it was, it made Archer mutter a *very* recognizable word under his breath before replying in the same language, the words sounding strange in his familiar voice. I heard the slapping sound of footsteps running off into the distance.

Archer dropped my wrists and braced his arms on the damp brick wall behind me, but I held my body stiff, afraid that if I relaxed even an inch, we'd inadvertently touch.

He sighed. "That makes, what? The second time I've saved your life? Third, if you count that thing in Defense with the Vandy. Speaking of which, you're still thrusting your elbow too high on Skill Nine."

I swallowed twice before I was able to answer. "I'll work on that."

I waited for him to move away. I *needed* him to move away, because I'd already started shaking. But he stayed right where he was, so close that I could see the violet shadows under his eyes, and how gaunt his cheeks were. I tried my hardest to keep my gaze at a spot somewhere over his right shoulder. I had pictured meeting Archer again so many times, and there were a million things I wanted to ask him, like why he had saved my life tonight, how long had he been working for The Eye.

If he'd only pretended to like me.

Instead, I just said, "So did The Eye come here tonight looking for me?"

"Actually, we came because we heard it was free corn dog night. Imagine our disappointment."

I jerked my head to look at him. That was a mistake. We were already so close that turning to face him meant our noses were about an inch apart. So I craned my neck away and addressed my words to the street. "The last time we saw each other, you pulled a knife on me. So if you could spare me the banter, that'd be great." Of course, the last time we saw each other, we'd also shared a kiss so hot it nearly set my hair on fire, but I wasn't about to bring that up.

Still, I wondered if he was thinking it, too, because I was pretty sure I felt his gaze on my mouth for just a second before he said, "Fine. Yes, we're here looking for you. What are you doing here anyway?"

I blinked at him. "Me? The Council wants to kill *you*

on sight," I hissed. "And where are you hiding out? In their freaking backyard."

"I'm not hiding out. London is where I was assigned. And you didn't answer my question."

This time, I figured out how to tilt my head back enough so I could avoid any face touchage as I looked at him. It still meant we were close enough for me to see my reflection in his eyes. I ignored the sharp drop in my stomach and said, "I'm here with my dad."

He quirked an eyebrow, and for just a moment looked a lot more like the Archer I remembered. "Demon family reunion?"

It was on the tip of my tongue to tell him about the Removal, but before I could say anything, the guy from earlier shouted some more Italian from somewhere in the distance. Archer closed his eyes briefly and took a deep breath before calling out a response. Then he reached into his pocket.

I didn't think it was possible, but I tensed up even more.

"Relax," he murmured as he pulled out a dull gold coin. "That was Raphael. In addition to being one of the youngest Eyes, he's also the one of the stupidest. He asked what was taking so long, and I told him I was wiping your mind before I sent you on your way."

"You can do that?"

He flashed a brief grin. "No, but he doesn't know that. That's why he's staying so far back. Scared of catching Prodigium germs." He said it lightly, but there was bitterness behind the words. For roughly the thousandth time, I wondered how on earth a warlock had become a member of L'Occhio di Dio, and I wished I had time to ask him.

He pressed the coin into my hand. "Are you staying in London?"

"No, Thorne Abbey. It's—"

"I'll find you," he said, closing my fingers over the coin. "Just keep that on you."

"No," I said, grabbing at the sleeve of his jacket. "Archer, the Council is at Thorne. Not to mention my dad, who put an execution order out on you."

"There's a lot we need to talk about, Mercer," he said, glancing back toward the other end of the alley. "I'll risk it."

I shook my head again, but he was already moving away from me. "Keep out of the light and get out of here," he murmured. "And Mercer, from now on, stay out of Prodigium clubs, okay? These people aren't your friends."

"What do you mean?" I made one more grab for his sleeve, but he ran back toward Shelley's. I could see Raphael now, and Archer was right: he was young.

Really young, actually. I guessed around fourteen. I kept myself close to the wall as Archer clapped his arm around Raphael's shoulder, saying something in a light, jovial voice. Raphael shook his head and kept looking in my direction. Then a burst of blue light exploded from the back exit, and both he and Archer turned toward it, giving me a chance to run out of the alley.

My head was still spinning, and my knees were shaking by the time I turned left out of the passageway. I braced my hand on the slimy brick and tried really hard not to throw up. I had no idea where the road would be. I only hoped that Daisy or Nick had left some sort of demon bread crumbs for me to follow.

But when I got to the end of the street, I saw that all three of them were waiting for me in front of a squat, concrete building. Daisy and Nick were smoking again, and Jenna was pacing back and forth, her fangs still out, her eyes still red.

When she saw me, her whole face lit up, making her look less like a vampire and more like a kid on Christmas morning. I staggered up to the three of them, and Jenna threw her arms around me. "I was so sure they caught you," she said, her voice thick.

I hugged her back, a lump in my throat. I'd sworn there would be no more secrets in my life, but there was no way I could tell Jenna about seeing Archer. Jenna was my best friend, but there were some things even she couldn't understand.

"It's these stupid boots," I told her with a shaky laugh. "They're not exactly the best running shoes."

Jenna pulled back and cupped my cheeks. Her eyes weren't red anymore, but they were wide and bright with tears. "I am so sorry, Sophie," she said. "If I'd had any idea that this place would be so dangerous for you . . ."

"Yeah," Daisy said, coming to stand beside Jenna. "Seriously, Sophie, nothing like that has ever happened to us at Shelley's, I swear. We never would've taken you there if we'd known."

Even Nick came forward, frowning with worry. "James would kill us if he found out. We're supposed to be helping you adjust to being a demon and instead we nearly handed you over to L'Occhio di Dio."

All three of them looked so genuinely sorry, so guilty, and I felt sick all over again.

"It's fine," I said, waving my hand as though demon hunters raiding clubs to kill me were something that happened all the time. "*I'm* fine. Now let's get out of here."

Daisy had said that the second road trip wouldn't be as rough as the first one, but she was either wrong or a liar. The second one seemed far worse, probably because I was so drained. Still, we made it back to the corn mill, and even though it felt like a dwarf with a chisel had taken up permanent residence in my frontal lobe, I managed to stagger all the way back to the house. Luckily, everyone appeared to have gone to bed, because the front hall was dark and silent as we let ourselves in. After more whispered apologies, Daisy and Nick headed for their rooms on the second floor, while Jenna and I went up to our hall.

At her door, Jenna stopped. "Soph, I really am—"

"Jenna, if you say sorry one more time, I'm going to punch you in your tiny pink head."

She gave a little smile. "Okay, okay. Still, the next time I suggest going to Prodigium nightclub, please smack me."

"Will do," I said.

I practically had to drag myself to my room. I put on a nightshirt and brushed my teeth in a daze, my mind replaying those minutes in the alley with Archer on a continuous loop. Six months ago, he'd pulled a knife on me in the cellar at Hecate. Tonight, he'd protected me from the other members of L'Occhio di Dio. Why?

My jeans were crumpled up on the floor, and before I got into bed, I reached into the front pocket. The gold coin he'd given me was still warm. It was old, the likeness stamped in the metal so faded that I couldn't tell if it was supposed to be a man or a woman.

Keep it on you, he'd said. *I'll find you.*

139

I should've thrown it out. I should've found which-ever one of the hundreds of bedrooms in this place was my dad's and told him what happened. I should've done anything but what I did, which was to close my fist over it and slide it under my pillow.

CHAPTER 16

Thankfully, there were no weird dreams that night, and I slept nearly until noon. I would've slept even later if my door hadn't opened.

"Go'way, Jenna," I mumbled into my pillow.

"I would if I were Jenna," a deep voice—a voice that was most definitely not Jenna's—replied.

All of last night's events came rushing back to me, and in my sleep-fogged brain I remembered Archer saying to keep the coin on me, that he would find me, and how I'd put the coin under my pillow.

I sat up so fast I practically broke the sound barrier, but it was Cal standing in my doorway, not Archer. I heaved a huge sigh, one of relief, and not even a little bit of disappointment.

Of course, once I'd wrapped my mind around the fact

that it was Cal and not Archer standing in my bedroom, it dawned on me that *Cal was standing in my bedroom.*

"Hey," I breathed, hoping my hair wasn't a huge tangled mess, even though I was ninety-nine percent sure that it was. I mean, I could see it out of my peripheral vision.

"Hey."

"You're, um, in my room."

"I am."

"Is that allowed?"

"Well, we are engaged," Cal deadpanned.

I squinted at him, shoving big handfuls of my hair away from my face. I had no idea if that was supposed to be a joke or not. You could never tell with Cal.

"Did you want to watch me sleep or something? Because if that's the case, this engagement is *so* broken."

Cal's lips quirked in what might have been a smile. "Do you have a smart-ass reply for everything?"

"If at all possible, yeah. So why'd you come in here, then?"

"To see how last night went."

My heart slammed painfully into my ribs, and suddenly all I could think about was that stupid gold coin currently burning a hole underneath my pillow. "It was good," I said, scooting against the headboard. "You know. Villagey. Hate that you had to miss it."

"Yeah." He ran a hand over his jaw. "It was weird. Your dad said there were only a couple of plants that I needed to look at, but it was like as soon as I finished healing one plant, another one started drooping and looking sick. I must've worked on every bush in that whole garden. Took me until nearly ten o'clock last night."

"That is weird," I said, even as a suspicion began to form in the back of my mind. I couldn't have been the only one to realize that Cal wouldn't have been cool with going to Shelley's.

"Did you learn anything about Nick and Daisy?"

Oh, right. That whole part of my mission had been a total bust. "No, not really. It was a pretty boring night, actually."

Despite all the practice I'd had over the past few months, I was a terrible liar, and Cal wasn't an idiot. He watched me intently for a second before saying, "Your dad got home early this morning. Apparently L'Occhio di Dio raided some Prodigium club in London last night."

"Wow," I said faintly. "That must've sucked."

"Yeah," Cal said, never dropping his eyes from mine. "It seems they heard that the head of the Council's daughter was there with two other demons and a vampire."

I felt the blood drain out of my face. "Crap. Is he mad?"

Cal shrugged. "That's one word for it. I'm not all that thrilled with it either."

I pushed the covers off and got out of bed, making sure my nightshirt didn't ride up. "Cal, I already have to deal with an angry dad today. Please don't pull some macho 'betrothed' thing on top of it, okay?"

He caught my wrist. "I'm not. And it's not you I'm pissed at. It's them. They shouldn't have taken you there."

His hand was warm on my skin. "I think they were trying to be nice," I told him. "And they said that The Eye had never been there before."

His fingers tightened, almost to the point of pain. "So they *were* looking for you."

"Yeah. Seems like it."

There was a light knock at the door. Cal let go of my arm and we jumped about six feet apart as Lara eased the door open. If Mrs. Casnoff had caught Cal in my bedroom back at Hecate—with the door closed, and me still in my pajamas—I had a feeling there would have been steely glares, pursed lips, and words like "wildly inappropriate."

But if anything, Lara looked . . . well, pleased. Her expression was slightly smug as she said, "Sophie, your father is waiting for you in the library."

Ugh. I nodded and said, "Right. Let me grab a shower, and I'll be right there."

"He also requests that you wear something other than jeans and sneakers."

That was irritating, but I didn't want to take it out on Lara. "I have a dress I can wear."

"Excellent," Lara replied, but she made no move to leave.

"I, uh, guess that's my cue to get out of your hair," Cal said, his neck turning slightly red. "See you later, Sophie."

I watched him and Lara leave before leaning my head against the window and sighing. Outside, the fountain sparkled in the sunlight, and I caught a faint whiff of the lavender Dad was so in love with. In the light of day, it was easy to imagine last night hadn't happened.

I felt a little bit better after I showered. Sure, Dad was going to be mad at me. There might even be some yelling. I could handle that. The only dress I'd brought was a white sundress with blue flowers on it. It was pretty, but I thought something a little more sophisticated might be called for. Using my magic, I changed it into a simple black, sleeveless sheath. I added a little black shrug jacket and pearls for good measure before it occurred to me that I was using my powers again.

Yeah, but just little powers, I told myself. *The chances of your magic going all scary and dark while changing clothes are probably pretty slim.*

Still, it bothered me how easy it was to slip back into the habit of using magic. So I wrestled my hair into a demure braid the old-fashioned way, even though it ended up looking pretty sloppy. I decided not to wear makeup, figuring the more innocent I looked, the harder it might be for him to ground me, or shoot hellfire from his eyes, or whatever it was that angry demon dads did.

Before I left, I grabbed the gold coin from underneath my pillow, then looked around the room. No hiding places immediately jumped out at me, so in the end I added a pocket to my dress and slipped it in.

Dad was standing in front of the big windows when I got to the library, his hands clasped behind his back in the classic "I am so disappointed in my offspring" pose.

"Dad? Um, Lara said you wanted to see me."

He turned around, his mouth a hard line. "Yes. Did you have a nice time with Daisy and Nick last night?"

I fought the urge to reach into my pocket and touch the coin. "Not particularly."

He didn't say anything, so we just stared at each other until I started feeling fidgety. "Look, if you're going to punish me, I'd really rather just get it over with."

Dad kept staring. "Would you like to know how I spent my evening? Well, not evening, really, so much as very early morning hours."

Inwardly, I groaned. Mrs. Casnoff sometimes pulled this maneuver: she'd say she wasn't mad, and then proceed to list all the ways my screwup had inconvenienced her. Maybe they taught it at those fancy schools non-reject Prodigium got to go to. "Sure."

"I spent those hours on the phone. Do you know with whom?"

"One of those psychic hotlines?"

Dad gritted his teeth. "If only. No, I was busy assuring no less than thirty influential witches, warlocks, shifters, and faeries that surely, my daughter—the future head of the Council, I should add—had not injured over a dozen innocent Prodigium while attempting to escape a nightclub during a raid by L'Occhio di Dio."

"I didn't hurt them!" I exclaimed. Then I remembered just how hard they had hit the wall, and winced. "Well, not on purpose," I amended.

Dad dropped his head and pinched the bridge of his nose between two fingers. "Damn it all, Sophia."

"I'm sorry," I said miserably. "Really. And I tried to help them. I dropped all of the Eyes that were coming after them."

"No," he said, raiding his head. "No, this is my fault. I should've dealt with this as soon as you arrived."

"With what?"

"Come with me. We have an errand to run." He swept his arm out like I was supposed to leave the library first, but I stayed right where I was. I felt totally confused

147

and off-center. When Mom was mad at me, she just yelled and got it over with.

I swallowed. "Wherever we're going, I want Jenna to come too." Whatever Dad had planned, I didn't think it was something I wanted to deal with alone.

But Dad gave this mysterious little smile and said, "I believe Miss Talbot has company."

"What are you talking about?"

"It was my understanding that she and Victoria Stanford had grown close while Jenna was in Savannah last year. Fortunately, Miss Stanford was granted a few weeks vacation from her duties for the Council. I thought she might want to spend some of that time here with Jenna."

"You flew Vix out here?"

He turned back to the window and nodded at something outside. "Her flight got in late last night."

I went to stand beside him. There on the front lawn, Jenna was walking arm in arm with a very pale, very beautiful girl, their heads close together. Vix looked sixteen, but since she worked for the Council, she was probably older. One of the perks of being a vampire, I guess. Jenna was laughing. My throat felt tight with a feeling that was part happiness for Jenna, part jealousy that I'd have to share her, and part anger.

I remembered the look on Dad's face on that first day,

when Jenna had leaped to my defense, and he'd said Mrs. Casnoff had called us what?

A formidable team.

"Well played, Dad," I muttered.

I expected him to deny it, but instead he said, "Yes, I rather thought so myself. Now come along."

I cast one more glance at Jenna and Vix, hoping to catch Jenna's eye and wave, but she never looked up.

CHAPTER 17

I'd thought I was getting a pretty good handle on the layout of Thorne Abbey, but as I followed Dad down one massive corridor, then another narrower hallway, and finally up a flight of stairs, I got disoriented all over again.

Dad finally stopped in a section of the house that looked like it hadn't been used since Alice was here. The furniture was covered in heavy drop cloths, and a thick layer of dust and grime coated the portraits on the wall. In front of us was a heavy oak door, and when Dad pushed it open, I half expected someone's crazy locked-away wife to spring out at us.

But as I looked into the dim room, the only person I saw was me. Well, lots of mes.

Nearly every square inch of wall was covered in mirrors of all kinds: huge mirrors in ornate frames that looked like they weighed three times more than me; tiny, round mirrors that only reflected little pieces of me; old mirrors, so warped and spotted that I could hardly see anything in them at all.

Dad crossed the room to open some gray velvet drapes, but when he tugged on them, the fabric fell away from the windows in a moldered heap.

"Oh, well," he said, surveying the mess. "It's my house anyway." He raised his eyes to me. "I'm sure you're wondering why I've brought you here."

I moved to the center of the room, my strappy sandals clacking on the marble floor. "I'm assuming this is where the punishment part comes in," I said. "So do I need to clean all these mirrors, or do I have to, like, stare at myself until I feel shamed or something?"

Surprisingly, Dad gave a tiny smile. "No, nothing quite that abstract. I want you to break one of the mirrors."

"Excuse me?"

Dad leaned back against the now-drapeless window and folded his arms over his chest. "Break a mirror, Sophie."

"With what, my head? Because I'm pretty sure that'd be corporal punishment, and Mom would not be cool with that."

"With your powers."

Ugh. I took in the dozens of mirrors and muttered,

"I think I'd rather use my head." When Dad didn't say anything, I sighed and turned to face him. "Okay, fine. Which one?"

He shrugged. "Doesn't matter. Just pick one."

I studied the mirrors on the wall. One of the bigger ones might be easier to "target," but when it inevitably exploded all over the place, there'd be a lot of flying glass to deal with. Best to pick one that might be harder to hit, but would cause less flaying and pain.

I settled on a mirror just to the left of Dad. It was about the size of my hand, and I focused all my concentration on it. *Break.*

The sound was nearly deafening as every single mirror in the room exploded outward in a sparkling spray. I screamed and threw my hands up, but the glass never touched me. It froze about three inches from my face, hovering there for a second, long enough for me to see my wide terrified eyes in thousands of bright shards. Then the pieces slowly began to slide backward toward the empty frames. There was a sound like a giant bubble popping, and suddenly the mirrors were whole again.

I whirled around. Dad was still standing at the window, but he was holding both his hands out, and there was a fine sheen of sweat on his face. When he dropped his arms, he sagged against the window seat and took a deep breath.

"I'm sorry!" I blurted out. "I told you, I suck at this. It's like any time I try to do a spell, it goes all big and scary and explodey, and—"

Dad rubbed his forehead. "No, Sophie, it's all right. That's what I'd hoped you would do."

"You hoped I'd commit mirrorcide?"

He laughed, but it sounded a little breathless. "No, I'd hoped to see just how powerful you really are." His eyes were bright, and there was something that might have been pride in them. "You exceeded my expectations."

"Well, yay," I said. "So glad my skill at blowing crap up impresses you, Dad."

"Your sarcasm is—"

"I know, I know, 'an unattractive quality in a young lady.'"

But Dad grinned and suddenly looked much younger and less like a guy who ironed his ties. "Actually, I was going to say it's something you must've gotten from me. Grace always hated sarcastic comments."

"Oh, I know," I replied without thinking. "I spent most of the seventh grade grounded because of it."

He snorted. "She once put me out by the side of the road in Scotland because I made a completely harmless joke about her map-reading skills."

"Really?"

"Mm-hmm. Had to walk nearly five bloody

kilometers before she stopped to let me back in."

"Dude. Mom is hard-core."

For a moment we smiled at each other. Then Dad cleared his throat and looked away. "Anyway, your powers are definitely impressive, but what you lack is control."

"Yeah, I kind of picked up on that."

Dad pushed himself away from the window. "Alice taught you spells." It wasn't a question.

"I sucked at those, too," I said, not looking at him. "Elodie was able to catch on a lot faster than I did."

Dad watched me very closely for a second before saying, "Cal says that you used a transportation spell to get close enough to Alice to kill her."

"Cal has a big mouth," I muttered.

"Did you?" he asked.

"Yes," I said, "but I literally moved like, five feet. It really wasn't that impressive. Like I said, Elodie was able to do it a lot sooner than I could."

"But Elodie was a witch," Dad said. "Focusing her powers would've been much easier for her."

"What do you mean?"

"Comparing your powers to Elodie's is like comparing a geyser to a water pistol. Your magic is much greater than hers was, but it's . . . unwieldy, let's say. Factor that in with the emotional distress you suffered at Hecate, and it's no surprise your spells have a tendency to go—what was the word you used? Explodey?"

I shook my head. "My spells were awful before I ever even went to Hex Hall, though. Remember the teacher who lost his memory? Or the whole prom disaster?"

"Same issue," Dad replied. "Tremendous power, but no idea how to control it. And the more upset and afraid this makes you, the harder your powers are to handle." He walked across the room and took my hands. Just like with Daisy and Nick, I could sense his power rolling through his veins. "I spent years feeling the same way, Sophie."

"Really?" My voice was barely above a whisper.

He nodded. "I wasn't much older than you when my mother . . ."

He trailed off, and his fingers reflexively tightened on mine. "After my father's death," he continued, "I would've ripped my powers out with my bare hands if I could have. Like you, I refused to use magic anymore because it scared me so much."

"I hadn't really thought about that. What it must have been like for you." I tried to imagine how I would have felt if, instead of Alice killing Elodie, my dad had killed my mom, but the thought was too painful to even wrap my brain around. "So what changed your mind about your powers?"

Dad sighed and gave a small sad smile. "It's a long story. Anyway, the point is that I eventually learned how to control my powers to a very precise degree. For example—"

He lifted one long-fingered hand and pointed at the tiniest mirror in the room, a square of silver glass about three inches high that I hadn't even noticed. "Break," he said in a low voice. I cringed, but only a hairline crack ran across the surface of the mirror.

"Okay," I said slowly, "that was very unexplodey. So how did you do it?"

Dad dropped his hand and turned back to me. "A combination of things. Concentration, deep breaths . . ."

"Demon yoga?" I suggested, and he chuckled.

"Something like that. The best way I can explain it is to say that you and I—Daisy and Nick, Alice, my mother—we have powers of gods, but the bodies, souls, and minds of humans. Both parts of ourselves have to work together, or the magic is too much."

"And then we go crazy. Like Alice."

He nodded. "More or less. Now, try to break the mirror again, but this time, focus more on the human side of yourself than the demon part."

"Um . . . how exactly do I do that?"

Dad pulled off his glasses and began cleaning them with a handkerchief from his front pocket. "There are several ways. You can think of a memory from before you came into your powers. Or focus on a time when you felt particularly strong human emotions: jealousy, fear, love . . ."

"What do you think about?"

Settling his glasses back on his nose, he replied, "Your mother."

"Oh." Well, if it worked for him, maybe it would work for me. I picked out another mirror, this one medium-sized and in a frame made up of little gilt cherubs. I felt my power rushing up from my feet, but instead of flinging it out like I usually do, I took a deep breath and pictured my mom's face. It was a memory from a year ago, just before everything went so wrong for us in Vermont. We were picking out my prom dress, and Mom was smiling, her green eyes bright.

Almost immediately, my heartbeat slowed, and I felt the magic move up more gradually. When it finally reached my fingertips, I focused on the mirror, keeping Mom's face in my mind. "Break."

The mirror and the ones on either side of it shattered, little slivers of glass raining to the dusty floor. But still, it was only three of them. And there had been a distinct lack of explosions. "Holy crap!" I breathed. A goofy smile spread across my face, and I realized it was the first time I'd felt magic drunk in months.

"Much better," Dad said, waving his hand. In a few seconds, the mirrors were repaired. "Of course, the more you practice, the better you'll get. And the better you are at controlling your powers, the less probable it is you will ever hurt anyone."

Now the euphoric feeling gave way to a nervous, fluttering feeling. "So you're saying that if I mastered this magical tai chi thing, I could keep from being like . . . like Alice?"

"I'm saying it greatly reduces the chances, yes. I told you, Sophie. You have many more options than the Removal."

Because I couldn't think of anything to say, I just nodded and wiped my suddenly sweaty hands on my thighs. Practicing deep breaths and picturing people I loved seemed a lot better than having magical runes cut into my skin, but it was almost too much to believe that it could be this easy.

"Of course, the choice is yours, and you don't have to decide anything today," Dad said. "But still, just . . . tell me you'll consider it."

"Yeah," I replied, but the word came out kind of squeaky. I cleared my throat. "Yeah," I said again. "Of course I will."

I expected Dad to do his usual brisk thing and say something like, "Excellent. I will anxiously await your pronouncement on this significant matter." Instead, he just looked relieved and said, "Good."

Thinking we were done, I moved toward the door, but Dad stepped in front of it. "We're not quite finished yet."

I blinked at him, surprised. "I could try to break some more mirrors if you really want me to, Dad, but I'm kind of wiped out. Between last night and today, there's been an awful lot of magic flyin' around for me, and—"

He shook his head. "No, not that. We have one more matter to discuss."

I didn't need my new psychic senses to tell me something bad was coming. "What?"

Dad took a deep breath and folded his arms. "I want you to tell me about Archer Cross."

CHAPTER 18

I stopped myself just before I reached into my pocket, but it still felt like the coin was burning a hole in there. My mind flew in a million different directions. How could Dad know that Archer was there last night? Did he know I'd taken the coin? Archer had said he'd use it to find me. Maybe Dad wanted to use it to lure him here.

But before I could have a mental breakdown, Dad said, "I know it's uncomfortable to talk about, but it's very important that I have a clearer understanding of what happened last semester."

"Oh," I breathed, hoping it didn't sound too much like a sigh of relief. "I told you. Mrs. Casnoff made me write a statement to the Council a few weeks after it happened. Everything's in there."

"I read that. And neither I, nor the rest of the Council, believe it contains the entire truth."

I made a sound that I'd like to say was a cry of indignant outrage, but it was actually closer to a bleat. Probably because Dad was right: that stupid statement didn't even begin to touch the whole truth.

"Your entanglement with Archer Cross—"

"We were never *entangled*," I spluttered.

"Listen to me!" Dad snapped, and I shut my mouth with an audible click. He lowered his voice as he continued. "Did you see Archer at Shelley's last night?"

For just a second, I thought about lying. But there was something in the way Dad was watching me that indicated he already knew the answer. Lie, and this whole thing would just get that much worse.

"Only for a minute." I said the words in a rush, like the faster I got them out there, the easier it would be. "But Dad, he protected me from the other Eyes. He could've given me to them, or killed me himself, but he didn't. And I think there's something weird with him being in The Eye, because he's still using magic—"

Dad grabbed my shoulders. His grip wasn't all that tight, and it's not like he shook me or anything, but something in his gaze made the words dry up in my throat.

"You can never see him again. I'm saying this both as

your father and as head of the Council. It is *imperative* that you have no further contact with Archer Cross."

I knew all of that. But there was something about having it actually said out loud that physically hurt. "I get it," I said, looking down. "I'm a demon, he's an Eye. If we got together, think of how awkward family holidays would be. Magic and daggers flying around, knocking over the Christmas tree . . ."

Dad didn't crack a smile at my joke, but I couldn't blame him. I think the fact that I practically choked out the words killed some of the humor.

"It's more than just that," Dad said, releasing me and stepping back. He sighed. "Sophie, Archer Cross is perhaps the greatest threat Prodigium have ever faced."

I stared at him. "Okay, I know that The Eye freaks everyone out, but I saw them in action last night, Dad. They're not *that* scary, and Archer's one of the youngest ones."

"Yes, but he's also a warlock. In the past, The Eye has used the element of surprise and sheer numbers to hunt us down, much like what you saw last night. But if they were also capable of using magic? We'd lose the only advantage we have. The idea that L'Occhio di Dio could recruit one of our own is terrifying to Prodigium. It's why Archer Cross has to be found, and dealt with."

"You mean killed," I said flatly.

"If that's the Council's ruling."

I walked over to the nearest window. It was warped with age, distorting my view of yet another garden. This one wasn't nearly as pretty as the others. The fountain was covered in moss, and one of the stone benches had cracked in half.

Dad came up behind me. In the glass, I watched his hands hover over my shoulders before coming to rest at his sides. "Sophie, I know this is difficult to understand, but these are very dangerous times for us. When we arrived, you asked why the Council was here at Thorne Abbey instead of in London."

"Lara said there had been some 'unforeseen events,'" I said without turning around.

His eyes met mine in the window, our faces wavy. "Yes. Namely, that L'Occhio di Dio burned Council Headquarters to the ground two months ago."

Now I did turn around. "What?"

"That's why there are only five Council members here at Thorne. The other seven died in the attack."

Even though I hadn't know any of the Council members, I felt his words like a punch in my gut. I couldn't think of anything to say but, "Why didn't we hear about that at Hecate?"

Dad turned away from me and walked over to one of the tiny gilt-and-velvet chairs that lined the walls.

He sighed as he sank into it. "Because we're working very hard to keep that knowledge secret. If it got out, it would cause panic, and we simply can't afford that right now."

He looked back at me. "Can I be brutally honest with you, Sophie?"

It would make a nice change, I considered saying. But I looked at his sagging shoulders, the naked fear on his face. Taking a deep breath, I nodded. "Please."

"Do you remember the war we talked about, between The Eye and Prodigium? It seems we are on the verge of another, but one that has the potential to be far, far worse. The Eye did not attack Council Headquarters on their own. They had help from the Brannicks." He paused, his eyes searching my face. "Do you know anything about the Brannicks?"

"Irish girls, red hair," I replied, remembering a picture of them from Mrs. Casnoff's "People Who Want to Kill Us All" lecture at Hex Hall last year. I also remembered Mrs. Casnoff saying that if the Brannicks and The Eye ever teamed up, we were screwed. "They're like white witches, aren't they?" I asked.

"Descended from one, yes. They don't have any powers anymore, not really. They heal more quickly than regular humans, and there's still the odd bit of magic that surfaces in some of them. Mild telekinesis, precognition, that kind of thing. Their numbers have diminished over the years, but they have a new leader, Aislinn Brannick. Apparently, she's a great deal more ambitious than her predecessors. And now it seems she's reached out to The Eye."

My magic buzz was completely gone now, and I leaned against the windowsill. "Why? I mean, what changed to make them team up and get so serious about killing us?"

"Nick and Daisy," he said flatly. "The knowledge that someone has started raising demons for the first time in sixty years has put them on edge. But of course, most Prodigium are equally distressed that one of our kind is part of their ranks. The entire situation is . . . well, I'm afraid *tense* doesn't begin to cover it. Combustible, let's say." He got up, coming to stand in front of me again. "Sophie, do you understand now why I will do anything to convince you not to go through with the Removal?"

Great. More about my duty, and great responsibility coming with great power and all that. "Sure," I said, trying to keep the bitterness out of my voice. "It's like you said the other night about Alice: demons make pretty awesome weapons, and if there's a big war coming, you guys will need me, right?"

Dad stared at me, frowning, and I tore my eyes away from his, biting the inside of my cheek.

"No," he said at last. "That's not it at all." He touched my shoulder until I looked at him again. "Sophie, I would never use you as a weapon. I want you to have your powers so that you'll be safe. The thought of you completely defenseless against The Eye and the Brannicks?" His voice shook on the last word. He cleared his throat. "It terrifies me."

I blinked against the sudden stinging in my eyes. "But if I went through the Removal, they wouldn't be after me anymore, right?" I hadn't meant for it to sound so much like a plea.

Dad shook his head. "It wouldn't matter if you had your powers or not. You're still my daughter. At least with your powers, you can defend yourself."

My hands were trembling, so I shoved them into my pockets. My fingers brushed the gold coin, and I jerked as though it had burned me. Dad glanced down, and I quickly said, "Why didn't you just tell me that in the first place?"

His eyes met mine. "Why haven't you told me the truth about you and Archer?"

"We were just friends," I said. "How many times do I have to say it?"

When he didn't say anything, I rolled my eyes. "Okay, so I liked him. I had a crush on him, and—" I wasn't sure if the heat in my face was from embarrassment or anger. "And yes, one time we kissed. But it was just the once, and about ten seconds afterward, I found out he was an Eye."

Dad nodded. "And that's it. That's the whole story."

Why oh why wasn't there a giant hole in the floor that I could plummet through, preferably to my death? "Yeah, that's it."

"Well, that's something," Dad said, running a hand through his hair. "At some point, I want you to add that to your original statement."

We were quiet for a long time before I wiped my sweaty palms on my dress and said, "Is there anything else horrible happening that I need to know about?"

Dad gave a humorless laugh as he ushered me toward the door. "I believe that covers all the current horror."

Another question suddenly occurred to me. "What about Nick and Daisy, Dad? I know you said you didn't want to use me as a weapon, but—"

"Never." His voice was quiet but steely. "What was done to them was a crime, and whoever did it is responsible for the dire situation in which we now find ourselves. Which is why finding out who changed them is so important."

We paused on the landing. "What do you mean?"

"There is one other way to rid a demon of his or her powers besides the Removal. That's for the person who originally performed the ritual to reverse it. Obviously, it's too late for the two of us, since we're third- and fourth-generation demons, and our maker is long dead. But it's still possible for Nick and Daisy."

I thought of them last night, so forlorn, talking about magic "pounding" inside their heads. "They'd like that."

"I know," Dad replied. "And I'm also hoping that doing so will . . . well, if not appease The Eye, at least remove some of their drive."

I looked at Dad. I mean, really looked at him. His suit was probably a size too big, and there were deep creases, like parentheses, on either side of his mouth. He was a handsome guy, sure, but he seemed more exhausted than I'd known a person could be.

"Look," I said. "Don't get super-psyched or anything, but maybe . . . maybe we could do this again tomorrow. You know, the demon yoga thing."

Somewhere in the house, several clocks began chiming. They rang out three times before Dad said, "I would like that."

We walked down the stairs in silence, and after making plans to see me at dinner, Dad headed back to his office while I went to my room to check my e-mail.

There was a reply from Mrs. Casnoff, but all it said was, "Thank you for informing me."

I leaned back in my chair and rested my crossed

168

forearms on top of my head. She didn't seem all that con-cerned. That had to be good, though. Especially since the last thing I needed was Elodie's ghost hanging around. I already had enough on my plate.

The gold coin was heavy in my palm as I pulled it out of my pocket. I studied it for a long time before getting up and slipping it in my bedside drawer.

CHAPTER 19

Later that afternoon, I went in search of Jenna. It wasn't hard to find her: she and Vix were still hanging out in the garden. When I approached, shading my eyes against the bright sunlight, they were sitting side by side on the edge of the fountain, their shoulders touching, bare feet dangling in the water. I half expected to see cartoon hearts floating over their heads.

"Hi," I called out, giving a particularly lame wave.

Jenna twisted around to look at me. "There you are!" she exclaimed, eyes bright and cheeks flushed. "Where have you been all morning?"

I kicked off my sandals and sat on the other side of her. The water in the fountain was cold enough to make me wince. "Hanging out with Dad mostly. You know, doing the father/daughter bonding thing."

"Your dad is a wonderful man," Vix said, leaning past Jenna. Her voice was low, and like Jenna's, held just a little trace of a Southern accent. She was also ridiculously pretty with big green eyes and silky brown hair. No wonder Jenna was so smitten.

"Well, he's definitely my favorite person on earth right now," Jenna said, reaching down to squeeze Vix's hand. "How cool was he, flying Vix out here?"

"So cool," I murmured in reply. I wondered if it had even crossed Jenna's mind that Dad had brought Vix here to distract her. Something about the starry look in Jenna's eyes told me no. "It's great to finally meet you," I said to Vix. "Jenna talks about you all the time."

She laughed. "Same to you. And of course, your dad was always talking about you, so between him and Jenna, I feel like I already know you."

Man, first Cal, then Lara and the other Council members, now Vix. Did Dad have a blog about me or something? "My Daughter Sophie and Why You Should All Follow Her and/or Marry Her."

"So what did you and your dad do?" Jenna asked.

I hesitated, but Vix pulled her feet out of the water. Bracing her hands on the edge of the fountain, she spun around so she was facing the other way. "I think I'll go unpack," she said. "I was so excited to see Jenna that I just threw my suitcase in my room." She grinned, two dimples appearing in her pink cheeks. I noticed the bloodstone around her neck, glinting in the sun. "Come find me later?" she asked Jenna.

"Okay," Jenna replied before shyly leaning over and brushing a brief kiss on Vix's lips.

We watched Vix practically skip back to the house. I bumped Jenna with my shoulder. "Your girlfriend is soooo dreamy."

Jenna turned back to me, her face glowing. "I know!" she squealed, and we both laughed.

When we'd settled down, Jenna pushed her hair out of her eyes and said, "Okay, so there are some deep thoughts going on in that head, Sophia Alice Mercer. What's up?"

"What's *not* up is a better question," I told her. "Things are getting . . . intense with The Eye."

Jenna watched me. "How intense?"

I sighed and kicked out one foot, sending up an arc of water. I didn't want to tell her about Council Headquarters, or the dead Council members. Apparently that was so secret even Vix didn't know about it, and she worked for the freaking Council. "Intense enough that Dad really, really doesn't want me to go through the Removal." I wiggled my fingers at her. "It seems demon powers might come in handy if a bunch of people decide to kill me."

"Don't say that," Jenna said sharply.

"Sorry," I replied, laying my hand on her arm. "I just . . . I'm really freaked out."

Her expression softened and she covered my fingers with her own. "I know. The joking in the face of death thing kind of gave it away. But, Soph, please tell me this means you're for sure not doing the Removal."

I had to look away as another image of Alice crouching by Elodie, her silver claws puncturing Elodie's neck, filled my brain. But then I thought of Dad's face, so sad and scared. For me.

Squinting up at the top of the fountain, I took a deep breath and thought of my first night at Hecate, giggling with Jenna in our room. I flicked my hand, and immediately, the water turned bright pink. "Nah," I said. "If I didn't have powers, how could I do cool things like that?"

I'd meant to make Jenna smile. And she did, but it was pretty wobbly, and there were tears in her eyes as she reached over and hugged me. "Yay."

"Yay," I agreed, squeezing her back.

When we pulled apart, Jenna scooped her hair off her neck with both hands and tilted her head back, eyes closed. "Did your dad say anything about Nick and Daisy?"

"He—" I started. Then I caught a blur out of the

corner of my eye, and something landed in the fountain with a resounding splash, drenching me and Jenna in a wave of pink water.

Nick surfaced, tossing his head back and sending droplets flying. If a demon and a vampire both staring at him with identical looks of "WTF, dude?" bothered him, he didn't show it.

Instead, he gave his usual creepy grin and asked, "Did one of you lovely ladies say my name?"

"Yeah," I said, glaring at him as I wrung water out of my braid. "We were just saying, 'Man, I wish Nick would fling himself into the fountain like a nut job and totally ruin our clothes.' So thanks for that."

"Sophie's right," Daisy said, coming to stand next to the fountain. Apparently, wherever Nick was, she was right behind. "Tell them you're sorry." Her words might have sounded sterner if she hadn't been looking at Nick like he was something tasty to eat. God, they were weird.

Nick sloshed through the water until he was right in front of me and Jenna. "That's actually why I came out here, my darling," he said to Daisy. "Sophie, I was a jerk to you yesterday."

He didn't actually say "jerk," but another word that was way more accurate. I just raised my eyebrows and waited for him to continue.

"I'd heard all these rumors about you and that Cross guy, and I got the wrong impression. But the way you dropped those Eyes last night . . ." He shook his head. "I was wrong about you. And I hope we can start over as friends."

He thrust his hand out at me. I hesitated before taking it. There was something about Nick that was like being around a wild animal. He was smiling and friendly now, but it felt like at any minute he could turn snarling and scary again. It reminded me of . . . well, Alice.

Still, I put my hand in his, meaning to shake it. But as soon as we touched, I felt magic crackle over and through me, so strong that I tried to jerk my hand back. But he held tight until, finally, the crackling sensation stopped. My hand slid out of his, and I leaped up from the fountain. "What the hell was—"

Then I looked down and realized I was completely dry. Not only that, but my demure black dress had been replaced with . . . well, another black dress, but this one was a lot shorter, sparklier, and also rocking a very low neckline. Even my hair was different, transformed from a soggy braid to silky brown waves.

Nick winked at me. "That's better. Now you look more like the Demon Who Would Be Queen." He heaved himself out of the water and grabbed Jenna's hand. Within seconds, she went from drowned rat to hottie, her soaked clothes replaced with—what else?—a pink sundress. Of course it showed a lot more skin than anything Jenna would have picked for herself.

"Oh, lovely, Nick," Daisy said, rolling her eyes as he wrapped an arm around her waist.

"What?" he asked once he laid a smacking kiss on her cheek. "They look better like that."

Without thinking, I reached out and grabbed Nick's free arm. His wet white T-shirt and jeans rippled, and suddenly he was wearing a Day-Glo yellow tank top and acid-washed jeans. "And you look better like this."

I wasn't sure if it was the ridiculous sight of Nick in those clothes, or the fact that I'd done a spell so easily— with absolutely no explosions—but I could feel my lips curving upward in a smile. As Daisy hooted with laughter, Nick narrowed his eyes at me. "Okay, now you're in for it." He waved his hand, and suddenly I was sweltering. When I glanced down, I saw that it was because I was now dressed like the Easter Bunny. But with the flick of one fuzzy paw, I'd transformed Nick's jeans and tank top into a snowsuit.

Then I was in a bikini.

So Nick was wearing a particularly poofy purple prom dress.

By the time he'd turned my clothes into a showgirl's costume, complete with a feathery headdress, and I'd put him in a scuba suit, we were both completely magic drunk and giggling.

My clothes shifted and slid until I was wearing a blue T-shirt and Capri pants. I sagged back to the edge of the fountain, the stone hot against my palms. Nick stood over me, back in his regular clothes. "Truce?" he asked, and I knew he wasn't just talking about our magic duel.

I shaded my eyes. "Yeah," I replied. "Truce." Something about Nick still bothered me, but as buzzed as I was feeling, it was hard to remember why.

I tipped my head back, sighing as my hair brushed the back of my arms. Magic rushed over and through me. With the water splashing pleasantly and the sun warm on my face, the threat of The Eye seemed very far away.

Someone's thigh brushed mine, and I opened my eyes to find Jenna sitting next to me. Nick and Daisy were sauntering back to the house, their arms around each other.

"You look like yourself again," Jenna said with a soft smile.

I closed my eyes. "I *feel* like myself again."

We sat there for a while in companionable silence. "I remember the last time I saw you this happy," Jenna said.

Dropping my head onto her shoulder, I said, "Yeah, the day you got to come back to Hecate was a happy occasion."

She snorted. "No, not that day. You were happy to see me, but you were also all freaked out and sad. I was thinking about the night before the All Hallow's Eve ball. Remember, we raided the kitchen and you turned all the mashed potatoes into ice cream sundaes?" She giggled at the memory. "And all the beets into maraschino cherries. God, I think I gained ten pounds that night."

"I was trying to cheer you up." That had been right after Chaston had been attacked, and most of the school had blamed Jenna for it.

Jenna rested her cheek on the top of my head. "I know," she said. "And it almost worked. But you were in such a good mood that night. Seriously, you were like, glowing."

That was because just hours before the kitchen raid, I'd been on cellar duty with Archer. On that particular night, one of the pieces of magical junk we were supposed to catalogue was a cursed pair of gloves that had a tendency to fly around like a demented bat. We'd chased those darn things for twenty minutes before wrangling them into a jar. It had taken both of us to hold the lid on, which meant we'd been standing very close to each other, our hands overlapping. I could still feel how warm he'd been, pressed against my side. We'd laughed through the whole thing, and I remembered how badly my cheeks ached as I'd smiled up into those dark eyes.

"If the spell on these gloves means I get to be this close to a pretty girl, I'm totally stealing them," Archer had said, waggling his eyebrows at me. We'd laughed again, and Archer had just been a boy I liked, and I'd thought the only secret between us was just how *much* I liked him.

This time when I closed my eyes, it was to keep tears from spilling onto Jenna's shoulder. "Yeah," I finally said. "That was a good night."

CHAPTER 20

Jenna and I hung out in the garden until early evening. Once we were back at the house, she went in search of Vix while I decided to go hang out in my room for a while. As I climbed the stairs, Lara met me coming down. "Oh, Sophie, I was just looking for you," she said, forcing a ginormous brown book into my hand. "Your father wanted me to give this to you. He asked that you read as far as you can tonight."

I read the title stamped on the cover: *Demonologies: A History*.

"Oh. Um . . . yay. Thanks for this." I tried to lift the book in a kind of salute, but it was way too heavy for that. In fact, when I got back up to my room and tossed it on the bed, the mattress creaked in protest.

I opened my laptop and mindlessly surfed the Internet

for a while, but my eyes just drifted over the screen without reading anything. There was something else on my mind.

Snapping the computer shut, I walked over to the nightstand and opened the drawer. I stared down at the coin, but before I could pick it up, Jenna came flying into my room, Vix in tow.

I slammed the drawer, hoping neither of them noticed my pounding heart.

But Jenna's attention was on the book on my bed. "Wow, Soph, that's some heavy summer reading right there."

"Yeah," I said, walking over to pick it up. I winced slightly as I hefted it into my arms. "Just some demon homework from Dad."

"We were just about to head down to dinner," Jenna said. "You wanna come with?"

I glanced back and forth between the two vampires. I'd had Jenna all to myself for most of the afternoon, so it's not like I minded sharing. Still, seeing them beam at each other and throw "we" around reminded me just how crappy my love life was. "Nah, I actually think I'll just chill up here tonight. Get started on some of this reading."

Jenna raised a pale eyebrow. "Sophie Mercer, turning down food for homework?"

"Yeah, it's the new, lamer, more Britisher me."

Jenna and Vix laughed at that and, after making me promise to hang out with them tomorrow, practically waltzed out the door. I felt like there should have been rainbows and rose petals in their wake or something.

Ugh. That was catty.

Jenna deserved rainbows and rose petals, I reminded myself as I flopped back on my bed, Dad's book bumping painfully against my sternum. After everything she'd been through, Jenna had earned an eternity of nothing but good stuff. So why did seeing her with Vix make me want to brain myself with *Demonologies: A History*? I looked at the nightstand again and sighed. Then I opened the heavy book and tried to make myself read.

For the next few hours I made a valiant attempt to get through Chapter One.

For a book that was supposedly about fallen angels running around and creating havoc with their super-awesome dark "magycks," it was awfully boring, and all the weird spellings definitely didn't help.

Sighing, I settled deeper into my pillows. As I shifted the book, trying to rest it on my upraised knees, a sheet of paper fell into my lap.

I cringed, thinking it was one of the pages, but then I realized the paper was a lot whiter, and not nearly as musty smelling.

It was a note.

I recognized Dad's handwriting immediately from all the impersonal birthday cards he'd sent over the years. They'd always been pink and glittery—and I now realized that Lara must have bought them—and he'd always just signed them "Your father." Never a little message or even his own "happy birthday."

This note wasn't much warmer. All it said was, "Be prepared to discuss this book and all that you have read tomorrow—Your father."

"Yeah, *Father*, I'll be sure to do that," I muttered, rolling my eyes. Did he really need to write me a note to tell me that? And why had he'd stuck it around page three hundred? Because if he thought I was reading that far tonight, that was pretty freaking optimistic of him.

I sighed and was going to crumple up the note, when suddenly the words on the page *moved*. Vibrated, actually.

I rubbed my eyes, thinking I'd been reading for too long, but when I looked back at the note, the letters were still shaking. And then they started sliding around. A lot of them slid down to the bottom of the page, but the rest gathered together to spell out an entirely different message:

The bookcase. Five a.m.

It was Dad's handwriting again, and as I watched, the discarded letters slipped up the page until the original message was back in place.

"Cryptic Dad is cryptic," I muttered. There was no doubt in my mind which bookcase he meant—the one holding Virginia Thorne's grimoire. But why the spells and secrecy? We'd hung out all morning. Was there no time in there he could have said, "Oh, hey, meet me at the magical bookcase at the butt-crack of dawn tomorrow, cool?"

And what the heck did he want to do at that bookcase?

By now, my eyes felt like I'd rubbed sand in them, and it occurred to me that between the Prodigium club, Archer, and everything with Dad today, this was turning out to be the least relaxing vacation ever. I looked around my palatial room, and for just a second I wished I were back at Hecate Hall, sitting on my tiny bed, laughing with Jenna.

But Jenna was down the hall, either hanging out with Vix or sleeping, and I was on my own.

I put the book on my nightstand, surprised that the weight of it didn't break the tiny piece of furniture. Mom always said there are few things in life that can't be cured by a hot bath, and I decided to test her on that advice.

A few minutes later, I was up to my chin in hot, soapy water.

I ran my big toe over the faucet, which was made to

look like a golden swan. I guess it was supposed to be classy, but it just looked like the swan was vomiting water into the tub, which was a pretty gross thought. Plus, baths always made me think of Chaston, nearly bleeding to death in one of the creepy tubs at Hecate.

Despite the heat of the water, I shuddered. I hadn't seen Chaston again after that night. Her parents had come to get her, and they'd pulled her out of school for the rest of the year. I wondered what she was doing now, if she even knew about Anna and Elodie.

I was just reaching for my towel when I heard a muffled thump from my bedroom. My fingers froze and the hair on the back of my neck prickled. In scary movies, this was always the part where the naked girl called out, "Hello?" or "Who's there?" or something equally stupid. But *this* naked girl wasn't announcing her presence to anyone. Instead, I soundlessly pulled my towel off the rack and wrapped it around me before creeping to the door and pressing my ear against it.

Other than my own heartbeat, I couldn't hear anything. I rolled my eyes as I grabbed my robe from the back of the door. Clearly, the bath—and thoughts of Chaston—had spooked me. If there was anyone in my bedroom, it was probably just one of the army of servants fluffing my pillow. Maybe leaving me a chocolate mint.

Knotting the robe's sash around my waist, I opened the door. My room was empty, and I blew out a long breath.

"Way to be lame, Sophie," I muttered as I crossed the bedroom to the dresser. This place was like the Prodigium version of Fort Knox. The idea that anyone would be in my bedroom, being all nefarious, was completely—

I heard the sound again—another thump, this one a lot louder. And then I realized that it was coming from my nightstand.

Blood pounded in my ears as I ran over to the small table and yanked open the drawer.

Sure enough, the gold coin was thumping around in there like it was alive. How the heck did this work? Archer had said he'd use it to find me, but it suddenly occurred to me that I had no idea what that actually meant. Maybe the coin was a type of portable portal, and he was about to poof into my bedroom in a cloud of smoke or something.

That thought—Archer literally putting himself in the middle of a whole bunch of people who wanted to kill him—was too horrible to contemplate. I closed my fingers around the coin, drawing in a sharp breath at how hot it was.

Suddenly, it was like a screen fell over my eyes, and I could see the abandoned corn mill. The alcove that led to the Itineris. Archer was sitting there next to it, in the low windowsill.

Waiting for me.

Dropping the coin on the bedside table, I turned toward the dresser. I'd grab a pair of jeans, that long-sleeved black shirt I'd brought. If I were quiet enough, I could probably get out of the house without even trying to come up with an excuse—

Then I thought of Dad, pale and serious, telling me how important it was that I never see Archer again. I thought of how proud of me he'd been today, of what might happen to him if anyone caught me sneaking out to see an Eye.

Of Council Headquarters, burning down with seven Council members still inside.

I reached into the open dresser drawer, but instead of my jeans, I took out my nightshirt. Once I'd slipped it on, I climbed into bed and flipped out the light, fumbling for the coin in the darkness. As I clutched it in my fist, I saw Archer again. He was standing up now, pacing and rubbing his hand over his jaw. He kept glancing toward the door.

Tears wet the hair at my temples.

At least I knew he was alive. At least I knew he hadn't been trying to kill me. That was enough. It had to be.

Archer waited for me a long time. Longer than I'd

thought he would. It was past midnight when he gave one last look at the door, then finally disappeared into the alcove. I held the coin even tighter, but as soon as Archer was gone, it went cold, and the vision faded to black.

CHAPTER 21

Five a.m. came very early the next morning, especially for someone who'd spent most of the night crying. And when I had slept, it had been fitfully. I kept jolting awake, sure someone was in the room with me. Once, I even thought I caught a flash of red hair, but I must have been dreaming.

My head throbbed, and I practically had to pry my swollen eyes open when my alarm went off. But despite that, I felt better—lighter—as I went down to meet Dad. Yes, it still hurt to think about Archer, but I'd done the right thing. I'd put Dad and Jenna and, heck, pretty much all of Prodigium society ahead of what I wanted, and if that wasn't showing "leadership ability," I didn't know what was.

So I was pretty proud of myself by the time I made

my way up the library steps and over to the bookcase.

Dad, sadly, was not feeling the same way. "I said five," he hissed as soon as I rounded the corner. "It is now five-fifteen." He looked like he hadn't gotten much sleep either. His suit wasn't wrinkled, exactly, but it wasn't as pristine as usual. Also, he hadn't shaved, which freaked me out almost as much as the intensity in his eyes.

Surprised, I blinked at him. "Sorry—" I replied, but he held up his hand and whispered, "Keep your voice down."

"Why?" I whispered back. We stood on either side of the bookcase, Virginia Thorne's grimoire looking every bit as ominous as it had that first day. "What are we doing in here?"

Dad glanced around like someone might be listening to us, before saying, "We're going to open this bookcase and remove the grimoire."

Now I wasn't surprised so much as shocked. "No way," I shot back. "This thing is enchanted to hell and back—maybe *literally*."

Dad closed his eyes and took a deep breath, like he was having to physically restrain himself from yelling. "Sophie," he said slowly. "I can't do this alone. The magic sealing this case is too strong even for me. But if both of us were to try . . . well, I think we could do it."

"Why?" I asked. "You said yourself that the grimoire is filled with the most ancient, darkest magic in the world. So what do you want it for?"

Another deep breath. "Academic reasons."

Anger rushed through me, and I felt my magic start to rise up. "If you want my help so much, tell me the truth."

"This is extremely dangerous business, and I think it's better for you if you know as little as possible. That way, if we're—if we're caught, you can honestly say you didn't know what I was doing."

"No," I said, shaking my head. "I am so sick of people lying to me, or only telling me half of what I need to know. You said yesterday that it was time I started learning about the 'family business,' and I gave up Ar . . . a lot for you, and for the Council. So tell me what's going on."

It was Dad's turn to look surprised. For a moment, I thought he might just call the whole thing off. But then he nodded and said, "Fair enough. I told you that the Council had been trying to raise a demon for hundreds of years before Virginia finally located this book." He gestured to the grimoire. "After Alice, the Council agreed that the magic was too dangerous, and the book was locked in this case. Ever since then, no one's been able to do a possession ritual. But now . . ."

"Daisy and Nick," I murmured.

"Exactly."

"So what? You think someone took the grimoire out and used that spell to make Daisy and Nick demons?"

Dad ran a hand through his hair, and for the first time, I noticed that his fingers were trembling. "No, it's not that. This case is exceedingly difficult to open. I just want to see the ritual itself, what's required for a possession spell. If I knew exactly *what* had been done to Daisy and Nick, then maybe it would help me figure out *who* did it to them. And why."

It sounded like a rational enough explanation, but, to be honest, it still scared the crap out of me. Unleashing a book that contained the darkest magic in the whole wide world could never be seen as a good thing, you know? But I didn't say that to Dad. Instead, I asked, "Okay, so how do we get it open if it's so 'exceedingly difficult'?"

Dad laid a hand on top of the case. "Brute strength, basically. The case requires all twelve of the Council members to unlock it."

I raised my eyebrows. "Okay, well, since there are only two of us, and only one of us is a Council member—"

Shaking his head, Dad cut me off. "No, technically, we're both Council members. You're the heir apparent to the head of the Council, ergo—"

"Dad, it is way too early to be using words like 'ergo.' And even if I am a Council member, that still leaves us ten people short."

"Yes, well, that's where the brute strength part comes in. Between our combined powers and the blood, it should open for us."

"Blood?" I echoed faintly.

Dad looked grim as he pulled a short silver dagger out of his suit jacket. "I told you, blood magic is very ancient and very powerful. Now give me your hand. We don't have much time."

The light from outside was beginning to turn more golden than blue-gray, and I knew the house would be waking up soon.

I also knew that I really, really didn't want to give Dad my hand.

"This is why you worked with me yesterday, isn't it?" I asked, my voice barely audible. "You wanted to make sure I could do this without blowing the library to smithereens in the process."

Something washed over Dad's face, and I hoped it was guilt. "It wasn't the only reason, Sophie," he replied.

"Okay, but please remember that I still broke a lot of mirrors yesterday. Shouldn't we wait until I've had a little more practice?"

Dad shook his head. "Yesterday afternoon, The Eye attempted a raid on Gevaudan."

It took me a moment to remember that that was the name of the fancy shapeshifter school in France. "Time is no longer a luxury we can afford," Dad said. Then he moved the blade over his left palm in one quick flash. I gasped, and he laid his now-bloody hand on top of the bookcase. His blood trickled over the runes carved into the glass, flowing into them. As it did, the markings began to glow with golden light. Inside its box, the book seemed to shudder a little.

I waited for my newfound psychic feelings to kick in, telling me what a horrible idea this was. But there was nothing. Yeah, I felt kind of sick, but I think that was more about the blood than any terrible feelings of dread.

"Sophie," Dad said, holding out the dagger. "Please."

I thrust out my hand before I had time to think about it, giving him the palm that was already scarred by demonglass. The pain was bright and quick, and not nearly as bad as I'd thought it would be. Following Dad's lead, I put my hand next to his on the case, even as I winced, remembering how hot it had been last time.

But there was no heat. I felt the magic covering it, and my powers surged in response. "Now what?" I whispered, unable to take my eyes off my own blood as it flowed into the runes. As it did, the golden light got brighter.

"Do what we did yesterday," Dad said, his voice low and even. "Picture a human memory. A human emotion."

Suddenly, I saw Archer sitting in the window of the

corn mill again, and a sense of longing flooded through me. Almost instantly, at least a dozen books flew off the shelf nearest to me, the force breaking their spines and sending pages fluttering all around us.

"Something else!" Dad hissed, raising panicked eyes to mine.

"S-sorry, sorry," I stammered, shaking my head like my brain was an Etch A Sketch that could erase Archer.

Think calm, happy thoughts. Mom. That time you went to the carnival when you were eight, and she let you ride the Ferris wheel over and over again. Laughing. The twinkling lights, the smell of funnel cakes.

My heartbeat slowed, and I felt my powers curl up inside me, safe, ready to be directed.

"Much better." Dad sighed with relief. "Now, focus on the case and just think *Open.*"

I took long slow breaths and did just that. My hand was starting to feel cold, and I had the unsettling sense that the case was somehow *drinking* my blood. My knees went wobbly at the thought, and I rapidly blinked my eyes, trying to clear the gray fog that was threatening to overwhelm me. I had teleported, and made things appear out of thin air. I had *flown*, for God's sake. I wasn't going to faint opening a stupid glass box.

Still, I'd never felt anything like this, even when doing those hard-core spells. My magic didn't feel like it was rushing from my feet so much as trickling. And even though my teeth were shattering like I was freezing, I was drenched in sweat.

My fingers were numb, and my hand looked awfully pale, but I kept pressing it to the box. But other than the glowing, bloody runes, nothing seemed to be happening.

Across the case, Dad didn't look quite as wrung out as I felt. "It's more than just the case," he said, his hand slipping on the bloody glass. His voice was ragged. "It's the book, too."

The gray spots were getting bigger. "What do I focus on, then?" I whispered. I wasn't trying to stay quiet; whispering was all I had the strength for.

"Both of them," Dad answered. "Picture the case opening, and the book in your hands. And don't lose sight of your human memory."

My head felt too heavy to hold up anymore, and I lowered my forehead to the case. "That's a whole lot of stuff to picture, Dad."

"I know it is, Sophie, but you can do it."

So I did. I kept Mom's face in mind, all the while focusing on the case, and the grimoire, and trying very hard not to focus on how woozy and drained I was feeling.

And then—finally—the glass started to move.

"That's it," Dad murmured, his eyes bright in his haggard face. "Almost there."

I'd expected the glass to open, or for maybe one side of it to fall off or something. Instead, it just vanished, like a bubble popping. It was so abrupt that both mine and Dad's hands fell to the wooden shelf with a loud slap.

Dad reached out and grabbed the book, which looked like any other old, dusty book now that it was out of its magical case. The black leather cover was dulled with age, and it smelled like ancient paper and mold.

As Dad flipped through the book, my knees gave out. I slipped to the floor and leaned against the nearest bookcase. I felt like I was watching Dad from a distance, or like I was in a dream. I glanced down at my hand and wondered if the rest of me was as chalky white as it was.

"Oh my God," Dad breathed. I felt like I should probably be alarmed by how freaked out he looked, but even that was too much effort.

"What is it?" I muttered drowsily.

He raised panicked eyes to me, but it was like he didn't even see me at first. "It's the ritual, it's—Sophie!"

As I lurched sideways and gave in to unconsciousness, the last thing I saw was the book falling to the floor, its cover opening to reveal a jagged edge of paper.

A page had been ripped out.

CHAPTER 22

When I came to, I was lying on one of the library couches near the big windows with a blanket on me, and Cal was holding my hand.

"Déjà vu," I said as I watched silver sparks of magic race over my skin. He gave a tiny smile, but his eyes were trained on the rapidly closing cut on my palm. I looked past him and saw Dad standing at the end of the couch, his face etched with worry. Suddenly, everything came rushing back to me. The case, the book.

The missing page.

Dad gave a barely perceptible shake of his head, but I knew better than to say anything in front of Cal. Still, now that I didn't feel like I was dying from blood loss, I felt every bit as disturbed about that missing page as Dad had looked.

Like he could read my mind—and for all I knew, he could—Dad said, "I want you to rest here for a little while, Sophie. Once you're feeling better, we can discuss the ramifications of that spell in my office."

"Must have been some hard-core spell," Cal remarked as he gently laid my hand down on the couch.

"Yeah," I said, my mouth feeling like it was full of sawdust. "Dad's been working with me on controlling my powers. Guess I overdid it."

Dad walked around the couch and, to my surprise, leaned down to kiss my forehead. "I'm sorry," he said softly. "But I am also very proud of you."

It was hard to talk around the sudden lump in my throat, so I just nodded.

"I'll be in my office. Come see me when you're feeling up to it."

Once Dad was gone, I flexed my hand, studying the place where the gash had been. There was no sign of it, and I could swear that even my demonglass scar looked a little better. "Okay, so the ability to heal people has to be the coolest magical power ever," I told Cal.

His lips quirked. "Yeah, well, I didn't always think so."

"What do you mean?"

"It's what got me sent to Hecate."

I perked up. I'd always wondered how someone as straight-and-narrow as Cal had gotten sentenced to Hex

Hall. "They sent you there for *healing* someone?"

"Making someone's leg magically unbreak itself kind of draws attention to you," he said.

"Yikes. I bet. So when you did it, was there a lot of screaming and pointing? That's what happened to me."

He laughed. "Yeah, she was nowhere near as happy to be healed as I'd thought she'd be."

We were sitting so close that our hips touched. He smelled nice, like freshly cut grass and sunshine. I wondered if he'd been outside already this morning, or if that's just the way Cal always smelled.

I was about to ask him more about this mysterious "she" with the broken leg, but he changed the subject. "So you're learning to control your powers," he said, studying me with those clear hazel eyes. "How's it working out?"

"Great," I answered, before I remembered that Cal thought I'd just been grievously injured during one of those lessons. "I mean, it's really hard," I amended, "but I think I'm getting the hang of it. Sure beats the idea of going through the Removal."

"Does that mean the Removal is out?"

I ran my finger around the paisley pattern on the couch. "I think so, yeah," I replied, leaning back against the cushions. The cut on my palm may have healed up, but I still felt pretty wiped out.

"I'm glad," he said quietly. The space between us suddenly seemed smaller, and when he covered my hand with his, it was all I could do not to jump. It took me a minute to realize that he was just using more magic on me. I could feel the weariness running out of me as silver sparks ran along my arm.

"Better?" The sparks faded, but Cal didn't take his hand off mine.

"Much." Of course, all that tiredness had now been replaced by a weird jitteriness that had me shoving the blanket off my legs and standing up. "What does it feel like, doing healing magic?" I asked, moving away to stand near one of the big windows. The early morning sunlight sparkled on the dew-covered grass.

"What do you mean?"

Rubbing my hands up and down my arms like I was cold, I shrugged. "It seems like it would be super draining, closing wounds and bringing people back from near death."

"It's actually kind of the opposite," he said, getting up off the couch. "It's like . . . touching electricity, I guess. You're handling someone's life energy, so it's intense, yeah, but there's like this *charge* from it."

"I'm not sure how I feel about you 'handling my life energy,' Cal."

He grinned, and I was taken aback by how different it

made him look. Cal spent so much time being stoic and solemn that it was easy to forget he even had teeth. "I'll buy you dinner first next time, I promise."

Okay, the grin was one thing, but that had definitely been flirting. Then, like I wasn't thrown enough, Cal leaned down and picked up a potted African violet on the low table next to the sofa and brought it over to me. For a second, I wondered if this was his socially awkward way of trying to give me flowers, but he said, "Any Prodigium can do it, really. Not on the same level I can, but still. You just have to be patient." He pushed the plant toward me, and I noticed a few brown spots on its velvety petals. "Wanna try?"

I looked at the droopy violet and snorted. "Thanks, but that poor little flower looks like it's suffered enough." Wiggling my fingers, I added, "I'm way better at the blowing-stuff-up part of magic. Healing is probably beyond me." Sure, I'd managed to make water pink and change Nick's clothes yesterday, but healing seemed a lot harder than that. Not to mention that my mind was still on that jagged piece of paper, and how Dad had covered up our stealing the grimoire.

Cal nudged my arm with the pot. "You said you were working on controlling your powers. No magic requires more control than healing. Try."

I thought about protesting that I was too worn out

from the spell with Dad earlier, but the truth was, thanks to Cal's magic, I felt better than I had in days.

And I'm pretty sure he knew it.

I took the terra-cotta pot. "What exactly do I do?"

Cal curled his fingers around mine and raised my left hand to the brownish flower. There was a callus on his thumb that should have been irritating against my skin.

"In a lot of ways, healing is like any other magic. You concentrate on what you want to change, and you make it happen."

"Or, in my case, explode."

Cal just shook his head and said, "But when you're healing something living, you have to take it into account, too."

"And I do that how?"

Cal's fingers tightened on mine, and my heart thumped in response. The library felt very quiet and very still around us. "You'll feel it."

I swallowed, which was hard to do what with my mouth suddenly drying out. "Okay."

I closed my eyes and felt my magic traveling up from the bottoms of my feet. So far, so good. I thought about those brown spots on the petals, all the while keeping Mom's face firmly lodged in my brain. *Heal*, I thought, feeling too self-conscious to actually say the word out loud. The flower stirred under my hand, but when I cracked my eyelids, it looked as brown as ever.

I closed my eyes and took more of those deep breaths Dad was so fond of, thinking that it was no wonder Prodigium were always getting their asses handed to them by humans. I mean, every time I had to do an intense spell, there was all this focusing, and relaxing, and picturing, and breathing. . . . It wasn't exactly the most effective battle strategy against something like The Eye.

I should've known better than to think about The Eye, though. As soon as the name popped into my head, my control shattered.

And so did the terra-cotta pot.

Black soil rained down on my feet, and the purple flower drooped even further. I could have sworn it actually bobbed accusingly at me.

"Ugh," I groaned, as Cal quickly scooped the jagged pot out of my hands. "Sorry, but I warned you I was destructo-girl."

"Don't worry about it," he said, even as his hand curled protectively around the plant. "You almost had it." He glanced down, probably to survey the damage. "Oh, wow," he said, surprised.

I wiped my dirty hands on my jeans. "That bad?"

"No, it's not that," he said. "Look."

He held the pot out to me. The flower was still awfully droopy, but just behind it were two other smaller, non-droopy flowers. And these were vibrant purple, without a brown spot to be seen. "Whoa. Did I make those?" I asked.

Cal nodded. "You must have. So much for destructo-girl."

I gave him a rueful smile. "Yeah, well, shiny new flowers or not, there's still a broken pot, and a very sad old violet."

"Maybe," he said with a nod. Then he paused, and I could tell that whatever he was going to say was really important. There was even a chance he might use more than five words to say it. "Or maybe your magic isn't that destructive after all. The rain of Doritos, the bed thing, this . . . Maybe it's just that you *create* too big, you know?"

When I could find my voice, I said, "Cal, that might be the nicest thing anyone's said to me since we got here."

He twirled one of the naked roots between his fingers, and didn't meet my eyes. "It's true." Then he glanced up and gave one of those half smiles I was really starting to like. "And it's also true that I need to find another pot for this guy. I, uh, guess I'll see you at dinner."

"Great. We can pick out our colors."

"What?"

"For the wedding. I'm thinking melon and mint. Supposed to be really hot next spring."

Cal laughed out loud, the first time I'd ever heard him do that. "It's a plan. See ya, Sophie."

"Later," I called after him, suddenly struck by a pang of sadness. Archer had called out, "See ya, Mercer," at the end of nearly every cellar duty. I'd never hear him say that again.

It sucks that we miss people like that. You think you've accepted that someone is out of your life, that you've grieved and it's over, and then bam. One little thing and you feel like you've lost that person all over again.

I thought about him sitting in the corn mill, waiting for me. What had he wanted to tell me so badly that he'd risk his life to say it?

I tightened my fingers around one of the jagged shards of pottery so hard that I nearly drew blood. "It doesn't matter," I murmured. The whole Archer thing was beyond done. And, I reminded myself with a glance upstairs, I apparently had way bigger problems than a messed-up love life.

CHAPTER 23

Dad's office was actually one of the smaller rooms at Thorne. Inside was pretty nice, though. There was a cherrywood desk and ivory carpets, plus comfortable leather chairs and sturdy-looking bookshelves. He also had nice view of the river.

Dad was at his desk when I opened the door, doing what all British people do when they're freaked out: drinking tea. I leaned against the door frame. "So . . . this sucks, right?"

He waved me into the office. "Close the door behind you."

Once I had, Dad opened one of the desk drawers. The grimoire looked even worse in the bright light of his office, but there was still a sense of menace coming off of it that made me want to cross my arms over my chest.

"I glamoured another book to look like the grimoire, and remade the glass," Dad said to my unspoken question. "Still, I'll need to get it back soon. The glamour won't hold forever."

He threw the book onto his desk, where it landed amid all the paper. "I've looked through it three times already. The possession ritual isn't in here."

Gingerly, I lifted the book and opened it. I'd felt the magic coming off of it even when it was in its case, but I still wasn't prepared for the wave of power that hit me. It felt like when you stick your face out the window of a fast-moving car. My lungs burned and my eyes watered just looking at it. My stinging eyes scanned the first page, but there were no words I could make out, only strange and unfamiliar symbols.

Still, I recognized one of them. It looked a lot like the mark Dad had put on the Vandy's hand when he'd banished her.

Before I could even turn the first page, I dropped the book back on the papers. "Holy hell weasel," I breathed.

Dad nodded. "Now you see why I had to let you do the majority of the heavy lifting while opening the case. There was no way I could have used that much magic *and* had the strength to search for the ritual."

"Now you tell me." I sank down into one of the leather chairs opposite Dad's desk. "How did you even know what you were looking for? There aren't any words in this thing."

"It wasn't easy. Even I didn't realize how powerful this book is." He opened the front cover, and I winced; but since I couldn't see the pages, I didn't feel the magic this time. Dad, however, visibly shuddered. "This grimoire was written in the language of angels."

"Shouldn't that be, like, harp music or chanting, and not hard-core hieroglyphics?"

Dad either wasn't listening to me, or he chose to ignore that. "What I don't understand is why just *that* ritual was taken," he murmured, almost to himself. "Of all the rituals, why that one?"

"And when did someone take it?" I added.

Dad blinked at me like he'd just suddenly remembered I was in the room. "What?"

"That book has been in that cabinet since, what, 1939? 1940? So did someone rip that page out sometime over the past seventy years, or was it torn out before the grimoire was even locked up?"

"I hadn't thought about that." He pinched the bridge of his nose and sighed. "Curiouser and curiouser."

Startled, I glanced at him. "I say that sometimes."

Even with his face tight with worry, Dad managed to look a little amused. "It's from *Alice in Wonderland.* Appropriate, don't you think?"

Yeah, except that our rabbit hole was a heck of a lot darker, I thought.

I pretended to study the bookcase in the far corner. I'd expected boring books about Prodigium history or shifter economy, and there were a few of those, but I also noticed some recent fiction, as well as several Roald Dahl books. Dad went up in my estimation another notch.

"Do you think whoever—or whatever—raised Daisy and Nick had that piece of paper?"

"They would've had to."

I turned back to him. "And that's bad."

"Worse than bad." He leaned forward. "Sophie, Virginia Thorne raised a demon to use as a weapon. I can only think that whoever raised Nick and Daisy had similar motives."

I blew out a breath. "Dad, this is a total cluster . . . um, a mess."

He flashed me a wry smile. "I think the word you were about to use is probably the best summation of the current situation."

"So what do we do?"

"There's nothing we can do right now except wait and see how it all plays out."

I tapped my fingernail. I'd never been very good at concealing my emotions, and fear was practically making my internal organs shake. Whoever had that ritual could technically raise a whole army of demons if they wanted to. And if Prodigium had that on their side in a war against The Eye? I fought back the image of Archer lying broken and bloody at the feet of some demon, of all that horror spilling out into the human world as it had before. Trying to keep my voice light, I said, "Well, waiting is lame-sauce."

"I'm not sure I know what that means, exactly, but I think I share the sentiment." Dad put the grimoire back in his desk, closing the drawer with a soft click.

I hoisted myself out of the chair. "Dad, do you really think finding out who did this can stop a war from coming?"

"I don't know," he said quietly. He was looking at me, but I got the feeling he wasn't really seeing me. "I hope so."

As far as reassurances went, it wasn't great, but it would have to do.

I was almost to the door when Dad said, "Before you go, Sophie, would you tell me why you've been carrying a Saint Anthony's medallion in your pocket for the past two days?"

"Huh?" Then I remembered the coin Archer had given me. Reluctantly, I pulled it out of my pocket and handed it to Dad. "It's just something I found. How did you know I had it?"

He turned it over in his fingers. "I could sense the magic." He glanced up at me. "Saint Anthony's medallions are very powerful objects. Witches and warlocks used them in the Middle Ages, usually if they were travelling. You could give them to someone and use them to telepathically show your location. Very useful if you got lost or captured, both of which happened quite often in those days." He flicked it back at me. "I'm actually not surprised you found one. We have dozens in the cellar at Hecate."

Well, that explained it, then. Secret demon hunter *and* thief. Man, did I know how to pick 'em.

I entertained the idea of going back to bed, but when I opened the door to my room, I discovered Nick and Daisy waiting for me. Nick was holding the picture of my mom, while Daisy lounged on my bed, flipping through my copy of *The Secret Garden*.

"Is this your mom?" Nick asked. "She's a hottie."

While Nick no longer set my teeth on edge, I still wasn't crazy about him—or Daisy for that matter—pawing through my stuff. "What do you guys want?"

Nick whistled through his teeth as he placed the photograph back on my nightstand. "We were just coming to check on you. Heard you got hurt doing a spell today."

"Oh," I said. "Uh . . . yeah, I was practicing with Dad. But I'm fine now."

Throwing himself down on the bed next to Daisy, Nick folded his arms behind his head. "Ah, yes, all the breathing and focusing stuff."

"Such a waste of time," Daisy murmured, tracing her finger over an illustration of Mary Lennox wandering the halls of Misselthwaite.

I let that go. "Well, as you can see, I'm fine. Thanks for worrying about me."

Nick made quite the production of getting off the bed. "I think we're being dismissed, my love," he said to Daisy before pulling her to her feet.

"But we didn't get to talk to Sophie about the party," she said, a hint of whine in her voice.

"What party?" I asked.

Nick smiled. "Your birthday party. Apparently, the Council is throwing quite the shindig."

Thanks to all the moving around Mom and I had done, I hadn't had a birthday party since I was eight years old. That had been at Chuck E. Cheese. Something told me the Council had something more elaborate in mind.

"They don't need to do that," I said, shoving my hands into my pockets. "Especially with all that's going on right now."

Nick flashed me a wolfish grin. "That's Prodigium

for you. Very 'fiddle while Rome burns.'"

Daisy looped her arm through his. "Besides, it'll be fun. They'll go all out for—" She broke off suddenly, and her smile turned into a grimace of pain. All the blood seemed to drain from her face, turning her ivory skin ashen. She dropped her head, and Nick caught her elbow.

"Daisy?"

Her hands clutched the footboard of my bed, and she took several deep shuddering breaths. Then she raised her head and opened her eyes. I half expected them to be violet-red, like Alice's had been the night she'd killed Elodie, but they were her usual light green. "I'm fine," she said, but her voice was tight. "Just a little . . . magic flare-up. Nothing to worry about."

Nick's face creased with worry, but Daisy waved him off. "I'm fine," she said again, steering him toward the door. "Now let's let Sophie get some rest. She looks a bit rough."

I couldn't have looked any worse than Daisy, but I didn't say anything as she and Nick left. Only once they were gone did I catch that familiar scent of burning wood in the air. But this time, it was no hallucination.

There, in the footboard of my bed, were two singed and smoking handprints.

CHAPTER 24

For the next three weeks, I kept a closer eye on Nick and Daisy. There were no more "magic flare-ups," but it seemed like both of them were drinking more than normal, and every time they sat in on "demon yoga" with me and Dad, they ended up leaving early. After one of the lessons, Dad gave them a copy of *Demonologies: A History*. I found it later, stuffed in a tall brass urn.

A couple of days before Vix was supposed to leave, Lara drove Jenna, Cal, Vix, and me into London—Dad put the kibosh on any more Itineris travel—and I finally got to do all the touristy stuff. When we went to the Tower of London, Lara gave us these little brochures that talked about the Prodigium history of the place, like how Anne Boleyn was really a dark witch (no surprise there), and that one of Queen Victoria's grandsons had been held in the White Tower after becoming a vampire.

It was a fun day, I guess. I mean, there was fish-and-chips, and a ride on one of those double-decker buses. But going to London made me realize how accustomed I'd gotten to only ever being around Prodigium. Hex Hall was super isolated, obviously, and so was Thorne. It had been nearly a year since I'd been around humans, and I was surprised by how nervous I felt. I kept waiting for someone to notice the weird brochures, or Vix's and Jenna's bloodstones, and realize what we really were. It was an unsettling sensation, and I wondered if that's how other Prodigium felt all the time. So I breathed a sigh of relief when our car turned down the gravel drive later that evening.

Our next trip to London came two days before my birthday. Not only did we have to take Vix back to the airport, but also Jenna, Nick, Daisy, and I had an appointment at Lysander's, a super-posh boutique. Lysander was a faerie, but he kept his shop glamoured so the rich human women who shopped there didn't know it. This day, however, the store was closed to everyone but us.

"The costume is great," I said to Lysander, "but a crown? Really?"

He glared at me, his black wings beating. I'd only been in his shop for thirty minutes, but I was pretty sure the guy already hated me. "It was my understanding that you were to go dressed as the goddess of witchcraft, and *Hecate* wears a crown."

"It's not really a crown, Soph," Jenna offered from her spot on a nearby white satin settee. "It's more like a tiara." She had her chin in her hand, and there was practically a little black rain cloud over her head. We had taken Vix to the airport, so Jenna was Sulky McSulkerton. Nick sat next to her, with Daisy on the other side. They'd tried on their costumes earlier, and while they'd both looked great—Nick in a white doublet, flowy shirt, and black pants; Daisy in a simple column of purple silk—I had no idea who they were supposed to be.

"Lysander's right," Lara added. She was sitting in a chair, her legs demurely crossed at the ankles. "The crown is an essential part of the costume. And besides, it looks lovely."

I turned around on the little raised platform and studied myself in the three-way mirror. It had been Lara's idea that my birthday party be "fancy dress." At first I'd assumed that meant black tie, kind of like the All Hallow's Eve Ball back at Hex Hall. But apparently in England, fancy dress means costume party.

It has also been Lara's idea that I go as Hecate, as a nod to the school. I thought that was kind of crappy—it made me feel like I was Hex Hall's mascot or something—but

Dad liked it, and since he was the one footing the bill for this whole thing, Hecate it was.

Still, as I took in my reflection, I couldn't help but wish I'd put up a little bit more of a fight. It wasn't that the costume wasn't gorgeous. Lysander was the go-to guy when Prodigium needed fancy clothes, and he had certainly outdone himself on this dress. It was made of a shimmery black fabric that sparkled with silver in the right light, and despite it covering pretty much every bit of me except for my shoulders, it was undeniably sexy.

And then there was the crown.

Jenna could call it a tiara all she wanted, but it was a filigree band of platinum topped with a diamond and sapphire crescent moon, and it definitely felt crownlike.

I fought the urge to pull at the dress where it fastened around my neck. "It's beautiful," I said for what had to be the third time. "It's just awfully . . . elaborate."

Lysander made a disgusted sound and threw up his hands. "It should be elaborate! You're meant to be a *goddess*!"

I had no idea how to reply to that, but Nick saved me. Leaping to his feet, he said, "And you do look like a goddess, Sophie." He took my hand and pulled me off the platform, spinning me. "See? Embrace your goddessness."

Nick may have been a weirdo and a half, but I chuckled.

218

Then he pulled me to him like we were going to dance, and the laugh died in my throat. For an instant, all I could see was another dance, another dress, another dark-haired boy holding me, and the sudden pain that lanced through me caught me by surprise. Before I could stop myself, I raised a hand to his chest and pushed him away.

An awkward silence descended over the room. Lara discreetly cleared her throat and said, "Nick, Daisy, why don't you come with me and let Jenna and Sophie get changed? Lysander, we can discuss your payment."

Nick and Daisy shot me unreadable looks as they followed Lara and Lysander.

"You okay?" Jenna said once we were alone.

I shook my head, but answered, "Yeah. Just a little freaked out about the party."

Which technically wasn't a lie. It seemed profoundly stupid to gather a whole bunch of very important Prodigium plus four demons in one place when things were so scary. But Dad had explained that it was a point of pride with the remaining Council members. "We can't let The Eye think they've cowed us," Dad had said. Then he'd given me a little smile. "Besides, this will be the first birthday party of yours I've ever been to."

I couldn't resist that. Still, I was uneasy about the whole thing.

Jenna stood up, coming to stand beside me. She had

decided to go as Mina Harker from *Dracula*, and she was wearing her own Lysander design, a pseudo-Victorian concoction of black lace and pink silk. It even had a cool little top hat and veil.

There were no changing rooms at Lysander's, probably because faeries tend to be really into their bodies and showing them off, so something like "modesty" is kind of a foreign concept to them. Luckily, Jenna and I had lived in close quarters for nearly a year, so it wasn't a big deal.

"You looked really beautiful in it, though," Jenna offered as I attempted to unsnarl the crown from my hair.

"Please. I look like an Evanescence album cover. *You* look fabulous." Jenna tipped her top hat at me, which made me smile. "I just hope no pictures of me looking like this ever get back to Hex Hall," I continued, turning toward the mirror. Maybe if I could actually see where the crown was snagged . . . "Can you imagine? Dressed as Hecate? And wearing this thing?" I gave another tug. "All my new social cachet would be gone like *that*."

I glanced at Jenna in the mirror, but she had her back to me. Weird. I thought that would've gotten me at least a chuckle.

"Sucks to think that we'll be back at Hex in, what, four weeks? Gonna be quite an adjustment after being"— I pulled hard, but my hair refused to let go—"a pretty, pretty princess all summer." I was joking, but even as I said it, my stomach sank. Thorne definitely had its own issues, but at least I could do magic here.

Jenna turned and met my eyes in the mirror. "I'm not going back to Hecate, Sophie."

My fingers stopped tugging, and the tiara dangled limply near my left ear. "What?" I whirled around to face her.

"I'm not going back," she said, her voice firmer now.

"But . . . you have to," I said stupidly.

For the first time in a long time, Jenna's face flushed with anger. "No, I don't. I don't have to do anything the Council tells me to. They're not—"

"The boss of you?" I finished, even as I cringed at how snotty that sounded. But Jenna couldn't leave Hecate. I was already dreading going back; how could I possibly do it without her?

"I don't belong there," Jenna said, pulling off her pink lace gloves. "Vix thinks it's time we were with our own kind, and so do I."

A very nasty comment sprung to the tip of my tongue, but I bit it back. In two days I would be seventeen, and I couldn't act like a toddler with hurt feelings. I touched the tiara and used my magic to make my hair uncurl itself from the platinum band. "But last year you said you didn't even want to be a vampire. That you wanted a normal life with algebra and prom, and all that."

"Last year changed both of us a lot, Soph," she said, not unkindly.

"Yeah." It was all I could think of to say. We got changed with our backs to each other, and neither of us said anything until we were back in our regular clothes, the costumes up on silk hangers.

"I don't get why you're so upset," Jenna said, taking me by the shoulders and turning me to face her. "This is something I have to do. I thought you'd get that, especially after everything with the Removal."

I stepped back, and her arms fell limply between us. "What does that have to do with anything?"

"Well, if you had gone through the Removal, I'd have been left on my own at Hex Hall, and that never seemed to bother you."

"Right, but I was going to do that so I wouldn't *kill anybody*," I said, trying not to get angry but failing miserably. "It wasn't like I was ditching you at Hecate to frolic with some guy."

Her eyes flashed, and I thought I saw a hint of fang. "Oh, really? So you're telling me Archer had nothing to do with why you wanted to get your powers removed, and ditch *me* at Hecate?"

I gaped at her, even as magic swirled up in me. "What?"

Jenna rubbed her nose with the back of her hand,

her voice thick when she said, "Like it never crossed your mind that you could be with him if you weren't a demon."

It had. Or at least I think it had. All the reasons I'd wanted to go through the Removal were too twisty and complex to sort out. But still, it hadn't been the main reason, and how could she . . . Something clicked.

"That's why you were all 'Sophie and Cal, rah, rah, rah!' isn't it? You thought if I found some new guy, I wouldn't want to go through the Removal."

She didn't have to answer. The blush that spread up her neck and her lowered gaze were enough.

"I watched Alice murder Elodie, Jenna. I thought I was a monster. That's why I wanted the Removal, not so I could be with Archer." My powers were racing around me now, curling inside me. A nearby mannequin rattled, and both mine and Jenna's hair was fluttering slightly. "The Removal could have killed me," I continued. "And you'd have to be a total moron to die for a *crush*."

Jenna recoiled like I'd slapped her, and I suddenly realized what I'd said. "Oh, Jenna," I said, taking a stumbling step toward her. "I didn't mean—"

"No," she snapped, backing up from me. "I get it. You're Demon Queen of the World, and I'm an idiot who let a monster kill me."

"That's not what I said."

223

"You didn't have to."

It seemed impossible to believe that just a few minutes ago we were laughing and joking about my dumb costume. "Jenna," I said, but she just shook her head and walked away.

CHAPTER 25

My seventeenth birthday party was held in the conservatory, that giant glass room filled with plants. The ferns had been decorated with tiny purple ribbons and white lights. A group of faeries were set up in the corner, playing some kind of elaborate clockwork instruments, but the music that came out of them was thin and wavering, and weirdly melancholy for a birthday party. Not that you could hear it that well, anyway. A storm had sprung up earlier in the evening, and raindrops were splattering loudly on the glass roof. I had staked out a spot on a window seat, and from there I watched the rain trickle down the glass like tears.

I thought about my last birthday party and decided that despite the ice sculptures, and the champagne fountain, and the giant cake shaped like Thorne Abbey, I preferred Skee-Ball and a guy in giant rat suit.

Of course, that could have had something to do with the fact that my dress weighed roughly fifty pounds, my crown was giving me a headache, and my best friend was currently not speaking to me.

I scanned the room, but I didn't see Jenna. She'd kept her distance ever since that day in the dress shop. Maybe it was easier this way. If Jenna was bound and determined to get her vamp on, it might hurt less if we weren't friends anymore. Still, telling myself that did nothing to lessen the ache in my chest.

There were maybe a hundred Prodigium in the room, all of them in fancy, glittering costumes, and they were all smiling at me, and coming up to wish me a happy birthday. They'd all brought gifts, too: a marble-top table near the door was rapidly piling up with brightly wrapped packages. Still, there was this heavy feeling in the air, like everyone was trying too hard to have a good time. Laughs were too loud, and smiles looked forced. Maybe they were afraid Dad and I would vaporize them if they didn't act like this was the best party ever.

I would have laid my forehead against the cool glass wall, but I didn't really want to see my reflection that closely. Lysander had brought the dress earlier that afternoon, and insisted on doing my makeup, too. Consequently, it looked like a glitter bomb had exploded on my face. Even my bare shoulders were dusted with sparkling blue powder.

There were dozens of waiters moving through the room, bearing trays of glasses that were filled with a glowing purple concoction. I wasn't sure if the waiters were Thorne's regular servants, or if they'd been specially hired for this party. They were dressed in simple white shirts and black pants, the upper halves of their faces covered with silver masks. One had already come up to me three separate times, and each time I took a drink, only to pour it in the nearest potted plant as soon as the waiter walked away.

"Why so glum, birthday girl?"

I turned to see Nick and Daisy, each holding an empty crystal-and-silver goblet. There was a purple stain on the lapel of Nick's doublet. From their pink cheeks and bright eyes, I guessed those weren't the first drinks they'd had tonight. "It's my party, and I'll sulk if I want to," I replied, heaving myself off the window seat.

"This party does kind of suck," Daisy said, reaching up to straighten the silver laurel wreath on her dark hair.

"You could always open a present, see if that makes you feel better," Nick said, nodding toward the gift table. A couple of the boxes were moving. One spun in slow circles above the rest, while another skittered about like

227

a spider, the trailing ends of white satin ribbon acting as legs.

I gulped. "Um . . . you know what, I'm good. Have either of you seen Jenna?"

A look passed between them, but before they could say anything, that same waiter headed our way again. Ugh. What was that guy's deal? Had someone paid him to get the head of the Council's daughter drunk or something?

Looping my arms through Nick's and Daisy's, I pulled them away from the window and out of the waiter's path. "What are you two fighting about, anyway?" Daisy asked.

I was about to tell her the whole story about Lysander's shop when a blond witch in a bright red dress stopped us. "Hello," she said, her voice breathless. "I'm sorry to interrupt you, but I wanted to wish you happy birthday, Sophia."

"Okay," I said. "Thanks."

I thought she'd move on, but she just kept standing there, smiling at me. Well, at all three of us, actually. "It's just such an honor to meet you," she enthused. "All of you. I hear . . ." she glanced around, and when she turned back to us, her cheeks were flushed. "I hear demons can make something appear out of nothing. Is that true?"

I blinked at her. *What the heck?* "Yeah," I replied. "But so can witches. It's just a matter of—"

Before I could finish, Nick bowed, and with a flourish of his hand, produced a huge bouquet of white roses. "It is indeed true," he said, handing the flowers to the witch. "Of course, that's only a little of what demons are capable of."

The witch nearly squealed. "That's amazing!"

There was a dangerous glint in Nick's eyes. "Oh, that's nothing." He leaned forward and whispered, "If I wanted to, I could bring this whole ballroom down before you had time to blink those pretty brown eyes. Or pull the fabric of time so that—"

"Okay, that's all really awesome, Nick," I said, tugging both him and Daisy away from the witch. "But I think I see my dad, so we should go. Bye! Thanks for coming!"

Once we were out of earshot, I turned to Nick. "What was that all about?"

He took another swig of his drink. "That was me giving them what they want. They want us to be these scary, powerful things that can kill The Eye for them. That's why they made us, right?"

I briefly pressed the heels of my hands against my eyes, which only had the effect of smudging the glittery gunk on my lashes.

Daisy patted Nick's arm, her laurel crown listing heavily to the right. "Sweetie, can we ease off on the killing talk? It's a birthday party." She punctuated that sentence with a little hiccup, and suddenly I was very tired of both of them. I wanted to talk to Jenna. Or Cal. Someone normal—well, as normal as my friends got— and preferably sober.

"Maybe I will go get a present after all," I told them. I had taken maybe four steps when that waiter made another beeline for me. "Drink, miss?" he asked, holding out the tray.

"Look, dude," I said, stumbling a little as I stepped on one of my draping sleeves, "I don't know if you're trying to suck up or what, but—"

I glanced up into his masked face, and our eyes met.

"You have got to be kidding me."

CHAPTER 26

Even though I couldn't see it, I had a feeling Archer was raising an eyebrow at me. "Who are you supposed to be?" he asked in a low voice.

I took deep breaths and tried to keep my face as impassive as possible. If anyone glanced over here, they had to think I was just talking to a waiter, not facing down an Eye in their midst. "Hecate," I said, plucking one of the glasses off his tray. "What are you doing here?"

He shrugged, managing somehow to look elegant even in his waiter's uniform. "Who doesn't love a party? Plus, I thought there might be a chance you'd wear that blue dress again."

My fingers tightened so hard on the crystal goblet that I'm surprised I didn't snap the stem. "You are a crazy person," I said, struggling to keep my voice calm. "Or an idiot. Or a crazy idiot person. Why aren't you at least glamoured or something?"

"No one here has ever seen me in person," he replied, making a show of rearranging the glasses on his tray, "so the mask is good enough. If I'd used a glamour, I just would've drawn attention to myself. Of course, I wouldn't have had to go to all this trouble if you'd just met me three weeks ago."

It could have been the dim lights or the mask, but I thought I saw real anger flash in his eyes for just a second.

"I couldn't," I said, smiling like he'd just said something funny. My heart was leaping around in my chest, and it was all I could do to keep my powers under control. "You should leave. Now."

Now there was no mistaking it: he was definitely pissed. "Do you have any idea what I risked to come here tonight?" he hissed. "Not only from your people, but mine?"

I glanced around, but no one seemed to be watching me. That would probably change once I started yelling at a waiter. I gave Archer what I hoped was a significant look, but thanks to all the sparkle, I wasn't sure he got it.

I walked away to the corner of the room and ducked behind a truly insane amount of potted plants. The light back there was dim and green, and everything smelled rich and loamy.

Archer parted the palm frond a few seconds later and leaned against the glass wall, his arms folded over his chest. "Why didn't you meet me?" he asked without preamble.

"I don't know, maybe because you're a demon hunter and I'm a demon, so us hanging out seems like a bad idea?" When he didn't reply, I sighed and said, "Look, basically, everyone in my life has told me to stay away from you. So that's what I'm doing."

It was weird talking to him while he was wearing that mask. I could see his eyes, but I couldn't read him at all. "Trust me," he said. "If there weren't something major going down right now, I'd never see you again. Happily."

Pain sliced through my heart, as bright and sharp as the dagger Archer undoubtedly had hidden somewhere on his body. I hoped I didn't let it show. "What do you mean, 'something major'?"

But he shook his head. "I don't have time to get into it, but it's about your little demon buddies back there. Can you meet me tomorrow night at the mill?"

My brain raced. If Archer really knew something about Nick and Daisy, maybe Dad and I could get a better grip on what was going on here. Or was I just telling myself that so I could spend time with Archer and not feel guilty about it?

"I can't tomorrow." Dad and I hadn't had any time

to research stuff about the grimoire, thanks to all the birthday madness, but we'd set aside all next week to work on it. That should have been all I said. That could have ended it, and I could've walked away. Instead, I heard myself say, "But my dad leaves for a business trip in nine days. It would be easier for me to get away then."

He nodded. "Good. Nine days, then. Three a.m."

"Fine. But if you pull a knife on me again—"

To my surprise, he laughed. "You keep bringing that up. First of all, I didn't pull the knife on *you*, I pulled it out so I could jimmy the lock on that window. Secondly, I was trapped in a cellar with a pissed-off demon. Of the two of us, who do you think was the most freaked out?"

I rolled my eyes, no easy feat, seeing as how my eyelids were weighed down with a thousand pounds of glitter. Archer moved past me, out of the plants. When I followed a few seconds later, he was nowhere to be seen.

As I walked over to the gift table, I kept looking around for him, but it was obvious he'd already left. I sighed and reached up to take off my crown. I was probably making a huge mistake, but Dad wanted to know where Nick and Daisy came from, and if Archer—or The Eye—had that information, why shouldn't we use it?

"There you are."

Cal appeared at my elbow, and it was all I could do

not to jump guiltily. Then I saw what he was wearing. "Where did you get that?"

Cal was dressed in a Hex Hall uniform. The blazer was a little tight on his broad shoulders, more so when he shrugged. "It was mine. Mrs. Casnoff brought it with her. I don't really, uh, do costumes. Figured this was a good compromise."

I'd thought no one but Archer could make that uniform look good, but Cal proved me wrong. The bright blue was nice against his tan skin and golden hair, and he looked younger. There was a dimple in his cheek as he smiled at me—something I'd never noticed before. "You make a good Hecate," he said.

I would have snorted and made a sarcastic comment, but there was something in his eyes that made me just say, "Thanks."

All of the sudden, something else he'd said clicked. "Wait, Mrs. Casnoff brought it? Is she here?"

"Yeah," Cal said, nodding over toward the ice sculpture, where, sure enough, Mrs. Casnoff stood. She was wearing a draping gown in the same bright blue as Cal's uniform.

When Mrs. Casnoff saw us, she walked over to us. "Sophie," she said, her voice warmer than I'd ever heard it. "Happy birthday. It's good to see you."

I actually believed she meant it, which was weird.

Weirder still was the smile she gave me as she said, "I was just talking with several of the guests about your decision not to go through with the Removal. We're all so pleased."

Great. Nothing better than my superpersonal decision being party chitchat.

"Well, that's probably a first for you," I tried to joke. When she just looked confused, I clarified. "Being pleased with me."

And then she completely freaked me out by laughing. Granted, it was a low, short laugh, but still. Before Mrs. Casnoff could blow my mind any more, Dad walked over, wearing a long black robe and carrying a staff topped with a dark red jewel carved to look like a pomegranate. Once again, I had no clue who he was supposed to be. He and Mrs. Casnoff just nodded at each other, so I guess they'd said their hellos earlier.

"Are you having a nice time?" Dad asked, and there was such a hopeful look on his face that I forced a bright grin.

"Yeah, best birthday party ever!"

I think I oversold it a little bit, but Dad seemed relieved. "Good. I know it's a bit much, but . . . well, it's the first time I've celebrated one of your birthdays. I wanted it to be special."

Guilt and other general yucky feelings bounced inside me. To keep Dad from noticing, I turned my attention to the gift table. That one present was still floating above the rest, spinning in lazy circles. As I looked at it, it drifted toward me, landing softly in my hands.

"I think that one wants you to open it," Cal observed.

The wrapping paper was a deep purple, and the silver ribbon curled and undulated around my fingers like it was underwater. It was a beautiful gift, but the magic coming off it felt awfully strong. Probably from the floating spell, I thought as I tugged at the bow.

It was the smell I noticed first, that weird metallic scent you sometimes get in a lightning storm. There was a sudden flash of red light, and a sound like a sonic boom. I heard Dad or Cal shout, and the next thing I knew, I was on my back, a painful stinging sensation in my shoulder.

My ears felt stuffed with cotton, but I had the sense that people were yelling, and I watched pairs of feet run by my head. It reminded me of prom, when I'd sat in that pool of punch, watching chaos erupt all around me. Then my shoulder stopped stinging and started burning, badly enough that I moaned. There was a crush of people around me, and I saw a tall figure wearing a mask push his way to the front of the crowd. His mouth was tight, and I thought I saw fear in his familiar brown eyes. I almost opened my mouth to tell Archer to get out of here before I realized how stupid that would be. Then the people shifted, and he was gone.

Cal's face swam into view. I couldn't hear him over the ringing in my ears. I'm pretty sure he mouthed for me to lie still, which seemed easy enough.

He held my hand, and while the pain didn't go away, a woozy sense of calm spread over me. So I was pretty dispassionate as I rolled my head to the side and watched Cal pull a six-inch shard of demonglass out of my shoulder. As soon as it was out, the burning faded, but I knew I'd have yet another scar. "That present sucked," I muttered.

Dad slipped an arm around my shoulder and helped me sit up. As he did, his sleeve fell back to reveal several slivers of demonglass embedded in his forearm.

"I'm fine," he said before I could ask. "Cal can get them out later. Are you all right?"

My shoulder was still on fire, but there was no pain anywhere else, and other than the shock of being blown backward and stabbed, I was peachy. "I think so. What was that, like a magic pipe bomb?"

The present lay in tatters on the floor, its ribbon coiling and snapping like a snake. Cal stomped on the ribbon, and it went still. "Seems like it," he said grimly.

"And it was ensorcelled to seek you out," Dad added. He looked so worried and angry that I decided not to give him a hard time for using a word like *ensorcelled*.

"Thank God they couldn't get their hands on very much demonglass," Lara said, and I glanced up, surprised to see her. She was wearing some sort of eighteenth-century gown, with wide hips and a square neckline. Her hair was hidden underneath a towering powdered wig. "It seems like that was the biggest piece," she continued, kicking the shard that had pierced my shoulder. Roderick was behind her, his black wings beating slowly, stirring the air. Lara turned to him and said, "Search the grounds. If Cross is still here, we'll find him."

My brain still felt woozy, and my voice was weak when I said, "Cross?"

It was Mrs. Casnoff who answered me. "Clearly, The Eye was behind this. Who else would do such a thing?"

"And since there's only one Eye who can do magic," Lara said, her voice sounding almost identical to her sister's, "it's obvious. Archer Cross just made another attempt on your life."

CHAPTER 27

The next nine days stretched out like taffy. Mrs. Casnoff went back to Hecate, which was kind of a relief. Having her at Thorne had been a little too "worlds colliding" for me. I spent most of my time in my room, recovering from my injury. But staring at the wall gave me lots of time to think, mostly about Archer. I'd seen the look on his face right after the explosion had gone off. He'd been scared. Shocked, even, and not in the "Whoops, my assassination didn't go off as planned" way. He hadn't known it was coming, which meant he couldn't have been the one who planted the gift. Which meant there was someone else who wanted to kill me, a thought that made me want to never leave the safe cocoon of my bed. Still, I decided to keep my meeting with Archer. I had a feeling that all of this was connected somehow. Nick and

Daisy, the attempt on my life, The Eye suddenly getting way more hard-core. The sooner I got to the bottom of it, the better.

There was one good thing that had come out of nearly being shish kebabbed; Jenna started talking to me again. She came by my room the morning after the party to check on me, standing uncertainly in the doorway. "How are you feeling?"

I scooted back onto my pillows and tried to shrug. That sent a fire bolt of pain through my whole upper body, though, and I grimaced. "Oh, you know. Like I got stabbed by glass from hell. But it's getting better."

Jenna took a couple of steps into the room, her expression grave. "You could've been killed."

"Yeah, but I wasn't."

A couple more steps and she was beside my bed, sitting on the edge. "Soph," she started, but I interrupted her. "Look, Jenna, can we just skip to the part where we both say we're sorry and hug?"

She gave a startled laugh, and for the first time, I noticed there were tears in her eyes. "Yeah, let's do that," she said with a sniffle, before gingerly wrapping her arms around me.

We sat there, our arms around each other, until I asked, "You're still not coming back, are you?"

She shook her head. "I can't." When she pulled away,

tears were streaming down her face, and even her pink stripe looked dimmer. "I have to do this, Sophie."

I wasn't sure if I could talk around the sudden lump in my throat, so I just nodded.

"But it's not like I won't be able to see you ever again," she said, squeezing my hand. "You could even come visit the nest at Christmas."

"*Nest*?" I asked, raising both eyebrows.

Jenna shrugged, embarrassed. "That's what you call it when a bunch of vampires live together."

I tried to think up a witty comment, maybe something about hippies and communes, but I was too sad to be snarky.

Between the thought of going back to Hecate alone and nervousness over meeting Archer, I was too much of a basket case to work with Dad. It wasn't until the day before he left that I felt up to working with the grimoire. No one seemed to have noticed that it was missing, and once I went to check on the glamoured book Dad had left in its place, I could see why. Even I couldn't tell it wasn't the same book, and the trace of magic coming off the glamour was so faint that you couldn't feel it unless you knew it was there.

We studied it in the same room where I practiced controlling my powers. The force coming off those pages still made my heart race and my head ache. Regardless, I sat down next to Dad on the floor, the book spread out before us, and listened as he explained every spell. He had been right: the magic contained within those pages was some of the darkest stuff I'd ever heard of. There were killing spells, and rituals that would bind another soul to yours so you could make someone your slave. Dad went over each one, his voice level and calm, no matter how bad the enchantments were. There was only one spell he didn't talk about, which was weird. The markings for it only took up half a page, and they looked pretty simple, but when we flipped to that page, Dad drew in his breath.

"What?" I asked, fidgeting on the cold marble floor. "It can't be any worse than that one about babies."

"It's not that," Dad said. He pushed his glasses farther up on his nose. "It's just that I didn't know this particular spell actually existed."

"What does it do?"

Dad paused before sliding the book over to me. "Touch it."

I raised my eyebrows, but did what he asked. I don't know why, but I pressed my whole palm to the page so that my hand nearly covered the markings. As soon as I did, I felt a weird thud in my chest, like someone had just punched me lightly in the sternum.

"Um, ow," I said, drawing back my hand. "Are you going to tell me what I just did?"

He pulled the book back. "No. Hopefully, you'll never need to know."

And apparently that was that, because Dad shut the grimoire and stood up. "I think it's time to put this back," he said. "There's nothing more to be learned from it, and I now see why the Council keeps it locked up." He glanced down at the book with disgust. "If it were up to me, we'd destroy it."

"So do it." After some of the stuff we'd read in that thing, nothing would make me happier than seeing it in flames. The thought of it in the wrong hands was truly shudder-worthy.

But Dad shook his head. "Alexei Casnoff wanted it kept intact as a reminder."

"Of course he did." I winced as I stood, and Dad hurried to help me up.

"How are you feeling?"

"Hard as it may be to believe, better. How's your arm?"

He absentmindedly rubbed it. "Stings, but it could've been much worse."

He slipped the grimoire inside his jacket, and we made our way back downstairs. I could tell there was something bothering Dad, but whether it was all that stuff in the grimoire or the birthday party incident, I didn't know.

We were all the way to the foyer before he said, "Sophie, I have to tell your mother about what happened."

I suppressed a groan. I'd known this was coming, but I was hoping we could put it off until after Dad got back. I had a lot going on, and the last thing I wanted was a worried mom on top of all of that.

"Dad, she's just going to freak. And probably come here and get me, and then you guys will start yelling at each other, and I'll have to act out by wearing lots of eyeliner and doing drugs. Do you really want to deal with that?"

Dad smiled and ran a hand over my hair. The gesture was so parental and normal that I didn't know how to react. "Perhaps it can wait until after my trip," he said. "I'm not quite ready to give you back yet."

His voice was full of affection, and I wondered if a person could actually choke on guilt, because it rose up in my throat as bitter and scalding as black coffee.

I looked away, hoping he wouldn't see it, and said, "Where are you going, anyway?"

"Up north, near Yorkshire. Another attack."

He didn't have to say by whom.

"While I'm there," Dad added, "I'm supposed to meet with a warlock in Lincolnshire. He's supposedly done some extensive research on demons, and I'm hoping he may be able to help me with tracing Nick's and Daisy's origins. Hopefully, when I come back, we can begin to resolve this matter."

When he got back, I might have news of my own about Nick and Daisy. Not that I had any idea how I was going to tell him what I'd found out. I didn't want to pursue that train of thought, what with it being all stomach-twisting, so instead, I asked him something else that had been bugging me. "Hey, Dad, remember earlier this week, when I got stabbed?"

"I have a hazy recollection, yes."

"Is it worth it? Being head of the Council? I mean, if people are always gunning for you, why not hand it over to someone else? You could go on vacation. Have a life. Date."

I waited for Dad to embrace his inner Mr. Darcy again and get all huffy, but if anything, he just looked rueful. "One, I made a solemn vow to use my powers to help the Council. Two, things are turbulent now, but that won't always be the case. And I have faith that you'll make a wonderful head of the Council someday, Sophie."

Yeah, except for that whole sleeping with the enemy part, I thought. Wait, not that I would actually be sleeping with . . . I mean, it's a metaphor. There would only be metaphorical sleeping.

My face must have reflected some of the weirdness happening in my brain, because Dad narrowed his eyes at me before continuing, "As for dating, there's no point."

"Why?"

"Because I'm still in love with your mother."

Whoa. Okay, not exactly the answer I was expecting.

Before I could even process that, Dad rushed on, saying, "Please don't let that get your hopes up. There is no way your mother and I could or will ever reunite."

I held up my hand. "Dad, relax. I'm not twelve, and this isn't *The Parent Trap*. But that's . . . it's good to know. I always thought you and Mom must have hated each other. I thought that's why Mom and I moved around so much—because she was trying to make sure you could never find us."

His eyes slid away from my face, focusing on a spot above my shoulder. "Your mother had her reasons," was all he said. Then he sort of sighed and turned away. "All the magic in the world can't simplify affairs of the heart," he murmured as he headed toward his office.

"Tell me about it," I said to his retreating back.

Two days later, he left for Yorkshire, and I prepared for what I'd come to think of as my "field trip" with Archer. Calling it that seemed safer and more business-like than "meeting" or, God forbid, "assignation." Still,

I spent most of the day in my room by myself because I was afraid Jenna or Cal would be able to tell something was up with me. I was so nervous that I was shooting off tiny flashes of magic like a sparkler.

I didn't even attempt to sleep, and I thought three a.m. would never come. Finally, at 2:30, I threw on a black T-shirt and some cargo pants, hoping that was an appropriate ensemble for meeting one's former crush who had turned out to be one's mortal enemy.

As I walked down the gravel path toward the mill, I tried to tell myself that despite my churning stomach, I had nothing to feel guilty about. I was doing this for a good reason. No, Dad might not understand that. And Jenna definitely wouldn't, but . . . no. No, I wasn't going to let the thought of Jenna make me feel bad about this.

When I got to the mill, Archer was waiting for me just as he had before, right by the doorway leading to the Itineris. His back was to me, and he was wearing a dark green V-neck shirt and a pair of worn jeans. That struck me as weird. I'd expected him to be all decked out in L'Occhio black, but instead he looked like any regular teenage guy.

Except for the giant sword in his hand.

"Is that really necessary?" I asked when I walked in, noting that his dagger was also hanging off his belt.

His head jerked up, and I thought he might have

been relieved to see me. But then he turned back to the Itineris, crouching down to pull something out of a black duffel bag at his feet. "Never hurts to be prepared," he said.

"It just seems like overkill when you already have a dagger and I have superpowerful magic at my disposal."

"'Superpowerful?'" He stood up, a gold chain dangling from his fingers. "Let me remind you of two words, Mercer: *Bad. Dog.*"

I rolled my eyes. "That was nearly a year ago. I'm way better now."

"Yeah, well, I'm not taking any chances," he said. For the first time, I noticed there was some sort of holster thing on his back. He slid the sword into it so the hilt rose over his shoulders. "Besides," he added, "I thought you might not come. After what happened the other night . . ." he paused, studying my face. "Are you all right?"

"I will be when people stop asking me that."

"You know I had nothing to do with that, right?"

"Yeah," I replied. "And if you did have something to do with it, I will vaporize you where you stand."

The corner of his mouth quirked. "Good to know."

He closed the distance between us, coming to stand entirely too close to me. "What are you doing?" I asked, hoping I didn't sound as breathless as I felt.

He lifted his hands, and with surprising gentleness, placed the chain around both our necks. Looking down at it, I saw that the links were actually tiny figures holding hands. I'd seen it somewhere before.

"This is the necklace one of the angels is wearing in the window at Hex Hall."

"It is indeed."

Reaching down to take my hands, he explained, "It's also a very powerful protection charm, which we're going to need."

I swallowed as we laced our fingers and stepped closer to the Itineris. "Why?"

"Because we're going a very long way."

I involuntarily squeezed his fingers with mine. The last time I'd traveled through the Itineris, I'd only gone a few hundred miles, and that had made my head nearly explode. "Where are we going?" I asked.

"Graymalkin Island," he answered. And then he yanked me into the doorway.

CHAPTER 28

Archer's necklace thing may have spared us the crushing headache and loss of breath, but it didn't make the landing any more graceful. We were tossed into a thick copse of trees as we came out of the blackness, and I immediately tripped over a huge exposed root, scraping my elbow on a branch as I went down.

Unfortunately, since the necklace was looped around both our necks, that meant Archer fell too. On top of me.

In another lifetime, that might have been kind of pleasant. And yeah, he still smelled nice, and as I grabbed his shoulders to push him away, I remembered that he was a lot stronger than his thin frame would suggest.

But none of that mattered. I didn't get to notice those things about him anymore.

The ground I was lying on was muddy, and I had a

feeling I'd be pulling leaves and twigs out of my hair for all eternity. "Get off of me!" I mumbled against his collarbone, shoving at him. He rolled over onto his back, his sword clanging against a rock or exposed root, but thanks to the necklace, that just pulled me half on top of him.

"And here I thought you were playing hard to get," he whispered. Moonlight glinted in his eyes, and he sounded a little out of breath. I told myself it was just from the fall.

I thwacked his chest with the palm of my hand, then ducked my head underneath the necklace. Once I was free, I scooted away from him. "Let me guess," I hissed, nodding at the chain. "Something else you stole from Hex Hall."

He pushed himself to his feet. "Guilty."

"Where the heck was I while you were playing Grand Theft Cellar?"

"I only took a few things, and most of those I grabbed during those last few weeks when you weren't talking to me."

I remembered that time now, right after the All Hallow's Eve Ball. Thanks to the weirdness of that night, Archer and I had spent a lot of cellar duties avoiding each other. No wonder he'd been able to stuff all sorts of magical things into his pockets.

"Is that why you defended me in Vandy's class?

Were you hoping to get cellar duty just so you could lift stuff?"

Dusting debris off his shirt, Archer shook his head. "Believe it or not, Mercer, I'm not quite that calculating. I stood up to Vandy because I felt like it. Getting to snag stuff out of the cellar ended up being a bonus." He turned his back on me and started walking away. "Now come on. It's a long walk."

"Why can't you just tell me what's going on?" I asked as we made our way out of the grove.

"Because I'm not sure you'd believe me. Easier to show you."

I'd never been on this part of Graymalkin before, and I was struck by how different it looked from the land surrounding Hecate. There was no thick, emerald grass underfoot, or majestic oak trees. The only plants were scrubby pine trees and unidentifiable bushes, and the ground was a mix of damp sand and rocks. From the smell, I knew we were close to the ocean, and sure enough, as we climbed a rise, the water suddenly spread out before us, lapping gently against the shore. The moon was nearly full, making a wide band of silver light on the black water.

"Where are we? Like, in relation to the school."

"We're on the other side of the island," Archer replied.

"It looks so different."

Archer glanced over his shoulder. "That's because there's a spell on the school grounds. Jessica Prentiss did it when she built the house. Apparently she was homesick, because she made it look like her family's place in Louisiana, right down to the landscaping." He paused. "Seriously, Mercer, didn't you pay attention in any of our classes?"

"Sorry, I was a little distracted, what with all the people dying."

He stopped suddenly. "To be fair," he said, his voice light, but his shoulders tense, "only one person died. Elodie."

We were both frozen now, standing several feet apart on the little hill overlooking the sea. "So you do know about that."

He nodded. "Yeah. We, uh, got a report about everything a few months ago." Rubbing the back of his neck, he turned so he was facing the sea. "I didn't . . . all of that was never real. Her and me. At least not on my part. And there were days when I thought if I had to spend one more second listening to her talk about beauty spells or shoes, I was going to go insane. Still, when I read the report . . ." He dropped his head and made a sound that would have been a laugh if it hadn't been so sad. "It was like being punched in the gut, you know?"

Even though he still had his back to me, I nodded. "Yeah."

"It's just hard to believe that someone like her could be gone."

I remembered Elodie's ghostly eyes looking into mine, the nod of her head, and thought about telling him that Elodie was maybe a little less gone than we all thought.

Then he shook his head and headed farther down the path and onto the beach. I followed him, gritting my teeth as sand filled my shoes. "So why were you with her?"

"She was my assignment."

"From The Eye?"

"No, from the Boy Scouts. That Witch Dating badge just kept eluding me."

"Well, you must have at least three Total Douchebag badges by now, so that has to count for something. What about Holly? Was that fake, too?" I was panting slightly, thanks to trying to keep up with him. Stupid short legs.

He had his hands in his pockets, and his head was slightly down, like he was walking against the wind. "You know, these were all things I was willing to tell you several weeks ago. Too bad you decided to stand me up."

I had caught up to him by now, and I snagged his elbow, doing my best to ignore the little thrill that went through me even at that innocent touch. "How is that you can go from decent human being to complete jackass in zero-point-two seconds? Do they teach you that in The Eye?"

He stopped, and his eyes glided over my lips. "Actually, I'm just trying to see if I can make you mad enough to kiss me again."

CHAPTER 29

My heart, which only seconds ago had been racing, suddenly seemed to stumble in my chest. I immediately dropped his arm and moved ahead of him. "I don't want to talk about that," I said as I walked quickly down the beach.

I had no idea where I was going, but at that point, walking straight into the sea didn't seem like such a bad idea. For months I'd been torturing myself, wondering if Archer kissing me had just been part of his act. But he was right, he hadn't kissed me. I had kissed him, and he'd just . . . responded. God, I was a moron.

Archer caught up with me, but I kept looking straight ahead.

"Mercer—"

"Look, forget it," I said. "Just show me whatever it was you dragged me out here to see."

"Fine," he replied, his voice clipped.

We walked down the beach in total silence. In the moonlight, our shadows stretched out before us, almost touching.

Finally we reached a small cove, and Archer turned right, back up the hill and into the forest again. Once more, the trees were so thick, I could barely see anything.

We were only a few feet into the woods when Archer said, "I just thought we should talk about it. Isn't that what you were getting at?"

I turned toward him, but all I could see was his silhouette. Maybe it was the darkness, the fact that I couldn't see his face, but suddenly, six months' worth of anger, confusion, and sadness spilled out of me. "No, Cross, it wasn't. Okay, so we kissed for, like, three minutes. I knew you for *months* before that. We—we were friends. I asked you all that stuff about demons, and you knew what I was. Don't you get why that might be a little upsetting?"

He didn't reply, but then, I didn't really give him a chance to. "All that time we were down there in the cellar, and I was telling you stuff—*real* stuff—about me, you were just, what? Lying? Casing the joint? Taking mental notes for your bosses? Is there any part of the Archer I knew that actually exists?"

Breathing hard, I stared at his dark form, trying to

read anything in his body language. He didn't move, but after a few moments, he blew out a long breath and said, "Okay. I've lived with The Eye for as long as I can remember. Ever since I was about two or three."

"What about your parents?"

He shouldered past me, walking deeper into the forest. "Killed, but no one knew by what. Whatever it was, it drew the attention of The Eye. They got word of a dead witch and warlock, and went to investigate. Found my parents' bodies, and then when they were searching the house, me. I guess no one felt comfortable about killing a toddler, so the team took me back to La Reina. That's what they call the leader of L'Occhio di Dio. Well, when it's a woman, at least. She saw the potential in raising a warlock as an Eye."

A branch brushed against my cheek, and I ducked around it. "Where did all this happen?"

I could practically hear him shrug. "Don't know. They never told me."

"So you don't know where you're from?"

"I don't even know what my real name is, Mercer. La Reina was the one who called me Archer, after an Eye who'd just been killed in battle. Anyway, she let me live, and gave me to a warlock she'd recruited, Simon Cross. He was the one who decided I should infiltrate Hecate, and—what are you doing?"

I had stopped as soon as he'd said "warlock she'd recruited."

"There are other Prodigium who work with The Eye?"

Now he went very still. "Why? You planning on telling Daddy?"

I scowled, even though I knew he couldn't see me. "No, the cone of silence has firmly descended over this entire night. I just . . . they think you're the only one. That's why they're so gung ho about killing you." It also meant that while Archer hadn't planted the exploding birthday gift, another Eye might have. Yay for more complications.

"There aren't many, but they're out there. Who do you think told us you were at Shelley's that night?"

Well, that certainly made things more interesting. And scarier. "Keep going," I said.

He started walking again, holding a branch out of the way so I could duck under it. "Simon trained me as a warlock and as an Eye, and I spent summers in Rome with L'Occhio di Dio, learning sword fighting, attack maneuvers, that kind of thing."

"No wonder you always kicked my ass in Defense," I muttered.

"The Eye had been looking for ways to get into Hex Hall for years, but the screening process for teachers was too intense, and they didn't have any Eyes young enough to get in as students. Until me. When I was fourteen, I turned my middle school gym invisible. Bam, instant ticket to Hecate."

"What did they want you to do there?"

"Nothing as awful as you're probably thinking. Listen, mostly. Observe and report back." He stopped and turned around. Even though I couldn't see his face, I knew he was studying me. "This is weird," he said. "I've never said this stuff out loud to anyone before."

"That's because I'm using a demon compulsion spell on you."

"Seriously?"

"No, you dork. So keep going. What about Holly and Elodie?" And me? I thought, and even though I didn't say it, I could feel the words hanging in the air around us.

"The betrothal with Holly was all aboveboard. Simon and her father arranged it." He took a couple of steps back, and I heard a faint metallic clunk as he leaned back against a tree. "It was part of my cover, but I liked her. She was sweet. Quiet. It's not like we had this great love or anything, and I obviously had no intention of actually marrying her, but . . . I don't know. It wasn't hard spending time with her. Elodie was a different story, especially after what she did to Holly."

"So when you left Hex Hall after Holly died, that wasn't because you were the grief-stricken fiancé. You were going back to The Eye."

"Yeah. I told them that I thought Elodie and her coven had raised a demon, so we decided I should get close to her, see what was really going on."

"And you decided to get *really* close to her."

He laughed softly. "I can't see you, but I have a feeling you're cute when you're jealous, Mercer."

Crossing my arms over my chest, I said, "It's not jealousy you're hearing, it's disgust. You dated a girl you didn't even like just to get information out of her."

His laughter died, and his voice sounded weary when he said, "Trust me, a lot of my brothers have done much worse."

There was so much more I wanted to ask him, but it's not like we could sit out here all night passing the sharing stick or whatever. Time to cut to the chase.

"So did The Eye tell you to get all Mata Hari on me too?"

There was a long pause before he answered. "I was supposed to watch you, yeah. They thought it was weird that Atherton would send his own kid to Hecate, so we wanted to keep an eye on you. No pun intended."

He kept doing that, using "we" and "they" interchangeably when he was talking about The Eye. Not like I could blame him for being all schizo. It had to be bizarre to live two lives for as long as he had.

He pushed himself away from the tree. "So yeah, you were part of the job. Don't get me wrong, Mercer, I like you. You're smart, fluent in sarcasm, and, Bad Dog incident aside, pretty kick-ass at magic. And it's not like you're hard to look at."

"Be still my beating heart."

"But to answer your question, no part of the Archer Cross you knew at Hecate exists. That day in the cellar, I kissed you back because it was my job to stay close to you. If that's where you wanted to take things, then that's where I was going to go. I kissed you because I had to. Not exactly the hardest assignment I've ever had, but an assignment nonetheless."

I stood there absorbing his words like blows, my heart aching. But it wasn't what he said that made me feel like I'd been punched in the chest.

It's that I knew he was lying. That speech came out way too quickly and way too smooth, almost like he'd been practicing it in his head. The same way I'd been practicing what I'd say to him if I ever saw him again.

I couldn't even begin to handle that right now, so instead I just said, "Okay, then. Yay for honesty. Now that we're done with the confessional part of the evening, why don't you tell me why we're here."

There was another pause, then he started walking again. I followed, leaves crunching under my feet.

"Like I said, Hecate Hall has always made The Eye nervous."

"Why? Are they allergic to plaid?"

I thought he might laugh, but instead, he said, "Think about it, Mercer. One place where Prodigium round up their most powerful members? Don't tell me that's not suspicious."

That had never occurred to me. I'd always just thought of all us at Hecate as giant screwups, but in a way, Archer was right. We'd all been sentenced to Hex Hall because of spells that were powerful and dangerous. I thought of Cal saying I created "too big." Wasn't that what just about everyone at Hecate had done?

Still, the idea that the place I'd called home for nearly a year was actually some evil farm for powerful Prodigium was unsettling to say the least. "Hecate isn't like that," I said weakly, almost more to myself than to him.

"Isn't it? Do some kind of illumination spell."

I raised my hand, and within seconds, a glowing orb of bluish light had appeared. It lit up the surrounding area, and I gasped. This section of forest looked like a meteor had landed here. We were standing at the edge of a crater that was about eight feet deep and thirty feet in diameter. All around us were flattened trees, lying broken like matchsticks. The trees that were still standing were scorched and blackened.

But it wasn't just that. Dark magic, darker than anything I'd ever felt, crackled over everything. It was like the whole area was marinating in it. It seeped up from the dirt under my feet, and I could practically taste it in the air.

There was a large flat rock at the base of the crater with something carved into it. I wiggled my fingers and the orb grew larger and brighter until I could see the markings.

I'd only seen writing like that one other place—the grimoire.

"Now you see why I wanted to show you this," Archer said quietly. "Whoever is raising demons is doing it here. At Hecate."

CHAPTER 30

"This is bad," was all I could manage to say.

"Yeah, I kind of picked up on that too."

"No, I mean really bad. Like, to a level I didn't know badness could reach."

Archer crouched down near the lip of the crater, the flickering blue light playing in his eyes. "It gets worse."

"What, does this pit also eat kittens? How much worse can it be?" I stared at the flat rock, blinking at the power radiating off the markings.

"Ever since I left Hex Hall, I've been looking into the history of the place. In the past eighteen years, six students have disappeared from the school."

I finally tore my gaze away from the depression and turned back to Archer. My knees were weak, and my stomach churned with dread, but I made myself play devil's advocate. "That's not that many. Have you ever been to a big human school, Cross? Some of those places lose six kids in, like, a week."

"Sophie, two of those kids were Anna and Chaston."

I knew he was serious because he hardly ever used my first name, and then I just went ahead and let my knees do their thing and give out. I thumped onto the ground.

"After the attacks, they both vanished," Archer said.

"No," I said, thinking of Daisy that night at Shelley's. How she'd kept insisting that The Eye couldn't be there. "No, their parents came to get them."

Archer stood up and moved closer to me. "Did you ever see them?" he asked quietly. "Did any of us?"

I racked my brain. Mrs. Casnoff had told us that their parents had come for them, and they were taking the year off. They were supposed to come back after the summer.

But no. I'd never seen either of them—or their parents—after Alice fed on them.

"I visited their parents," Archer continued. "All four of them were under some heavy spells, Mercer. They were convinced their daughters were spending the summer at Hecate. Said they talk to them once a week. But none of our guys have been able to locate either Chaston or Anna anywhere."

My brain was spinning. Demons, missing students . . .

Why had my life suddenly become a Nancy Drew mystery from hell?

"Okay, but that would mean . . ." I could hardly say the next words. They seemed unbelievable to me. "That would mean Mrs. Casnoff is in on it, and if that is the case, my dad would know something about it."

"Not necessarily," Archer said. "Hecate Hall and Graymalkin Island are completely Mrs. Casnoff's domain. Your dad signs off on all the kids who're sentenced here, but past that, he leaves it all to her."

Way to be screwed over by delegating, Dad.

I stood up and paced a few feet around the basin. "So you think Chaston and Anna were taken so they could be made into demons?"

"It seems to fit. Daisy and Nick are both teenagers; so was Alice back in the day. Maybe Mrs. Casnoff figured they'd be easier to turn because they'd already been up close and personal with the dark side."

"Why, though? Why would Mrs. Casnoff, of all people, be raising demons?"

"It might not be just her," Archer suggested. "After all, her sister works for the Council. Their father used to be the head. I think this goes way deeper than we can even guess."

I kicked a clump of dirt, and it tumbled down the sides of the crater, landing on the slab. For a second,

I thought I saw something move, but it was probably just a trick of the light. "Cross, my dad thinks if he can catch the people who changed Nick and Daisy, he can get them to reverse it, and stop a war between The Eye and Prodigium. But if it's the Casnoffs who are doing this?"

Archer stood up, dusting his hands on his pants. "Yeah. As we've established, it's bad."

"So . . . why did you want to show me this? You guys could handle this on your own. Why risk getting kicked out of your He-Man Monster-Haters Club?"

"Because we *can't* handle this on our own. At least I don't think we can."

"You said yourself you already have some Prodigium working with you. Why not go to them?"

"We have a handful," he said, frustration creeping into his voice. "And most of them suck. Look, just consider it a peace offering, okay? My way of saying I'm sorry for lying to you. And pulling a knife in your presence, even if it was just to open a damn window to get out before you vaporized me."

Most girls got flowers. I got a dirt pit used for demon raising. Nice.

"Thanks," I replied. "But don't you want in on this?"

He looked at me, and not for the first time, I wished

269

his eyes weren't so dark. It would have been nice to have some idea of what was going on in his head. "That's up to you," he said.

Mom always liked to say that we hardly ever know the decisions we make that change our lives, mostly because they're little ones. You take this bus instead of that one and end up meeting your soul mate, that kind of thing. But there was no doubt in my mind that this was one of those life-changing moments. Tell Archer no, and I'd never see him again. And Dad and Jenna wouldn't be mad at me, and Cal . . . Tell Archer yes, and everything suddenly got twistier and more complicated than Mrs. Casnoff's hairdo.

And even though I'm a twisty and complicated girl, I knew what my answer had to be.

"It's too much of a risk, Cross. Maybe one day when I'm head of the Council and you're . . . well, whatever you're going to be for L'Occhio di Dio, we could work on some kind of collaboration." That brought up depressing images of me and Archer sitting across a boardroom table, sketching out battle plans on a whiteboard, so my voice was a little shaky when I continued. "But for now, it's too dangerous." And not just because basically everyone in our lives would want to kill us if they found out, I thought. But because I was pretty sure I was still in love with him, and I thought he might feel something similar for me, and there was no way we could work together preventing the Monster Apocalypse/World War III without that becoming an issue.

Not that I could say any of that.

Archer's face was blank as he said, "Cool. Got it."

"Cross," I started to say, but then his eyes slid past me and went wide with horror. At the same time, I became aware of a slithering noise behind me. That just could not be good; in my experience, nothing pleasant slithers.

Still, I was not prepared for the nightmares climbing out of the crater.

CHAPTER 31

There were three of them, and they had been human once. Many humans. Their bodies, as they hoisted themselves out of the pit, were like patchwork quilts of human flesh and mismatched limbs.

They lumbered toward us, and the one nearest to me reached out one meaty, thick-fingered hand. His other arm, I noticed as hysteria bubbled up inside me, was slender, pale, and tipped with bright red nails.

"Ghouls," I heard Archer say. His voice was low and tense, like a person who's being confronted by a wild animal. "Reanimated human flesh, used as guardians. Seriously dark magic. Someone obviously didn't want us finding—"

"Oh my God, less talking, more stabbing, please." My voice was squeaky with fear, and I knew my eyes were huge when I swiveled around to look at Archer.

He already had the sword in his hand, and he was crouching slightly. "I can slow them down, but ghouls can't be killed by blades. You're the one who has to stop them."

"Come again?" I nearly squeaked.

"You're a necromancer," he said. "They're dead."

Oh, right. One of the many "perks" of having a lot of dark magic at my disposal. But I'd never seen the point in boning up on my necromancer skills. When was I ever going to need to order around the dead?

The things were getting close enough now that I could smell them, and it was all I could do not to gag. "I don't know what to do," I said, panicked.

"Well, think of something fast," Archer replied. There was a burst of movement out of the corner of my eye, and suddenly, he wasn't beside me anymore, but in the thick of them, sword flashing. He caught one of the ghouls under the chin with the point of his blade, but there was no blood. The thing stopped moving, but it didn't fall. Instead, it swept a hand at Archer like he was an annoying mosquito. But Archer ducked and swung again, piercing the side of the second ghoul. This time, a thick black substance poured from the wound, but the thing just looked irritated. No matter how much Archer hacked and stabbed, the ghouls showed no signs of pain.

By now I had drawn up as much magic as I could possibly hold, but I was afraid to start sending big bolts of it into the fray. The last thing I wanted was to hit Archer, who, I was beginning to realize, had definitely held back in Defense. I'd never seen anyone move like he did, his movements fast and sure. Too bad they weren't doing any good.

Finally, one of the ghouls got a grasp on his hair, and he winced as the thing jerked his head back. I think I might have cried out, but it was hard to hear anything between my heartbeat and the whirring of magic in my veins.

"Could we start with the necromancing now?" Archer shouted at me.

I held my hands out in front of me, pointed toward the ghouls, and did my best to stop panting, something that was hard to do when the smallest ghoul turned his head. I caught a glimpse of his face, which must have taken each of its eyes, its mouth, and its nose from different "donors."

Taking deep breaths, I gathered my power until I could feel it crackling in my fingertips. "Let him go!" I commanded in what I hoped was my most "I am a powerful demon" voice. Probably would've been better if my voice hadn't cracked on the last word. I released the magic in my hands, which felt kind of like snapping a giant rubber band.

A bolt of power flew from my fingertips, crashing into a nearby tree with a thunderous crack. There was a bright flash like lightning, and a branch fell to the ground. The ghouls startled, which meant the one holding Archer jerked his head back even farther. The smallest one made a noise that might have been distress, but they certainly didn't seem under my control.

And they weren't letting Archer go.

Okay, so my first experiment with necromancy was an epic fail. Take two.

I fought panic and frustration. Shooting off my magic at the ghouls was no good, but what else was I supposed to try? "Think, Sophie," I muttered under my breath,

"Yeah, please do that," Archer replied, his voice slightly strangled. The ghoul holding him had wrapped a hand around Archer's throat. The thing's expression wasn't threatening, just curious, like he was little kid trying to see what would happen if he just kept squeezing.

I slammed my eyes shut. Okay, they were dead. Yucky dead things. That smelled like—okay, those thoughts were not helpful.

Except . . . they were dead. They'd come from the ground, crawled out of the dirt at the base of the crater. I thought of how my magic always felt like it was rushing up from my feet, and wondered if maybe that could be reversed.

This time, instead of sending my powers out, I sent them down, snaking through the earth. "Release him," I said again, quietly this time.

I heard a muffled thump, and when I opened my eyes, Archer was lying at the ghoul's feet, rubbing the back of his head. The ghouls watched me with blank gazes, clearly awaiting their next order.

"What do I do now?" I asked.

Archer got up and came to stand next to me, his gunk-covered sword dangling from his hand. "You can put them back," he said. "Or you could let them go."

"What, like set them free to roam around the island? I don't think so."

Archer shook his head. He was breathing hard, and sweat gleamed on his brow. "No, draw the magic out of them and let them be dead. Really dead."

"Okay," I said, hoping I sounded confident, like taking the life force out of ghouls was one of my favorite hobbies, right up there with knitting and sudoku. But the weird thing is, as soon as I thought about it, I could actually feel the magic keeping the ghouls alive. I could almost see it shimmering like a black thread among my own powers. And in the end, it was a simple thing to use my own magic to "cut" that thread.

As soon as I did, the ghouls slumped to the ground. I stared at their prone forms and said, "They look kind of pitiful."

Archer snorted, and I saw the ring of purple bruises beginning to circle his neck. "Forgive me for not feeling too sympathetic, Mercer."

I think he would have said more, but just then we became aware of something bobbing in the distance. A light.

With a flick of my fingers, I extinguished the blue orb. I think both of us wanted nothing more than to turn and run, but crashing through the forest wasn't exactly the stealthiest way to escape. Instead, we backed up until we were out of the "blast zone" and into the shelter of the trees. Then, even though it was agonizing and I'm pretty sure I'd never been more scared in my life, we walked quietly away from the crater, taking care with every step not to make any noise. I could hear the low murmur of voices, but we were too far away for me to make out how many people were behind us. That was the worst part: knowing that if I could just turn around and try to hide, I would know who was behind all this. But I couldn't risk it. The best plan right now was to get back to Thorne and tell Dad what was going on.

Only once we'd made it back to the beach did Archer and I break into a run, and by the time we got back to the copse of trees that housed the Itineris, I thought my lungs were going to explode.

Archer braced his hands on his knees, leaning over and taking deep breaths. "I never thought I'd have to make that run again," he said when he could finally speak.

"You used the Itineris to get off Graymalkin," I said, finally understanding how he'd managed to vanish without a trace.

He just nodded before pulling the necklace out of his pocket and slipping it over our heads. "You ready?" he asked, holding my hands.

I glanced over my shoulder, wondering how so much could change in so short a time.

"As I'll ever be," I muttered before we stepped into the doorway.

CHAPTER 32

The sun was just beginning to rise when we reached the corn mill, which surprised me until I remembered that A) England has freakishly early sunrises in the summer, and B) we'd been gone nearly two hours. I was pretty sure I'd never been so wiped out in my entire life. I felt hollow and exhausted, and as I looked at Archer, almost unbearably sad. I tried to tell myself that it was just because I'd been nearly squished by the space-time continuum, but I knew that wasn't it.

I think Archer was feeling something similar, because his hands shook slightly as he lifted the chain from around our necks. It hit the floor with a heavy thump, sending up a cloud of dust motes. They sparkled in the shaft of pale pink light that fell between us, looking surprisingly pretty for dirt.

Archer's face was streaked with sweat, and there was a smudge above his left eyebrow, as well as a dark stain on his torso that was probably ghoul blood. I had a feeling I looked just as rough.

"Well," he said at last, his voice slightly hoarse. "That was the worst first date I've ever been on."

Despite being so tired that I thought I might dissolve right there on the grimy floor, I laughed. So did he, and once we started, it was like we couldn't stop. I knew it was just that weird mix of relief and fatigue, but it felt so good to laugh with him, I didn't care.

Tears dripped down my cheeks, and my sides ached, and for just a moment, I could forget I'd gotten myself involved in yet another potentially deadly mystery. I could forget that if anyone found out I had conspired with an Eye, I'd probably be killed in some sort of nasty, magical way.

But as I stood across from Archer, I couldn't forget that I was completely, stupidly in love with the one person I could never have.

The laughter died on my lips, and I dashed at my eyes with the back of my hand. "I need to get back," I said.

"Right," he replied. He was still holding his sword in his right hand, and he twirled the hilt, the point scratching the wooden floor. "So this is it. We're done."

"Yeah," I said, my voice cracking. I cleared my

throat. "And I have to say, the world's first and last Eye-demon reconnaissance mission went pretty well." It was a struggle to meet his eyes, but I managed it. "Thank you."

He shrugged, his dark gaze full of something I couldn't quite read. "We were a good team."

"We were." In more ways than one, I thought. Which is why this sucked so bad.

I stepped back. "Anyway, I should go. See ya, Cross." Then I laughed, only it sounded suspiciously like another sob. "Except I won't, will I? So I guess I should say good-bye." I felt like I was about to shatter into a million tiny shards, like the mirrors I'd broken with Dad. "Okay, well, best of luck with the whole Eye thing, then. Try not to kill anyone I know." I turned away, but he reached out and caught my wrist.

I could feel my pulse hammering under his fingers. "Mercer, that day in the cellar . . ." He searched my face, and I could sense him struggling for what he wanted to say. Then finally, "I didn't kiss you back because I had to. I kissed you because I wanted to." His eyes dropped to my lips, and it was like the whole world had shrunk to just me and him and the shaft of light between us. "I still want to," he said hoarsely. He tugged my wrist and pulled me into his arms.

My brain registered the sound of his sword clattering to the ground as his other hand came up to grab the back of my neck, but once his lips were on mine, everything else faded away. I clutched at his shoulders, raising up on my tiptoes, and kissed him with everything I had in me. As the kiss deepened, we held each other tighter, so I didn't know if the pounding heartbeat I felt was mine or his.

How stupid, I thought dreamily, to have ever thought I could give this up. Not just the kissing, although, as Archer's hands cupped my face, I had to admit that part was pretty awesome. But all of it: joking with him and working beside him. Being with a guy who was my friend and could still make me feel like this.

"Oh, Mercer," he murmured against my temple once we'd come up for air, "we are so screwed."

I pressed my face against his neck, breathing him in. "I know."

"So what do we do?"

Reluctantly, I tried to move away. It was hard to think when he was so close to me. "If we were good people, we'd never see each other again."

His arms locked around my waist, pulling me back. "Okay, well, that's not happening. Plan B?"

I smiled up at him, feeling ridiculously giddy for someone on the verge of ruining her entire life. "I don't have one. You?"

He shook his head. "Nothing. But . . . look. I've

spent basically my whole life pretending to be someone I'm not, faking some feelings, hiding others." Reaching down, he clasped my hand and lifted it so that our joined hands were trapped between our chests. "This thing with us is the only real thing I've had in a long time. *You're* the only real thing." He raised our hands and kissed my knuckles. "And I'm done pretending I don't want you."

I had read a lot about swooning in the romance novels Mom had tried to hide from me, but I'd never felt in danger of doing it until now. Which was why a snarky comment was definitely called for.

"Wow, Cross. I think you missed your calling. Screw demon hunting: you should clearly be writing Hallmark cards."

His face broke into that crooked grin that was maybe my favorite sight in the whole world. "Shut up," he muttered before lowering his head and kissing me again.

"Why is it," I said against his lips several moments later, "that we're always kissing in gross, dirty places like cellars and abandoned mills?"

He laughed, pressing kisses to my jaw, then my neck. "Next time it'll be a castle, I promise. This is England, after all. Can't be too hard to find one."

We didn't talk for a long time after that, and when we finally managed to break apart, the light in the mill was slightly brighter. "I have to go," I said, resting my head against Archer's chest. It occurred to me that my cheek was probably right over his tattoo. Without thinking, I lifted my face and tugged at the neckline of his T-shirt. This time, the stark black-and-gold mark wasn't hidden. No need for that spell anymore, I guess. Still, I covered it with my palm. Archer's hands clutched reflexively on my waist. Our eyes met. "It doesn't burn this time," I whispered.

His breathing was ragged. "Beg to differ, Mercer."

Magic was rushing through me, and when Archer covered my hand with his own, there was a little blue spark. Slowly, he moved my hand off his chest, then gripped both my shoulders. I thought he was going to kiss me again—and with the way we were feeling, there was a chance we might set the whole mill on fire—but instead, he gingerly pushed me away. "Okay," he said, closing his eyes. "If you don't go now, we're . . . You should go now."

Once we were several feet apart, the lust-fog cleared a little. "We still have no idea what we're going to do."

Archer opened his eyes and took a couple of steps backward. "Right now, you're going to go back to Thorne and check in with your dad. I'm going to go back to my people and do the same. Then tomorrow night, we'll meet here. You'll stand over there"—he pointed at a corner—"and I'll stand over *there*"—the complete opposite corner—"and there will be no physical contact until we've figured something out. Deal?"

I smiled, even as I shoved my hands in my pockets to keep from grabbing him again. "Deal. Midnight?"

"Perfect. So." That grin again. "See ya, Mercer."

Happiness flooded through me as warm and bright as sunlight. "See ya, Cross."

CHAPTER 33

The corn mill was just out of sight when reality sunk in. Now I knew that Archer wanted to be with me just as much as I wanted to be with him, but there was a lot of major stuff standing between us. Namely, the fact that basically everyone I knew wanted to kill him, and everyone he knew wanted to kill *me*. As far as obstacles went, that had to be the ultimate. And it wasn't just what other people thought. I'd gotten kind of used to the idea of being head of the Council one day, and at Thorne, I'd felt less like a freak with crazy powers, and more like . . . well, someone useful. Valuable, even.

As soon as Archer and I went public, that would be gone.

I made my way through the garden maze, the tall hedges making deep shadows in front of me.

Also, there was Cal to think about.

I stumbled slightly at the thought of him. It's not like I thought he'd be heartbroken or anything; Cal and I were friends, and sure, maybe he was a little interested in me, but I think that was just a result of the betrothal. I mean, hadn't I tried to make myself crush on him just because it would be easier?

The closer I got to the house, the more my happy feelings began to deflate. The Eye was Archer's family. And, I thought as Thorne Abbey loomed above me, the Council had become mine. I wasn't willing to give that up. Was he?

Ugh. Why did I have to have so many thoughts? Why couldn't I just be a normal girl and bask in the glow of finally knowing that the boy I wanted wanted me back?

I slipped in the back door, and as I did, one of the maids gave me a quick curtsy. Ah, right. Because I wasn't a normal girl.

I had hoped to get back to my room without seeing anyone else, but I met Cal on the landing. Wonderful.

"Hey," he said, taking in my disheveled appearance. "Why are you up so early?"

"Oh, I was just, you know, exercising." I jogged in place for a second before realizing that I probably looked like a mental patient.

"Okaaay," Cal said slowly, confirming my suspicions. "Well, I was about to go for a walk. You wanna come with?"

You couldn't actually die from guilt, right? No matter how stabby it felt in your chest?

"I'm actually fitnessed out," I told him. "But can we hang later?"

"Sure," he agreed.

As I watched him walk away, I told myself it was stupid to feel bad about Cal. It's not like he was going to be heartbroken when I called off our betrothal. Pissed, maybe, but not devastated. He didn't like me like that. If he did, surely he would have made a move by now.

I walked up the rest of the stairs to my room, the house hushed around me. Opening my door, I flipped on the light and started to sigh with relief.

But the breath caught in my throat when I saw who was standing in the middle of my bedroom.

Elodie.

Well, her ghost, obviously. She was much more translucent than she'd been at Hex Hall, and I could barely see her, but it was definitely Elodie. Her red hair waved out from her face, and she floated several inches off the ground.

I was so shocked to see her that it took me a second to realize she was trying to say something.

"What are you doing here?" I asked in a harsh whisper. I'd never heard of a ghost leaving Hecate. As far as I knew, it was impossible.

I couldn't be sure, but I thought she rolled her eyes. A horrible thought occurred to me: "Is this about Archer? Please don't tell me you're upset about us, because . . . I mean, you're dead."

She floated closer to me, until she was right in my face. At first I thought she was going to spit ectoplasm on me or something, but then I saw her lips moving again. I wasn't an expert lip-reader, but she was close enough and speaking slowly enough that I was able to make out what she said. "I told you," her pale lips mouthed, "that I'd haunt your ass."

I stared at her mouth, horrified, as she smirked. And then, just like that, she was gone. The air near my face wafted slightly, like someone had just opened a window.

"I don't need this!" I said to the empty room. "Seriously, plate? FULL."

But there was no reply.

I'd planned on getting my nap on for most of the day, but instead, I ended up spending most of it in the library, researching ghosts and demons. It was not exactly the lightest reading, and none of it did me any good.

All the books on spirits and haunting said the same thing: ghosts are tied to the place where they died, not to people. As for *Demonologies: A History*, I was beginning to think it would have been better employed as a door-stop. There was nothing in there that shed any light on the Daisy/Nick situation.

I thought about asking them at dinner—quietly, and hopefully somewhere in private—if either of them had any weird memories that might correspond to what I'd seen at Hecate, but they didn't show up in the dining room that night. I also couldn't find them the next morning, which was weird. Missing dinner was one thing, but Nick and Daisy always showed up for breakfast. No one seemed that concerned about it, though. "You know those two," Jenna said. "They're probably off doing their weird Kurt and Courtney thing somewhere."

Still, when they didn't turn up for dinner again, I was worried. I hovered around the hallway where their rooms were until nearly ten that night, but there was no sign of them. I was still hanging around when Roderick found me to say that Dad was back.

"That was fast," I said, following him inside, even as my stomach started doing jumping jacks. I had to tell Dad what I'd seen at Hecate, but I didn't have a good excuse for how I'd come by that information. I'd thought I'd have a few more days to cultivate one.

By the time I crossed under the marble arch leading to Council Headquarters, my mouth was completely dry, and my knees felt wobbly.

I wanted nothing more than to flop into one of Dad's leather chairs and tell him everything. For the first time, I understood why soldiers who go on dangerous missions have to be debriefed. I wanted to get the whole story out as quickly as possible, mostly so I could erase it from my memory. I thought again of that ghoul with the mismatched features, and was suddenly afraid I might hurl all over the diamond-patterned carpet.

But when I opened the door to Dad's office, he wasn't alone. Lara was in there, and even though they were speaking in low voices, the magic in the room was so intense it made me dizzy. They were both so busy glaring at each other that they didn't even notice me standing there, which was good. It gave me a chance to study Lara. I knew I wasn't going to figure out what she was up to just by reading her face; I seriously doubt there's an expression that says, "So me and my sister are raising demons at Hecate Hall." Still, I thought there might be some hint as to whether she already knew someone had found the demon spot.

But there was nothing. She was every bit as good at hiding her emotions as Mrs. Casnoff was. Must run in the family.

"So that's it then," Lara said, crossing her arms. "You're not going to do anything."

"What can I do," Dad said in that deceptively calm voice, "if neither you nor Anastasia will tell me what exactly has happened at Graymalkin?"

Well, there was my answer. I'd known that Lara and Mrs. Casnoff had to have had something to do with whatever was going on at Hecate, but to have it confirmed like that still blew my mind. How? How could these women who worked so closely with Dad be up to something so heinous without his knowing?

"The school is our domain," Lara snapped. "And so this is our affair."

"And yet you ask for *my* help."

Lara sprung forward suddenly, slamming her hand down on Dad's desk. "There was an intruder on a forbidden part of the island, and the security system was compromised." Another image of Archer's sword slicing through a ghoul came to mind. Yeah, compromised was one word for it.

Suddenly she changed tactics. "You swore. You swore to my father that you would do everything in your power to protect Anastasia's and my interests in Hecate."

Even I could have told her that was a bad move. Dad just looked pissed. "Don't bring him into this, Lara."

Dad finally noticed me then, and as he looked over

Lara's shoulder at me, she whirled around. Immediately, her face softened, and she even smiled. Her eyes, however, were every bit as hard and shiny as the varnish on Dad's desk.

"Sophie, there you are! Where have you been the past few days? We've hardly seen you."

"A–around?" I stuttered, inwardly cringing. Oh, that was an awesome alibi. "Dad gave me a bunch of reading to do. Am I interrupting something?"

Lara waved her hand. "Just some boring Council business. Nothing that concerns you." She glanced at Dad. "We can finish talking about all this later. I'll leave the two of you to chat." As she left the office, she patted my hand in that familiar way she always did. It took everything I had in me not to wince away from her touch.

The door clicked behind her, and I gave a sigh of relief. Dad gestured for me to sit. Once I had, he said, "I'm afraid my trip wasn't quite as successful as I'd hoped. Aislinn Brannick continues to—"

"They're raising demons at Hex Hall," I blurted out. "I went there the other day—I took the Itineris—and I saw it myself. That's where it's happening, and six students have disappeared from the school in the past eighteen years. Two of them were Anna and Chaston, the girls Alice attacked last year." It felt good getting it all out like that. It didn't give me time to be scared that there were holes in my story.

Dad just stared at me like I'd started speaking Greek. Of course, Dad probably spoke Greek, so maybe it was more like I was talking Martian. In any case, he looked equal parts freaked out and confused.

"What?"

I made myself slow down as I went back through the story, leaving out Archer's part in it, of course. I told Dad that I'd remembered seeing something weird at Hecate, so I'd gone back to check it out, then described the pit, the rock in the middle, even the ghouls.

By the time I was finished, Dad looked older and sadder than I'd ever seen him. "None of this makes any sense."

"I'm beginning to think I should make that the title of my autobiography."

"Lara and Anastasia are two of my most trusted allies," he said, rubbing his hand over his jaw. "Why on earth would they be behind all this?"

"That's the million-dollar question. Is there any way to check and see if Nick and Daisy were ever at Hecate? They must have had different names or you'd remember them."

I don't know why I was holding out hope that Dad would be all, "Why, yes, let me check the Hecate

Enrollment Roster 9000 computer database." Those lists were probably written on pieces of parchment with quill feathers. Still, I was disappointed when Dad shook his head and said, "No, Anastasia keeps all those records. And if what you say about Anna's and Chaston's parents is true, then Nick's and Daisy's own families would never have reported them missing."

Dad got that faraway look in his eyes, the one that said he was about to go in search of really ancient books and cryptic passages. Sure enough, he got up from his desk and walked over to his bookshelf.

He pulled out one of those giant leather tomes he was so fond of and started paging through it, so I decided I was dismissed. Fine by me. I heaved myself out of the chair and shuffled for the door.

Just as I turned the knob, Dad said, "Sophia."

"Yeah?"

When I looked back at him, he said. "I'm very proud of you for what you did. I have no idea what the far-reaching consequences of your actions may be, but—"

I held up my hand. "Let's leave it at the proud part for now, okay, Dad?"

Especially since a lot of that pride would probably dissolve once he found out about Archer, I thought with a pang of sadness.

He smiled. "Very well. Good night."

"Night, Dad."

I walked out into the lobby. It was nearly empty, for once, except for the two vampire guards standing watch. The whole house seemed quiet as I walked down the massive staircase. Glancing at my watch, I saw that it was nearly eleven. Less than an hour until I was supposed to meet Archer, and I had no idea what I would say to him when—

"Sophie?"

I glanced over my shoulder and saw Daisy standing at the top of the stairs, just inside the archway. There was something weird about her posture: her hands were clenched at her sides, and her head was tilted slightly to the right. Her face was blank. Alarm bells clanged in my head, but I raised my arm in a halfhearted wave. "There you are," I said, as I backed up. "We haven't seen you—"

I didn't get the chance to finish my sentence. Daisy started moving toward me, and then I noticed her eyes.

There was nothing human in them.

Everything seemed to slow down as nearly every hair on my body stood on end. I had seen eyes like that before, and I knew what they meant.

I raised my hands, and despite my fatigue, the magic came, clean and pure. I thought of Mom, and with one flick of my wrist, sent a burst of power crashing into

Daisy's shoulder. I didn't want to hurt her, just slow her down. But even though she stumbled on the steps, she kept coming.

"Dad!" I yelled, even though I knew he couldn't hear me.

Daisy snarled at me and lunged, her hands curling into claws, and this time I shot a bolt of magic big enough to knock her to the ground. She hit her knees, whimpering with pain, and even though I was terrified, guilt shot through me. She wasn't Daisy, I reminded myself. There was no trace of her in the thing that staggered to its feet, rage gleaming in its eyes. Then she looked up. I saw her lips move, but I wasn't sure what she was saying. Only when I heard the horrible screeching of metal on stone did I realize I was standing right under one of the huge statues that had so impressed Jenna our first day.

A statue that was about to land on my head.

CHAPTER 34

This may sound weird, but the first thing I thought as I watched that ten-feet-tall bronze lady plummet toward my face was, "Well, at least it can't kill me." Only demonglass could do that, after all, but I wasn't sure even Cal could heal the amount of broken I was about to be.

Without really thinking, I closed my eyes. I felt my powers surging through me, and then a strange sensation of cold wind rushed over me; something I hadn't felt since that night in the clearing with Alice.

As if from distance, I heard the deafening crash of the statue on the marble floor. I opened my eyes.

I was standing several feet away, on the staircase behind Daisy. For the first time in over six months, I'd teleported.

Daisy whirled around, confused, but apparently, the sound of a ginormous metal statue hitting the floor got everyone's attention, because I suddenly heard running footsteps. "No!" someone shouted. It was Dad, standing at the top of the stairs. He was breathing hard, one hand held out toward Daisy.

"This is not you," he told Daisy, and I could tell it was a struggle to keep his voice calm. "You can fight this. Remember what I taught you."

But not even the smallest hint of understanding flickered on Daisy's face. That was the scariest part. Even Alice, as insane as she'd been, had seemed human. Daisy was nothing but a monster, her face twisted with rage.

Moving so quickly we barely had time to react, Daisy reached into her waistband and pulled something out. It was the same piece of demonglass that had hit me at my birthday party. The substance sizzled in her hand, burning her, but Daisy didn't flinch. She charged us, her eyes the same violet-red Alice's had been that last night.

The next few moments were a blur. Daisy rushed at me, demonglass hoisted high, and then there was a flash of light from above me—Dad—but once again, it was like Daisy couldn't feel any pain. Dad was suddenly beside me, throwing his body between mine and the jagged, black shard, and I think I screamed.

Suddenly, a shout rang out, a word I'd never heard

before. In fact, I'm not even sure it was a word, but whatever it was, there was power in it that made my head feel like it was splitting open.

Daisy went very still, her eyes wide. The demonglass dropped harmlessly from her fingers, and for just a second, she looked like the Daisy I knew. Then her eyes rolled back and she crumpled on the stairs, rolling down several of them before coming to a rest on the landing. Somewhere in the house, one of the clocks rang out eleven bells, and I realized with shock that it had been less than four minutes since I'd walked out of Dad's office.

Dad ran down the stairs and over to Daisy's inert body, pressing his fingers into the hollow beneath her jaw while I stared at Lara. She stood next to the fallen statue, breathing hard.

"What the heck was that?" I asked her, my voice sounding very loud in the silence.

"A simple immobilization spell," she replied as she crossed the hall, her heels clacking.

"You're lying."

Dad spit those words out with way more venom than I'd thought he was capable of. Lara must've been shocked too, because her face paled. "Excuse me?"

Rising to his feet, Dad stared her down. "There is no immobilization spell that can stop a demon that has crossed over."

Dad sounded so scary that I shuddered a little bit, but Lara didn't even blink. "Clearly there is, because I just used it successfully." She gestured to Daisy. "That girl was going to kill you, James."

I moved down to stand next to Dad. "What will happen to her now?"

Dad never took his eyes off of Lara. "She'll have to be contained somehow. One of the cells in the lower level, I should think."

"Contained?"

Dad looked at me, his eyes sad. "She's gone, Sophie. The Daisy part of her, at least. Once the magic takes over . . . there's no reversing it."

Daisy groaned, her eyelids fluttering, as if there *were* some tiny sliver of her left in there that had heard and understood. "Someone has to tell Nick," I murmured.

Dad sighed and loosened his tie. "Of course. Jenna." I glanced up, surprised, to see Jenna standing a few feet behind Lara. She must have heard all the commotion. Her face was pale, her eyes wide as she hurried across the hallway and grabbed my hands. "Are you okay?"

"Yeah," I said, but seeing her made tears spring to my eyes. I wasn't sure if it was from guilt or from seeing the fear on her face.

"If you wouldn't mind, go find Nick and have him meet me in the conservatory," Dad said to her. She looked up, surprised, but said she would, then headed off toward the back hallway.

Crouching down again, Dad brushed Daisy's black hair from her forehead. He murmured something I couldn't understand, and she stilled, seeming to fall deeper asleep. "I'll see that she's taken care of," he said. "And Lara, after I meet with Nick, I want to talk to you. Is that understood?"

She gave a tiny bow, but her mouth was tight with anger. "Of course."

Once she was gone, I gave in to my wobbly knees and sat down on the steps. Roderick and Kristopher showed up a few minutes later. They picked up Daisy with surprising gentleness, and carried her off to one of those mysterious cells in the bowels of Thorne Abbey. The thought of Daisy, even a demoned-out murderous Daisy, locked away, sent a fresh wave of sadness rolling over me.

I rested my head on folded arms and tried to process what had just happened. "Dad," I said at last, "Daisy was going after me."

I expected him to do his usual thing of "Oh, Sophie, but that is impossible because of this big word, and that big word, and also this abstract concept." But for once, he didn't. He just sat down next to me and said, "Go on."

"She called my name right before she attacked. And all that with the dagger. You were the bigger threat. I was

302

too wiped out from teleporting to fight her off. But she only went for you when you got in front of me."

Dad took off his glasses and rubbed the bridge of his nose. "I told you my trip was unsuccessful. That was true with regards to the Brannicks, but not for the entire trip. The warlock I visited in Lincolnshire, Andrew Crowley, had some very useful information. Do you remember the section on controlling demons in *Demonologies*? I believe it's in chapter five."

"Um . . . no."

Irritation flashed over his face. "Honestly, Sophie, I gave you that book for a reason."

"And I'm really sorry, but it's long and boring, and can we just skip to the part where you tell me what it says?"

"There are legends of witches and warlocks summoning demons in ancient times and manipulating their powers."

"Like what Elodie's coven was trying to do with Alice."

Dad shook his head. "No, that was trying to summon a demon and hold it. That's different. Had their ritual worked, they would have been able to use Alice, to some extent, but they wouldn't have controlled her. She still would have had free will." He studied me, and then said, very carefully, "But according to Mr. Crowley's research, in order to truly control a demon, you have to be its maker—the witch or warlock who performed the possession ritual."

"Lara. That word, or sound, or whatever it was. It stopped Daisy dead in her tracks."

Dad released a shaky breath. "Yes."

Everything started clicking into place, but that only made me feel worse. "So it *is* her. She's the one who made Nick and Daisy." My thoughts kept rolling, like a particularly awful snowball. "She knows I was on Graymalkin, Dad. I don't know how, but she does. And she sicced Daisy on me because of it. She only called her off because Daisy was about to hurt you." Sweet, friendly Lara. Bizarro World Mrs. Casnoff, Jenna and I had called her. And she had just tried to kill me.

"So what now?" I asked him. "Do you go magically arrest her?"

"I can't."

That was just about the last answer I'd been expecting, and I stared at Dad in shock. "Dad, she just tried to kill me. Not to mention she's raising demons and using them as weapons."

"You don't understand," Dad said, weary. "Lara, Anastasia, and I are bound by blood oaths. If I throw them both in a dungeon with no proof, it could look like a political power play."

"But you have proof. The place on Graymalkin. Trust me, Dad, anyone would be able to tell there was hard-core stuff going down there."

"It wouldn't be enough. And Anastasia does have complete control over everything that happens at Hecate. She could easily come up with a plausible excuse."

Frustrated, I shook my head. "But Daisy and Nick—"

"Daisy in completely insensible now, and Nick has no memory of anything that happened before he became a demon. They're of no help in this."

I shot to my feet, then immediately regretted it. Too much magic and too much stress had made me dizzy. Still, I leaned against the railing and said, "So you're not going to do anything?"

Dad stood up, too. "Sophie, I told you once that being head of the Council required a great deal of sacrifice. That woman has lied to me, destroyed a young woman for her own purposes, and just attempted to murder my daughter." Magic was rolling off him so strongly that I felt like I should probably sit down again. "Believe me," he continued, "I want nothing more than to smite her out of existence. But I can't. Not until I have concrete evidence."

Smiting sounded good to me, but, as much as I hated it, I knew he was right. "Man, politics suck," I muttered.

Dad took my hand. "Sophie, I swear, we will get to

the bottom of this. And when we do, Lara and Anastasia and anyone else who had part in this madness will be punished."

"Thanks, Dad."

I wanted to wait for Nick to show up, mostly to lend Dad some moral support, but he told me to go on up to my room. "You look like you're about to fall over," he said, walking me across the hall to the back staircase. "I could get Cal—"

"No," I said quickly. "I just need some alone time."

Dad nodded. "All right. Go get some rest."

Those were the easiest directions I'd ever been given. But as I turned to go, Dad added, "And I am calling your mother now."

There was no use in arguing with him. I knew a determined face when I saw one. He would call Mom, and she'd fly out here ASAP and drag me back to . . . well, I didn't know where. It wasn't like I could go back to Hex Hall.

Those thoughts were way too tired-making, so I dragged myself upstairs and then took the longest, most scalding shower known to man. I knew it would take a lot more than hot water to wash away all the dread and sadness that threatened to overcome me, but it still helped. And I was meeting Archer in just a little bit, so I definitely wanted to clean up for that.

I was feeling a little better when I opened the shower door, but that immediately vanished when I saw Elodie standing in my bathroom. She looked a little more solid this time and a lot more freaked out. Her lips were moving fast and furiously, and I couldn't make out a thing she was trying to say. "I know," I muttered as I wrapped a robe around myself. "I probably need to hit the gym more often or something, but honestly, if you're going to haunt me, we need to establish some boundaries."

She threw up her hands and floated up higher, her face a mix of anger and anxiety. Something told me that whatever she was trying to say was more important than the ten pounds I could stand to lose.

A sharp rap at my bedroom door made me jump, and even Elodie's head swung toward the noise. "Stay right here," I said, pointing a finger at her. She responded by flipping me off. Lovely.

It was Lara at the door, her face every bit as worried as Elodie's. "Have you seen Nick?"

My skin prickled. "No, why?"

She twisted one of her rings. "We still can't find him. And after everything that's happened with Daisy, you can see why that's very troubling."

Out of the corner of my eye, I could see Elodie hovering outside the bathroom door, waving her ghostly arms for all she was worth.

"I'll keep an eye out for him," I said before shutting the door—gently—in Lara's face.

"What?" I whispered, turning back to Elodie. She floated back into the bathroom, gesturing for me to follow.

But when I got in there, she was gone. "Oh, great," I said out loud. "Even in death, you're a pain in my—"

But then writing began to appear on the steamy mirror. It was slow and painstaking, but finally, one word appeared.

ARCHER.

Two more words appeared, and dread curled in my stomach, heavy as a brick.

MILL. NICK.

"Oh, God," I murmured.

GO.

CHAPTER 35

As I ran out the front door in my bathrobe, it occurred to me that someone would surely ask me where I was going. Panic surged through me even as magic coiled up from my feet.

The teleportation spell. I'd never been able to move more than ten feet, and the mill was at least half a mile away. Still, I had to try.

I closed my eyes and took a deep breath, drawing my powers deep inside myself, trying to calm down. It probably only took five seconds, but it felt like hours until I felt the frigid wind wrap itself around me, felt my blood slow in my veins.

I was almost afraid to open my eyes when the cold subsided, but when I did, I found myself standing right in front of the corn mill. Any relief I might have felt over the spell working faded the instant I stepped inside. I could feel the residual charge of magic in the air. Dark magic.

"Archer?" I called out, my heart pounding so loudly I was afraid I wouldn't be able to hear anything else.

But then, from the back of the mill, I heard a faint and wheezing, "Mercer."

A sob burst from my throat as I ran to the alcove. Archer was lying on his back, his hands on his chest. In the moonlight he looked like he'd been splashed all over with ink.

But the substance covering his chest and spreading out in a large pool underneath him wasn't ink or black paint, or any of the other things my desperate mind tried to tell me it could be. There was a faint metallic smell that reminded me of when Jenna would feed in our room.

I dropped to my knees beside him, touching his cheek. It was felt cool and clammy under my hand. "This is . . . what I get . . . for coming early," he gasped out, trying to smile at me.

"Please don't joke and bleed at the same time," I said as I gently lifted his hands from his chest. It was too dark to see the extent of his injuries, which was probably a good thing. Still, his shirt was shiny and slick with blood, and his breathing was shallow.

"It was this guy," he murmured. "Came . . . out of nowhere. Think he had . . . claws."

Oh, God. That explained the gashes, but the thought of Nick, every bit as savage as Daisy had been, slicing into Archer made bile rise up in my throat.

I breathed in through my nose until the feeling passed. "You're going to be okay," I said, but my voice was wavering and I was shaking. "It's probably not even that bad, and you're just being a big drama queen as usual." My magic was crashing around inside me like a choppy sea, and I was too upset to focus on anything. Still, I tried. I stroked his forehead and tried to channel my powers through him, tried to close all the gaping wounds on his chest and stomach.

The bleeding slowed a little, but that was the best I could do, and he'd already lost so much blood. I sat back on my heels, wanting to scream in frustration. What was the point of having the powers of gods if you couldn't help the people you loved?

Shivering, Archer grasped one of my hands with his. "Lost cause, Mercer."

"Don't say that!" I cried.

He shook his head. His teeth were chattering so hard he could barely speak, but he managed to say, "This was always going to happen . . . sooner or later. Wish . . . it had been . . . later."

I wanted to tell him no again, that he would be fine, but there was no point. Even in the darkness I could see how white he was, and how scared his eyes were. The pool of blood under him was so huge it was hard to believe there was any blood left in his body.

He was dying, and we both knew it. There was nothing I could do.

But there was someone who could.

I leaned closer to him and whispered in his ear, "Cross, please, just hold on for a few more minutes, okay? You promised to make out with me in a castle, and I'm holding you to it."

He tried to laugh, but it just came out a weak gurgle. I pressed the back of my hand to my mouth to keep from crying out, and stood up.

His fingers grabbed for the hem of my robe. "Don't leave me," he whispered.

It killed me to do it, but I stepped out of his reach. "I'm coming right back, I swear."

There was more I wanted to say, but we were wasting time. If he died before I got back . . . I couldn't think about that. Before I had time to second-guess myself or weigh the risks, I closed my eyes and vanished.

I reappeared in the hallway just outside my room, and dashed down to Cal's room.

When he opened the door, he looked rumpled and

sleepy, and pleasantly surprised to see me. That was the worst part.

As soon as he realized I was covered in blood, however, his smile faded, and he clutched my arm. "Sophie, what happened?"

"It's not my blood," I said quickly. "Someone is hurt, and I need you to get to the mill as fast as you can. Don't tell anyone. I'll meet you there."

He frowned, confused, but I teleported back to the mill before he had a chance to ask any questions.

I didn't know if it was all the practicing I'd been doing with Dad, or what, but it hardly took anything out of me to do such a huge spell. When I flashed back to the mill, I felt clearheaded and not even a little bit dizzy. But fear raced through me as I made my way back to Archer. Thank God his chest was still rising and falling when I reached him, but he seemed to be breathing faster, and his eyes were closed.

"See, told you I'd be back," I said as I crouched at his side. I tried to keep my voice light, like if he thought I wasn't afraid, he wouldn't be either. I'm not sure it worked, but he took my hand and, without opening his eyes, pressed my palm to his lips. I held his other wrist so I could feel his pulse.

I focused on that, each steady beat underneath my fingers, until at long last I heard Cal call out, "Sophie?"

"Back here!"

I could hear him stepping over the loose rocks and fallen beams, and when he finally appeared in the doorway, I thought he might be the most beautiful thing I'd ever seen. "Oh, thank you," I breathed, but whether I was talking to Cal or to God, I couldn't have told you.

"What happened?" he asked, moving toward me.

And then he saw.

A mix of emotions crossed his face. He looked shocked at first, but that gave way to a cold, quiet anger. His eyes went hard and his mouth tightened.

"Cal," I said, but it came out like a whimper.

"Move," he said tersely. I scrambled to my feet, walking around to Archer's other side as Cal knelt where I'd been. He grabbed Archer's arm with none of the gentleness I'd seen him use healing other people, me included. It was like he was trying to touch him as little as possible. I had one horrible moment of doubt, but then Cal dropped his head, and little silver sparks started running over Archer's skin.

So I sat on the grimy floor of an eighteenth-century corn mill and watched my fiancé heal the guy I loved.

"Wow," I muttered. "I'm gonna have one messed-up 'How I Spent My Summer Vacation' essay when I get back to Hex Hall." I lowered my forehead onto my knees, debating whether I should burst into tears or hysterical laughter.

After a few minutes, I heard Cal say, "There."

When I looked up, the blood underneath Archer was completely gone, and even though he was still unconscious, his breathing was slow and regular. I scrambled over to them. "Thank you so much," I said, laying my hand on Cal's arm.

But he threw it off as he stood, and turned away from me. Fury was etched in every line of his body, from his tense shoulders to his clenched fists.

I followed him and started to say, "I'm sorry," but he cut me off.

"Don't. I knew you could be naïve, but I never thought you were stupid. He's *an Eye*, Sophie. They kill our kind. What part of that don't you understand?"

All I could do was blink at him.

"And this one is worse than any of the others," he continued, "because he's technically one of us. He's a traitor to his own race, and you just keep letting him in, and pushing . . . everyone else away." He looked up at me, and what I saw in his eyes made me flinch. Cal was so good at hiding his emotions that I'd never realized . . . God, how could I have been such an idiot?

"I am so sorry," I said again. "I-I never meant to hurt you, Cal."

As quickly as it had appeared, the flash of pain was gone. "This isn't just about me," he said. "You're supposed to be head of the Council one day. Prodigium have to trust you, and that's never going to happen if you have one of *them* in your bed."

A combination of anger and embarrassment rushed through me, burning my cheeks. "Okay, first of all, no one is 'in my bed.' Second, Archer has saved my life more than once. He's not what you think he is."

Cal made a sound of disgust. "Oh, come on, Sophie. Don't you get it? He's L'Occhio di Dio's ultimate weapon. They used him as a spy at Hecate for years, so what makes you think that's stopped now? This is probably just his new assignment, getting close to you so he can use you for information about the Council."

"Actually, I was just going to use her for her body, but that's a good idea, too."

Cal and I whipped our heads around to see Archer sitting up against the back wall, his dark eyes glittering. He was still pale, but other than that, there was no sign that he'd been at death's door only a few minutes ago.

"So if you're so convinced I'm a spy, why did you heal me?" Archer asked, wincing as he pushed himself to his feet. "You could've just let me bleed to death and saved yourself a lot of hassle."

Cal scowled at him. "I did it for her."

Archer's smirk faded. "Fair enough," he said softly. "Thank you."

They stared each other down, and while the dorky eleven-year-old in my soul kind of hoped that two hot boys might fight over me, the rational, seventeen-year-old knew that Archer needed to get out of here, fast.

"Okay, look, we can talk this out later," I said, walking over to Archer. He slipped his hand into mine and squeezed it.

Cal's glance fell on our joined hands, and he turned away. "I'm heading back to the house," he muttered, but when he turned to go, the doorway was blocked.

Dad, Lara, and the other three members of the Council were standing there, staring at Archer and me.

CHAPTER 36

My memories of everything after that are a little jumbled. I remember Kristopher storming forward and kicking Archer's sword out of reach, before jerking his arms behind his back and securing them with that black cord that always hung from his waist.

I know that Lara grabbed Cal's arm and shouted something at him, while Roderick crossed his arms and scowled at me, his black wings making him look like the angel of death.

But mostly I remember my dad standing there, staring at me with a completely unreadable look. And when I tried to talk to him, he abruptly raised his hand and said, "Do not even attempt to explain this, Sophia."

The walk back to the house was the longest and most miserable half-mile of my life. I wasn't sure which to worry the most about—what they would do to Archer, or if Dad would ever forgive me. Up ahead, Dad and Lara conferred in hushed tones, and I tried to absorb the enormity of the trouble I was in. I had been caught with one of Prodigium's greatest enemies. Something told me that punishment would be a lot worse than writing a thousand words on some obscure topic.

Thorne Abbey was dark and silent as we marched inside. Only once we'd been led all the way back to the main foyer did Dad finally say something.

"We're calling an emergency meeting of the Council for first thing in the morning. Sophie, Cal, the two of you are to go to your rooms and stay there until someone comes for you. Kristopher, secure Mr. Cross in one of the cells downstairs."

My gaze locked with Archer's as Kristopher began dragging him away. "It's okay," he mouthed, but it wasn't. It never would be.

After he was gone, I walked over to Dad. He still wouldn't look at me, and was holding himself with that same rigidness Cal had shown in the mill. "Dad, I know 'I'm sorry' doesn't even begin to cut it."

Breathing in deeply through his nose, Dad said, "Until your testimony is over, I can't speak to you. Please report to your chamber until tomorrow morning."

My eyes flooded with tears. "Dad—"

"Go!" he shouted, and I clapped my hand over my mouth to keep from crying out loud.

He walked away without even glancing at me.

"Come on," Cal said. "There's nothing you can do right now."

"Did you tell them?" I demanded. "Is that why they came to the mill?"

All of Cal's earlier fury seemed to have completely drained out of him. "No," he said. "I have no idea why they showed up when they did. Unless it has something to do with those tests they've been running on me. Maybe they traced my magic. Who knows?"

He turned to go, and even though I wanted nothing more than to run after Dad, I followed Cal away from the foyer and up the back stairs to our rooms. Our footsteps were muffled by the thick carpet, and the dim light from the sconces made our shadows waver on the walls. I felt the eyes of all the portraits lining the staircase, like they were judging me. All those nameless Prodigium, hunted through the centuries by Eyes, and Brannicks, and God knows what else.

I did it for a good reason, I wanted to tell the painted faces. *And Archer isn't one of them, not really.* Somehow, I didn't think the portraits would believe me.

"What do you think they'll do to us?" I asked Cal, my stomach icy with fear.

"It won't be as bad as you think," he replied, but he didn't sound wholly convinced. "You're James's daughter, and you're important to them. They aren't going to throw you to the wolves over something like this."

I wondered if being thrown to the wolves was a literal punishment in this case. I really didn't want to know.

"They may stretch your sentence at Hecate by an extra year or so, but I think that would be the worst of it," Cal continued. "With me—"

"You were just helping *me*," I said as we turned down our hall. "Tell them that, okay? Tell them that you were, like, honoring our betrothal vow or something. They'll go easy on you, I bet."

We stopped outside his door and he studied me. As usual, I had no idea what was going on in his mind. "Maybe," was all he said. Then, after another long pause, "I know you think they're going to kill him, but they might not. Archer Cross is just as valuable to The Eye as you are to the Council. He'd make a good hostage, and they know it."

I forced my face not to crumple. If I cried any more tonight, I'd probably turn into a dried-out husk. "So what now? We just go to our rooms and sleep and try to pretend like everything is going to be all right?" Another thought occurred to me. "Or pretend that Nick isn't out there right now, completely crazy *and* superpowerful? Because there's no way I can do that."

"Yes there is." He reached out, startling me, and pressed his palm to my cheek.

Almost immediately, a sense of well-being flooded through me, a blissful numbness that started at the top of my head and spread all the way to my toes. "Seriously, best powers ever," I mumbled drowsily.

"Go to bed, Sophie," he said, dropping his hand as if my skin had burned him. "Tomorrow will be a long day."

But today wasn't over yet. As I turned to go, I saw Jenna standing outside my door, her face a mask of hurt and anger.

"I was downstairs getting some blood," she said, her lips barely moving. "I . . . saw them come in with you. And Archer."

Cal's spell, which had seemed so helpful only a few moments before, was a nightmare now. My brain felt too soft and sleepy to come up with any explanation, and when I tried, I couldn't get the right words out. "He was helping me."

She made a sound somewhere between a gasp and a sob. "Helping you? Sophie, he's one—"

"Of them," I finished, suddenly irritated. "I know. You're not the first person to say it tonight. But Jenna, please." I reached out for her, curling my fingers around her wrist. "Cal is mad at me, my Dad probably hates me . . . I can't have you hate me, too."

Two tears dripped from her eyes, splashing on the back of my hand. Her bloodstone shimmered slightly in the light from the sconces, and after a long, long moment, she covered my hand with hers. "Okay," she said, sniffling. "But tomorrow, you're going to tell me everything."

"Everything," I echoed, feeling my own eyes sting. And when she finally wrapped her arms around me and hugged me, it was all I could do not to sob all over her. "You are a way better friend than I deserve," I mumbled against her shoulder.

She hugged me tighter. "I know."

I laughed through my tears, and just a little bit of the weight on my heart lifted.

Early the next morning, I heard a knock at the door, and jerked awake in an instant. Cal's spell had totally faded by that point, and all the anxiety and despair came flooding back. In less than twenty-four hours, my whole life had been turned upside down. Nick and Daisy had demoned out, Archer was a prisoner of the Council, and the fragile relationship I'd built with Dad had been blown completely to smithereens. It didn't seem fair that so much bad could happen in so short a time.

Or maybe I was just using up all the horrible now. Maybe the next eighty years would be full of nothing but Yahtzee and collecting various cats. That might be nice.

The knock sounded again, and I realized it wasn't my door, but Cal's down the hall. I sunk back to my pillow. Would I be next, or would they take Archer first?

Or maybe they'd already taken Archer.

I shook that thought away and got cleaned up and dressed. My clothes from last night still lay on the floor in a stiff heap, and I shuddered as I tossed them into the little brass trash can under the bathroom sink. It wasn't the first time I'd had blood on my clothes, but I dearly hoped it would be the last.

When they came for me, I was sitting on the edge of my bed, wearing the black sheath dress Lara had gotten for me at Lysander's. I opened the door to find Kristopher.

"Sophie, they're ready for you," he said.

I nodded, my heart fluttering in my chest, and my mouth completely dry.

He led me down the stairs, but instead of turning right toward Council headquarters, we went left, into yet another section of Thorne Abbey that was completely foreign to me. This hall was darker, with none of the marble and gilt that seemed to cover the rest of the house. Here, there was just wood paneling and thick iron cages over the lightbulbs. Finally, we stopped at a heavy, scarred door.

The room wasn't like any other space at Thorne. It was relatively small, for one thing, and dim. There were no windows, and the only light came from a thick metal chandelier ringed with candles. Everything smelled dank and slightly mildewed, and there were dark stains on the worn wooden floor. I didn't want to think about where they'd come from.

Up front, a long wooden table ran nearly the length of the room, with five high-backed wooden chairs. The chairs were filled with Council members. I saw Lara first, and then, surprised, I realized Mrs. Casnoff was sitting next to her.

I was so shocked to see her back at Thorne, it took me a second to realize that Dad was not sitting at the table. Lara looked up and saw me, and gestured for me to come forward. In front of the table was a low bench, made of the same dark wood as the rest of the room. It was like being locked inside a huge oaken cask.

Archer was sitting on the bench, his elbows resting on his knees. His wrists were still tied together with Kristopher's cord, and his clothes torn and stiff with blood. But when I sat next to him, he raised his head and tried to smile at me. It was more of a grimace, though. I wanted to reach out and touch him, but I knew that would just make things worse. My magic flooded through me, and I let myself envision, just for a moment, unleashing it on that table of five grim faces.

I could have. My powers were stronger than all of theirs combined.

But then what? Make a run for it, destroy everything Dad had worked for, and spend the rest of my life hiding out? No thanks. Whatever the Council had in store for me, it couldn't be as bad as that.

"Sophia, as you've no doubt noticed, your father is not seated with us," Lara said as Kristopher made his way to sit on the other side of her. "We decided, and he agreed, that he could not maintain the necessary objectivity to participate in your sentencing."

I glanced around and finally spotted Dad leaning against the back wall, nearly hidden in the gloom. His arms were crossed, but I couldn't see his face. Then it occurred to me that Lara said Dad hadn't participated in my sentencing. Had he had a role in deciding what would happen to Archer?

"But since Council law requires we have five members at all rulings, Anastasia agreed to fill the vacant seat. The two of you face very serious charges." Lara's voice should have been big and booming, the sound of a judgment coming from on high. Instead, it was low and quiet, almost intimate. "Archer Cross, you infiltrated Hecate Hall as a member of L'Occhio di Dio. Do you freely admit to this?"

Never in my life had I wished so hard for telepathic powers. *Please don't be a smart-ass, please don't be a smart-ass,* I thought, trying to will the words into Archer's brain. Either it worked, or Archer had more sense than I'd thought.

"I do," he said softly.

It was as if a sigh rippled through all five Prodigium. Then, as one, their eyes swiveled to me. "Sophia Mercer, you intruded in a forbidden area on Graymalkin Island and plotted with a member of L'Occhio di Dio in order to do it. Do you freely admit to this?"

A million arguments and explanations leaped to my tongue, namely that I'd only been at that part of Graymalkin because the Casnoff sisters were up to some evil crap there, but I bit them all back. I just wanted this over with. "I do."

Lara nodded, and I think I saw a flicker of relief on her face. She scribbled something on a long piece of parchment in front of her. She didn't even look up as she said, "Mr. Cross, since you admit to the charges before you, we shall now pronounce your sentence."

My heartbeat slowed, and I suddenly felt very cold,

like I was about to teleport. But it wasn't magic, just fear.

"It is the ruling of this Council that you shall be taken onto the grounds of Thorne Abbey tomorrow at dawn and executed."

It was like all the air rushed out of my lungs. Out of the room. I thought the chamber started to vibrate, but it wasn't the room. It was me, shaking so hard I couldn't see straight. Tomorrow. Dawn. That was less than twenty-four hours away. In less than a day, Archer would be dead. The words screamed in my skull, the pain in my head almost as intense as the pain in my heart.

Next to me, Archer drew in a deep breath, and I dug my nails into my palms to keep from taking his hand. If I touched him now, I was afraid of what might happen. My powers churned inside me, the way they had last night when I thought he was dying. I didn't think there was anything I could picture that would keep me from blowing this place to smithereens if I released even an iota of magic.

"As for you, Sophia," Lara said, drawing my attention back to the table. "You are an entirely different matter."

I'd been so focused on how they were going to kill Archer that I nearly forgot I still had to be punished.

Lara frowned, a vertical line forming between her brows, and said, "This is merely the last in a long line of troubling events where you are concerned. There was the situation at Hecate in the fall. You injured several Prodigium at Shelley's several weeks ago. You were able to open the case holding Virginia Thorne's grimoire almost single-handedly."

I shook my head. How did she know about that? I wanted to turn to Dad again, but it was like my eyes were glued to Lara, watching her lips as she calmly continued, "And perhaps most disturbing of all is the strength of your necromancy skills. There has literally never been another Prodigium as proficient in those as you."

"What, you mean the ghouls?" I asked, confused. "Because, I mean, yeah, I could control them, but it took nearly everything out of me."

Mrs. Casnoff settled back in her chair, hands folded on top of the scarred table and spoke for the first time. "Not the ghouls, Sophie. We are speaking of Elodie Parris."

CHAPTER 37

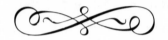

Her words fell on me like stones. "You told me that she had attempted to communicate with you at Hecate. Is this true?"

I could feel every eye in the room on me, even Archer's. "Yes."

Mrs. Casnoff leaned forward. "And has she done the same here at Thorne?"

My fingers were icy as I curled them in my lap, but I didn't say anything. Still, Mrs. Casnoff nodded as if I had. "There's never been a case of a ghost communicating with a Prodigium, much less following one across the Atlantic Ocean. Elodie should be haunting Hecate. Instead, she's haunting *you*." She shook her head slightly, like she couldn't believe it. "It's possible that it's an after-effect of her sharing magic with you as she was dying, but again, there is no precedent for anything like it. When we take that into account with both the powers you've already displayed, and your heritage, I'm afraid it leaves us with no choice."

My mind felt like an oversaturated sponge. There was just too much information to even begin to make sense of it all. I had somehow bound Elodie to me, and despite all the work I'd done this summer to not be scary-powerful, that's exactly what the Council was saying I was. And what did she mean, "heritage"?

Mrs. Casnoff dropped her gaze, and Lara once again scrawled something across her parchment, then spoke. "It is our ruling that you be subjected to the Removal."

As one, the Council murmured something, a word or phrase in a language that wasn't remotely familiar. Whatever it was, there was power in it, so much that my hair blew back off my shoulders while I sat dumbly, glued to my seat. Archer's hand landed on mine, warm and heavy, and I was reminded of the first time we'd ever touched, the night of the assembly at Hecate. From the back of the room, I heard Dad say something, his voice sharp as a blade. As stupid as it sounds, I wanted to laugh. Looks like I was finally going to get what I'd come here for after all.

Dad was beside me now, his fingers clamped on one of my shoulders. "Sophie was at Graymalkin with Archer on my orders," he said, and I immediately grabbed his hand.

"Dad, no!"

But he didn't even glance at me. He kept his gaze locked on Mrs. Casnoff. "I suspected you were the one who had raised Daisy and Nick, and I sent Sophie and Archer to investigate. If anyone should go through the Removal, it should be me." He nodded at Lara. "Being head of the Council has always been your chief desire. I cede it to you freely." He said the same phrase they'd used when handing down mine and Archer's sentences, and once again, a pulse of power went through the room.

This time, the surge felt stronger, and as I watched, the candles in the room guttered, nearly blowing out. Lara took a deep breath and rolled her shoulders, like something heavy had landed on them. Dad seemed to deflate a little as he said, "Just let Sophie go back to her mother unharmed."

"Oh, James," Lara said, almost sadly. "Your sacrifice is noble, if pointless and predictable."

Kristopher, Roderick, and Elizabeth were staring at Dad with the same look, a strange combination of pity and disdain. The dread that had been swirling around in me for over a month suddenly came crashing down, strong and heavy, stealing my breath. This was it. The thing I'd felt coming was finally here.

"You've been such a disappointment to us." Lara's gaze flicked to me. "Both of you."

The whole room was silent, but Lara didn't need any encouragement to continue. This was clearly the moment she'd been waiting for. "When my father and Virginia Thorne transformed Alice, they thought they'd created the perfect weapon—a being containing more power than dreamed of, yet completely under their control. Instead, they ended up with a mad, hysterical girl who had to be put down like a dog. Of course, Father still had such high hopes for Lucy, but she refused to work for the Council. So the Council simply waited until you were old enough, James, and then disposed of your parents."

It took me a second to realize what she was saying. Alexei Casnoff had been Alice's maker, so he'd had control over the whole bloodline. He'd made Lucy kill her husband. My grandfather. And then he'd had her killed, too. I was surprised I could hear anything over the sudden rushing of blood in my ears, but Lara was still talking.

"Father saw the value in using demons in our war against The Eye. Sadly, your grandmother and your mother proved . . . incapable of being used as weapons. Father had higher hopes for you."

I didn't think it was possible for Dad to look any paler, but as what Lara was saying sunk in, his skin went papery white. Rage and horror coursed through me, and

I waited for my magic to surge up, too. But while my powers were swirling in my blood, it was like they were locked in a glass box. I could feel them, but I couldn't access them. "Don't bother," Roderick said to me. "As soon as you were sentenced to the Removal, your powers were locked away from you. Your father's, too, once he'd spoken the spell of binding. Very useful piece of magic. Otherwise, a witch or warlock could attempt to fight their way out of the Removal."

Next to me, Archer sat up straighter, and I saw tiny blue sparks on his fingertips. I caught his eyes and shook my head. Archer was an amazing fighter, but he wasn't the strongest warlock. If he tried something now, he'd just end up as another stain on the wooden floor.

Lara was still looking at Dad. "However, my father was a smart man. He kept the ritual used to raise Alice just in case you did not prove yourself to be what we needed. Sadly, you have not. Nor has you daughter. But we have others."

Dad gave a humorless laugh. "Nick and Daisy? They're too feral to be of any use to anyone."

"No," Mrs. Casnoff said, speaking for the first time since I'd been sentenced. "Nick and Daisy are simply the ones you know about." If it hadn't been Mrs. Casnoff, I would have said her eyes seemed pleading. "You were never going to move aggressively enough against our enemies, James. I know you have personal reasons for that, but we simply couldn't allow ourselves to be vulnerable any longer."

"This is madness," Dad said, his voice trembling. "You have given The Eye and the Brannicks, the whole damn lot of them, more reason than ever to exterminate our kind."

"They have infiltrated our kind, James," Lara said, pursing her lips. "We need every weapon at our disposal."

She was wrong. I could feel it in my bones, but I didn't know if that was the psychic thing or just common sense. Raising demons would be seen as an act of war. There was no doubt in my mind of that. Despair crashed over me as I thought about all the evil this one family had done. Alexei Casnoff had destroyed Alice, Lucy, my grandfather . . . and now his daughters wanted me and Dad out of the way, too. The whole thing was so insane, I didn't know whether to laugh or scream.

But that decision was made for me when Lara nodded toward the back of the room and two of the vampire guards, maybe the same I'd seen last night, stepped out of the shadows and grabbed Dad.

"No!" I shouted, but the guards were already dragging him to the door.

"I'll be fine," Dad said, holding my gaze. His voice didn't shake, but I saw fear in his eyes.

I stared at him, my panicked mind trying to come up with something, anything, to say to him. After all, this could be the last time I saw him. But my brain was full of too much terror, and all I could say was, "Dad."

And then he was gone, the slamming of the door echoing in the dark chamber.

CHAPTER 38

Archer and I were taken to the lowest part of Thorne and put in one of those cells Dad had mentioned the other night. They weren't anything like what I'd imagined; I'd been picturing steel bars, a narrow cot—like a prison. Instead, they were just caves with iron doors. We were thrown into one of the larger ones, the white rock walls slick with moisture, the only light coming from an orb like the one I'd made the other night, hovering high overhead. Power crackled throughout the room—a spell, Archer informed me, that kept anyone held in the cell from doing magic. Apparently he'd discovered that last night.

For a long time, we just sat on the damp floor, holding hands. Somewhere in the house, my dad was being put through a ritual that might kill him. I was next, and by this time tomorrow, Archer would be dead. It was too much to think about, much less talk about, so we didn't speak for the longest time.

I watched the light flicker on the limestone walls until Archer said, "I wish we could go to the movies."

I stared at him. "We're in a creepy dungeon. There's a chance I might die in the next few hours. You *are* going to die in the next few hours. And if you had one wish, it would be to catch a movie?"

He shook his head. "That's not what I meant. I wish we weren't like this. You know, demon, demon-hunter. I wish I'd met you in a normal high school, and taken you on normal dates, and like, carried your books or something." Glancing over at me, he squinted and asked, "Is that a thing humans actually do?"

"Not outside of 1950s TV shows," I told him, reaching up to touch his hair. He wrapped an arm around me and leaned against the wall, pulling me to his chest. I drew my legs up under me and rested my cheek on his collarbone. "So instead of stomping around forests hunting ghouls, you want to go to the movies and school dances."

"Well, maybe we could go on the occasional ghoul hunt," he allowed before pressing a kiss to my temple. "Keep things interesting."

I closed my eyes. "What else would we do if we were regular teenagers?"

"Hmm . . . let's see. Well, first of all, I'd need to get some kind of job so I could afford to take you on these completely normal dates. Maybe I could stock groceries somewhere."

The image of Archer in a blue apron, putting boxes of Nilla Wafers on a shelf at Walmart was too bizarre to even contemplate, but I went along with it. "We could argue in front of our lockers all dramatically," I said. "That's something I saw a lot at human high schools."

He squeezed me in a quick hug. "Yes! Now that sounds like a good time. And then I could come to your house in the middle of the night and play music really loudly under your window until you took me back."

I chuckled. "You watch too many movies. Ooh, we could be lab partners!"

"Isn't that kind of what we were in Defense?"

"Yeah, but in normal high school, there would be more science, less kicking each other in the face."

"Nice."

We spent the next few minutes spinning out scenarios like this, including all the sports in which Archer's L'Occhio di Dio skills would come in handy, and starring in school plays. By the time we were done, I was laughing, and I realized that, for just a little while, I'd managed to forget what a huge freaking mess we were in.

Which had probably been the point.

Once our laughter died away, the dread started seeping back in. Still, I tried to joke when I said, "You know, if I do live through this, I'm gonna be covered in funky tattoos like the Vandy. You sure you want to date the Illustrated Woman, even if it's just for a little while?"

He caught my chin and raised my eyes to his. "Trust me," he said softly, "you could have a giant tiger tattooed on your face, and I'd still want to be with you."

"Okay, seriously, enough with the swoony talk," I told him, leaning in closer. "I like snarky, mean Archer."

He grinned. "In that case, shut up, Mercer." Then he pressed his lips to mine. I was very aware of the fact that this was probably the last time we'd ever kiss, and I think he was, too. The kiss was different than any of the others we'd shared, slower and tinged with desperation. By the time it was over, we were both breathing hard, our foreheads pressed together.

"Sophie," Archer murmured, but then the heavy iron door opened with a screech.

Kristopher was standing there, his hair blue in the orb's light. He barely seemed to register me and Archer, turning over his shoulder to someone behind him and barking, "In here."

Two dark figures walked into the cell, carrying a bundle between them.

Dad.

He was dressed in a black robe, similar to the one he'd worn the night of my birthday party, and his head lolled back as the two men—vampires, I realized—lowered him to the ground. At first, all I could see were those marks twining up his neck, spiraling over his cheeks and forehead like poisonous vines. In the gloom, they looked black, but I guessed they were the same dark purple as the Vandy's.

But I didn't care about any of that. All I cared about was the steady rise and fall of his chest and, when I grabbed his wrist, the thread pulse that beat there. "Dad," I said softly, but he didn't wake up. I squeezed his hand harder. Something about him felt different, and it took me a minute to realize that what I was feeling were his lack of powers. I'd been so used to tuning in to Dad's magic, like a low-frequency radio station that only I could hear. Now there was just silence. My own powers, locked inside of me, seemed to beat against their invisible case in sympathy.

Tears dripped from my eyes, landing on his robes.

Rough hands grabbed my shoulders as the vampires pulled me to my feet. Kristopher stood in the doorway, his face impassive. "Come along, Sophia."

I looked frantically from Dad to Archer and back again. No, this couldn't be it. These couldn't be the last few seconds that I'd see them. There was still so much I had to tell them.

"I'll look out for him," Archer said, kneeling next to Dad. "And I'll see you when you get back."

"Right," I said, licking lips that were suddenly, painfully dry. "I'll see you when I get back." I said it like it was a mantra, or a vow. And I kept repeating it in my head. *When I get back, when I get back.* If Dad could live through it, I could, too.

I shook off the vampires. "I can walk," I said. Even though my knees were wobbling so badly it was a wonder I didn't slide to the floor, I made myself move toward Kristopher.

I followed him out of the cell, keeping my back straight and my head high.

But when we got to the base of the steps leading up to the rest of Thorne Abbey, my resolve wavered.

Standing there, waiting for me, was Mrs. Casnoff.

CHAPTER 39

I could barely bring myself to look at her as she gestured for me to follow her up the stairs. I had never been her biggest fan, but I had trusted her. All I could think of was that night she and Cal had come for me after Alice, how she'd sat by my bed and held my hand. How she'd told me I had a destiny to serve the Council. Too bad she'd neglected to mention that they'd kill me if I didn't live up to their expectations.

We made our way up the twisting stone steps. "Sophie, I know you feel betrayed."

"Betrayed, pissed off, terrified . . . I have a lot of emotions going on right now, actually."

She stopped, placing her hand on my arm. "There are very valid reasons for all of this."

I threw her hand off. "Your sister already did the

'villain explains it all' speech. I don't need another one."

"But that's just it," she insisted. "We are not villains. We are doing what's best for all Prodigium. Our numbers are getting smaller as factions like L'Occhio di Dio and the Brannicks increase. You and your father were meant to protect us, and yet you both seem to prefer the company of our enemies."

"That's not what's—wait, what do you mean 'both'? Since when is Dad all cozy with The Eye? Or the Brannicks, for that matter?"

She shook her head and continued walking upstairs. "It's of no concern anymore."

We'd reached the top of the stairs, but we were still underground. There were no windows in the long corridor. Suits of armor lined the walls, but these looked different from the ones I'd seen in other parts of Thorne. The dimensions were strange, and many of the suits were freakishly huge. Fear raced over me and through me, and once again, I felt my magic thump pitifully, uselessly, inside me.

"If you'll follow me," Mrs. Casnoff said, but before we got even three steps, a voice cried out, "Anastasia!"

It was Elizabeth, running down the corridor on her tiny grandma legs, her long skirt flapping around her.

Mrs. Casnoff looked annoyed. "What is it?"

Elizabeth reached us, panting, her round cheeks flushed. "Lara needs to see you immediately."

Frowning, Mrs. Casnoff said, "I'm taking Sophie to the Removal chamber. Tell her I'll be there shortly."

"No!" Elizabeth shook her head. "She said to come now. It's"—she glanced at me—"it's about Nick."

Even in the near-dark of the hallway, I could see the blood drain out of Mrs. Casnoff's face. "Is it—"

"It's like before," Elizabeth said. "With his parents, but this time—" Her words dissolved into a strangled sob, and she pressed her hand to her mouth before saying, "Oh, God, Anastasia, it's happened again."

I had no idea what Elizabeth was talking about, but Mrs. Casnoff spit out a word I never thought I'd hear her say. She whirled on me. "Come with us, Sophie. And if you make any attempt to escape, so help me, I will kill you myself. Is that clear?"

I nodded dumbly, too relieved that I wasn't being taken to the Removal chamber to feel scared. I followed Mrs. Casnoff and Elizabeth down the corridor, my brain whirring. If something bad had happened, maybe everyone would be distracted enough so I could formulate some plan for escape, Mrs. Casnoff's death threats notwithstanding. First I'd need to find Jenna. It startled me to realize that I hadn't even thought of her during all of this. Did she even know what had happened? Of course, if she'd heard about the Archer part, she might not want to leave with me anyway. I shook that thought away. Not helpful. And then there was Cal. I needed to find him and see what they'd done to him, if anything. Then maybe somehow, Cal, Jenna, and I could find a way to get Archer and Dad out of that cell, and we could make for the Itineris like the hounds of hell were at our heels.

Which they probably would be.

We finally reached the main foyer, and even from there, I could hear shouting coming from upstairs.

As Elizabeth and Mrs. Casnoff ran up the stairs, I thought about making a run for my room, hoping Jenna and Cal were in theirs. I'd barely made a quarter turn in that direction when a bolt of magic hit me squarely between the shoulder blades, sending me to my knees. I'd been hit by an attack spell before—Alice had done it as part of our training—but it hadn't hurt like this one. I felt like I'd been electrocuted and slammed in the back with a bat all at the same time.

When I lifted my head, I saw Mrs. Casnoff standing on the landing, her hand held out toward me. "I warned you," she said. "Now get up here."

I did as I was told. Truthfully, I'm not sure if I could have done anything else; I could barely walk.

The rest of the Council was gathered in the hallway

outside Dad's office. A couple of palms were overturned, spilling black soil on the red carpet. On the floor, I noticed small bits of broken glass and two dark stains. Lara and Roderick stood in the middle of the lobby, shouting at each other.

"You assured us this wouldn't happen. You swore that he was completely under your control."

Lara's hands were clenched into fists at her sides as she glared up at Roderick. "He is. Clearly this is some sort of aberration. We can fix this."

"No," Elizabeth cried, "we can't! Lara, he killed nearly twenty people tonight. *Twenty*, in just a few minutes."

My stomach lurched. So that was the emergency. Their pet demon had gone rabid. I felt a fierce dark joy at that. Serves you right, I thought. This is what you get for turning kids into monsters. But then I remembered Nick, and how sweet he'd been with Daisy, how his smile had reminded me of Archer, and any satisfaction I felt withered immediately.

"And The Eye knows we have Cross," Elizabeth continued, her voice shrill. "They're coming to Thorne. Oh God, it will be just like before!"

"No," Lara barked, her face manic. "Not this time. We still have Daisy. We can fix this."

Kristopher appeared under the marble arch, his blue

eyes bright with anger. "It's too late for that. Elizabeth is right. They're coming, Lara. I can feel it. I know you can, too."

But Lara stood there, her dark blond hair falling out of its bun. There was a wild look in her eyes. "Let them come, then. Anastasia, let Daisy out of her cell."

But Mrs. Casnoff stayed where she was. "If we unleash Daisy on them . . . Lara, what if we can't control her?"

I felt invisible standing there, watching. In a weird way, I felt almost sorry for them. They'd done a stupid and dangerous thing because they were scared, and now they were paying the consequence. But that consequence was a war that was going to kill a lot of Prodigium, and probably a lot of humans, too.

It was stupid, but I tried one last time to summon up my powers. I don't know what I would have done with them if they'd worked, but once again, there was nothing. Just that helpless sense that my magic was right there, within reach but untouchable. Still, there had to be some way to get to it. If there weren't, why would the Removal exist? Maybe the binding spell wasn't permanent.

In the silence, I glanced down at the carpet, and something shiny caught my eye. Those broken bits of glass. But no, it wasn't glass that was sparkling in the light. It was a thin golden chain.

A choking sound, somewhere between a sob and a shout, forced its way out of my throat as I knelt down and realized what I was looking at.

A shattered bloodstone.

CHAPTER 40

"W here is she?" I asked Mrs. Casnoff. "This is Jenna's." I held up the chain. "What did you do to her?" My voice rose to a scream on the last few words, and I was shaking. If they had destroyed Jenna's bloodstone in the daylight, she would have died. Worse than died, she would have burned alive, screaming. I thought of the premonitions I'd had, that Cal, Jenna, and I would never go back to Hecate together.

The smell of smoke.

My fingers tightened on the chain until I was digging my nails into my palm. Lara looked at me with disdain and said, "It was time to clean house in more ways than one."

I gave a cry of rage and leaped to my feet. I might not have had any powers left, but that wouldn't stop me from killing her with my bare hands if she'd hurt Jenna. I don't know what would have happened if a loud crash hadn't reverberated through the house at that exact moment. But as soon as it did, all eyes swung away from me and toward the marble arch.

Another crash, then another, and then the horrible, screaming sound of cracking wood.

Without a word, Lara vanished in a faint rushing of air that told me she'd just teleported. Probably down to the cells to release Daisy. Mrs. Casnoff was murmuring something over and over in a language I didn't understand, and as I watched, Elizabeth's grandmotherly attire rippled and flowed until she was covered in gray fur, her face stretching into a muzzle. Her glasses fell off, revealing yellow eyes.

I think they were expecting someone to walk in through the arch, maybe offer "parlay" or whatever. That was the weird thing: they somehow expected this to go down in a formal, civilized manner. So they were caught by surprise when a silver dagger flew through the archway, hitting Kristopher squarely in the chest. He fell back soundlessly, his eyes staring at nothing.

What happened next was like something out of a nightmare.

The werewolf that had been Elizabeth howled and launched itself out of the lobby, headed for the stairs, Mrs.

Casnoff and Roderick right behind her. I stood, frozen. What the heck was I supposed to do in the middle of a giant magical battle with no freaking magic?

All I could hear from downstairs were screams and howls and things breaking. Dad and Archer were still trapped in their cell, and God only knew where Jenna was. Or Cal, for that matter. I couldn't stay here, waiting for more of those killing flashes of light to snake their way to me. And if any of The Eye downstairs found me, something told me they wouldn't care that I could no longer do magic, or that I was in love with one of their members.

I was going to have to make a run for it, and the only way out of Council Headquarters was out that marble archway and into an epic monster battle.

I took a deep breath and slid Jenna's chain into my pocket. If I wanted to find out what had happened to her, if I wanted to save my Dad and Archer, if I wanted to find Cal, then I had to get out of this alive, magic or no. "Elodie, if you're around and can offer any ghostly assistance, that would be great," I said. I was half joking, but before I even had time to blink, she was floating in front of me, a vaguely irritated expression on her face.

"Whoa," I murmured. "So . . . what they said, about me binding you to me. That's true?"

She crossed her arms and nodded, scowling.

"Okay. Well, sorry about that. But I promise, if you help get me out of this, I'll do whatever it takes to, uh, unbind us."

She studied me and then her lips moved. I'm not sure what she said, but it looked like, "You better."

She drifted over to one of the portraits. Her fingers moved around the edges of the frame like smoke, and after a moment, it swung open, revealing a passageway. She nodded toward it, and I could swear she looked smug.

"Thank you," I said, but she'd already vanished. I hesitated at the entrance until a deafening crack sounded from downstairs. I had no idea what it could be, but it sounded like the whole floor had split open. There was another rush of magic, and even if I didn't have my powers anymore, I still knew what it was. Lara had freed Daisy. I didn't know what she'd done, but the screams that followed were inhuman.

Dad, I thought. *Archer. Jenna. Cal. Get out so that you can help them.*

The tunnel was small enough that I had to hunch over, and once I'd moved a few feet down, it twisted so I could no longer see the opening into Council Headquarters. That meant everything was pitch-black. Instinctively, I lifted my hand to summon an orb before remembering that I couldn't anymore.

As I walked, moving as quickly as I could, I heard sounds of the battle raging inside the house. There were distant thumps and crashes like thunder, and once I thought I heard screams. I made myself keep moving even as I desperately wondered what was happening behind me. *Dad, Archer, Jenna, Cal,* I kept repeating. *You can't help them if you're dead.*

The roof got lower as the tunnel twisted upward, and I had to drop to my knees and crawl the rest of the way up. Finally, my head thunked against something solid. I felt around with my fingers. A door.

I pushed up on it, and a shower of gravel and dirt rained down on me as it opened. I could see the tall hedges of the garden maze towering over me, so apparently I'd crawled right out the back of the house.

Pulling myself out, I squinted. The light outside was so bright that for a disorienting moment, I thought the sun must be up. But no, it had been dark when I'd rushed through the house with Elizabeth and Mrs. Casnoff. Surely not enough time had passed for it to be sunrise. And the light wasn't the soft lemon yellow glow of sunlight, but the harsh orange glare of fire.

I rose to my feet and turned to face the house.

It was burning.

As I watched, tongues of flame broke out windows on the upper stories, licking at the building. An acre of roof, Lara had told us that first day, and now it seemed that the whole acre was on fire. Heat blasted my skin, and the smoke nearly choked me. Smoke.

Well, at least now I knew.

One of the massive wooden front doors crashed off its hinges. The house where Alice had been made a demon. The place where my father had lived his whole life. Council Headquarters.

It was gone.

And Dad and Archer were still inside.

I wanted to drop to my knees right there in the grass and sob, but a hand grabbed my arm. I screamed, swinging with everything I was worth. For the first time, I realized how vulnerable I was with no magic. My blows felt weak and ineffectual, and my powers screamed inside me.

"Sophie, it's me. It's me!"

Cal.

"It's okay," he was saying, pulling me closer to him. "It's okay."

I collapsed against his chest, too weak with fear and worry to cry. "Where have you been?"

"After my testimony, the Council sent me back to Hecate. But I . . . I don't know, I just felt like something was wrong here, so I used the Itineris to come back. What the hell happened?" he asked.

I looked up at him, his hazel eyes reflecting the

inferno in front of us. "It's the Council. They're raising demons. They raised Nick and Daisy, and now Nick has killed a bunch of people. They sentenced Archer to death, and—" I broke off on a sob. "L'Occhio di Dio attacked the house because of it, and Lara is using Daisy against them. And . . . and my dad is still in there. And Archer. And they did something to Jenna, but I don't know what," I finished, just as one of Thorne's many chimneys crumbled in a plume of fire and smoke. It sounds strange, but until I said all of that out loud, the full magnitude of what I'd lost hadn't really hit me. No more magic. Jenna missing, maybe dead. Archer and Dad trapped inside a burning building.

"Okay," Cal said softly. Then, more firmly, "Get to the Itineris. I used that chain Cross had to get to Hecate and back, so it's still there. Use it and get out of here."

"How?" I asked, trying to focus. "I don't have my powers anymore."

Cal shook his head. "You don't need them. The Itineris has its own magic. It doesn't need yours."

"Where am I supposed to go? I have no idea where my mom is." My throat tightened to the point of pain. Dad had said he was going to call her. What if she was on her way here right now? What if she walked into the middle of this? "You were at Hecate. Is she there?"

Cal shook his head. "No." There was another crash

from inside, and Cal's eyes darted back to Thorne. "Go to the Itineris and tell it you want to go to Aislinn Brannick. That should be enough to get you there, or at least close enough."

If he had told me to climb around the back of the mill and go to Narnia, I'm not sure I could have been more shocked. "What?" I shouted over the roar of the flames. "Why would I go there?"

"Because that's where your mother is," he said, his gaze boring into mine.

My hands clenched the front of his shirt. "Oh my God, did they capture her or something?"

He shook his head. "No, but I don't have time to explain. Just trust me. She won't hurt you, and it's the only place I can think of where you'd be safe. I'll see what I can do for your dad. And Cross."

I clutched his arm. "Cal, that's suicide," I said. God knows I wanted Dad and Archer safe, but the thought of Cal plunging back into that madness made my chest constrict with fear.

He gently pried my hand off his arm. "I have to," he said softly. He went to turn away, and then stopped, like maybe he was reconsidering. But instead of agreeing to come back to the Itineris with me, he reached out, cupped my face, and brought his lips to mine.

I was so shocked that I literally froze in place, one

hand hovering in the air next to Cal's shoulder. The kiss was brief—just a little too long to be considered chaste—but when he pulled away, all I could do was stare at him, my mouth slightly agape. He ran his thumb over my lower lip, sending a tiny flurry of sparks through me. "Good-bye, Sophie."

Then he jogged toward Thorne, disappearing into the blazing house. One more name I could add to my list of the lost.

I've heard people say that when you go through a lot of trauma, your brain just shuts off, goes right into survival mode. That must have been what happened to me, because I felt like I'd been dosed with a giant shot of mind-Novocain.

I turned away from Thorne Abbey and began walking toward the mill. Not running, not sprinting. Just walking. One foot in front of the other. *Go to Aislinn Brannick,* he'd said. *Your mother is there.* Okay, then. I'd go to Aislinn Brannick.

Once I reached the mill, I found the chain pretty quickly. Lying just a few feet from it was Archer's sword. That's right; he'd left it here that horrible night.

My fingers were as numb as the rest of me when I reached down and picked it up, its weight heavy and solid in my hand. I would take it with me, just in case I ever saw Archer again.

And just then, that feeling washed over me again, the strange psychic impulse I'd been feeling since I left Graymalkin. But this time, it wasn't dread that washed over me, or fear.

It was happiness. Hope.

I *would* see him again. I can't tell you how I knew it. I just did.

My magic flared inside me, futile but still there, and I felt the numbness slide away from me, steely determination taking its place. If Archer could live through this night, maybe that meant Dad and Cal could, too. And Jenna, wherever she was.

And together, maybe we had a chance of stopping all this. I clutched the sword tighter with one hand, and used the other to slip the chain around my neck.

"Aislinn Brannick," I muttered under my breath. "Wherever you are, I really hope Cal is right about you."

Then I stepped through the doorway.